'A funny, sassy, page-turning debut' Jenny Colgan

'Heaps of fun! ****' *Heat*

'I am in LOVE with Florence Love – she's flawed, feisty and funny as hell' Mel Giedroyc

'Plenty of twists, and a fresh, funny new voice that made me laugh out loud' *Woman & Home*

'A cracking read' Lorraine Kelly

'Clever page-turner' *Woman*

'With a smart, feisty heroine like Florence Love this is sure to be a great series' *The Book Magnet*

'Hugely entertaining' *Linda's Book Bag*

'Please hurry up and publish [book two] so we can find out what happened to Bambi' *That Thing She Reads*

'A fascinating insight into the world of detection' *Prima*

'A sassy, feisty heroine to die for . . . She's smart, she's sexy, and she's very, very funny' *Reader's Digest*

'A gem from start to finish, I absolutely cannot wait to read the second book in the Florence Love series' Samantha, *Goodreads*

'Delightful' *he Block*

By Louise Lee and available from Headline

A Girl Called Love (*previously* The Last Honeytrap)

In the
NAME of
LOVE

LOUISE LEE

HEADLINE

First published in Great Britain in 2017 by
HEADLINE PUBLISHING GROUP

First published in paperback in 2017 by
HEADLINE PUBLISHING GROUP

1

Cataloguing in Publication Data is available from the British Library

ISBN 978 1 4722 2458 3

Typeset in Garamond MT Std 12.25/13.5 pt by
Palimpsest Book Production Limited, Falkirk, Stirlingshire

Printed and bound by CPI Group (UK) Ltd, Croydon CR0 4YY

Headline's policy is to use papers that are natural, renewable and recyclable
products and made from wood grown in well-managed forests and other
controlled sources. The logging and manufacturing processes are expected to
conform to the environmental regulations of the country of origin.

HEADLINE PUBLISHING GROUP
An Hachette UK Company
Carmelite House
50 Victoria Embankment
London EC4Y 0DZ

www.headline.co.uk
www.hachette.co.uk

For Nan Lee – the cherry on my cake

Retired Entrapment Specialists 101 – Tip #1:
Never be yourself

Be this woman instead. The one who's thirty-three, uses the same name, day in, day out, and must contemplate a 'normal' job. Ideally, out of the public eye. In a morgue, for example.

Do not affect a show-stopping walk. Certainly don't glide as though your head's being pulled up and away from your shoulders by an invisible rope. You're a laughing stock to your profession and the whole human race; your penance is a repentant deportment – bent neck, splayed feet and saggy babaloos.

Beware of falling back in to the old entrapment habit: imagining you're French. Its connotations are dangerously attractive. They top-trump every physical shortcoming. People will stare, regardless of your posture. (*See* Gerald Depardieu.)

Get a new golden rule. Mine is this: live as invisibly as a radio wave. The alternative: I'll be explaining my side of the story for the rest of existence. Florence Love fact: I am incurably defensive.

Finally, find your motivation. By God, you'll need one. Wherever you go, whatever you do, never soliciting attention results in a life half lived. Try mine if you like, it's a time-honoured certainty . . .

The past doth *love* an arse to bite.

Part I

Part I

Kidnap, technically

The gun in my mouth belongs to Father Massimo Satori. Its barrel reflects the amber and gold of a stained-glass window to my left; I strain my eyes towards it. The Fourth Station of the Cross – Jesus heaving his crucifix to Golgotha and encountering his Blessed Mother, Mary. Me dying beneath this particular one is God's little joke.

The ache in my jaw is excruciating – it leaks into my eyeballs and down into my shoulder blades. Plus, Father Massimo keeps digging the piece at my tonsils and it's making me gag. That, and the saccharine smell of incense.

Sage advice: never puke on an assassin's gun; it irritates them no end.

I've no option but to enlist Transcendental Meditation.

An excellent mechanism in stressful situations, skilled practitioners can efficiently hop into their happy place at will. I could tell you how to do it, but that's bad form, spiritually. You have to have been trained by a resurrected yogi. Plus, I'm hopeless at alternative therapies – about to be murdered, and I fail to remember my mantra.

Instead, I attempt deep-breathing. In through the nose, out through the nose. But the air is a hundred degrees. I might as well inhale a hairdryer.

It was only a matter of time before my old foe arrived. Panic is her name, and the bitch jabs a bony elbow at my adrenal glands, draining my face of its blood.

Basic field survival techniques: I remember some of them . . .

When confronted with a life-threatening situation, present an appeasing stance . . .

I am cross-legged in a pool of my own piss. Check.

Maintain thoroughly friendly eye contact throughout . . .

This is tricky. My mouth is full of Colt 45. The gun's cylinder obscures his face. Desperately, I tilt my head to the left, show him my eyes, make them wide, beseech him to examine my irises. Because irises are a precise indicator of character, and mine contain densely packed crypts: people with densely packed crypts talk far too much, yet they're loyal and valiant.

But Father Massimo's not your usual priest. He's uninterested in whether or not I have a nice personality.

Honour your enemy's personal space . . .

Panic reminds me that, once upon a time, this priest was awarded an unambiguous nickname. The Eradicator, they called him, with no irony whatsoever.

I lose control of the situation.

Whipping my head away from the gun, I shuffle frantically backwards, my bare heels scraping angrily at the flagstones. I'm gasping at hot oxygen, a final treat before my goodnight slug in the head. Because it is coming. Oh boy, it's coming. Eyes squeezed shut, I wait for wrap-up. Total fact:

I knew this would happen one day. Death, I mean.

Aged eight, I discovered I was mortal. The hush of night. Listening to the heartbeat in my temples, an ancient clock clunking in the hall downstairs – my chest, its chest, producing an interminable beat that marched me in one dreadful direction. Death. The night frights didn't give an arse that I was too immature for the subject matter – they still laid the gaff:

Florence Love, you are not special. You will die. Nobody

avoids it. Not even Jesus, who is actually God, avoided it. Expiration is a devastating blip in the Big Guy's masterpiece.

Eight is too young to have a light-bulb moment about death. I've wasted too much life anticipating it.

Father Massimo cocks the trigger. I hear it clicking. Two metal snaps, quick as an old clock dying. Yet it seems to last an hour or so.

To be fair, I had suspected my death would be sooner than most. What I'd not anticipated was the abject disappointment. The anticlimax of dying. The appalling realisation that I, Florence Love, didn't have a big enough role.

That awful possibility had never crossed my mind.

The bullet itself takes a day or two to arrive. Its journey is so long and so silent, I begin to wonder if I have actually passed over. Eventually, I allow one eye to relax into the smallest slit.

Father Massimo's head is tilted to the left. He studies me from behind the gun then – quite suddenly – loses the will to kill. I watch him clean the gun's nozzle on his cassock. Polish my bile from its tip.

'It's blasphemous getting killed in a church,' I mumble. 'I'm not ready to die. I'm only twenty-nine.'

In truth, I'm thirty-three, but that is none of his business. Things I still have to do . . .

Write a book, star in the film of my life, have an Indian head massage, swim with dolphins, come to a definitive conclusion about an awful lot of things, all while being entirely invisible.

I certainly cannot die before finding my mum.

'*Chiudi quel cazzo di bocca.*'

The priest suggests I put a cork in it.

Secretly, I give him the Death Stare, even though you can't actually give it in secret – it's too powerful a weapon. And, by God, I wish I hadn't started it. I clock his irises – they are alive, every shade of black squirming within.

This is a very bad omen indeed. The genes responsible for the eye's development play a critical role in the formation of the frontal lobe, thus providing scientific proof that our eyes are the windows of the soul; and Father Massimo has the contraction furrows of a sociopath.

Other things about the priest:

He looks nothing like the man in the photo I'd found at the Biblioteca Città di Arezzo. In that snap, the priest is thirtyish, with a mop of blond hair and a cracking set of teeth. Now sixty-something, he's let himself go. Marlboro-ecru dentures. Bald as a balloon. A cassock that smells of yeast infections and communion wine. His long nails are packed firm with filth, very possibly with other people's DNA. And his wrinkles – they're likely to have been etched into his forehead and cheeks with a machete, each groove a nod to another man's expiry.

He takes a step back. Waves the gun at me. Gesticulates that I'm to sit on the front pew. I stumble to my knees. Pull myself up on to the wooden bench. But the priest becomes agitated once more. Urgently, he points the gun at my knees.

I look down at them. Back up at him. At the altar ahead.

A life-sized Virgin Mary gazes back, her blue stone head confusedly cocked . . .

You were brought up a Catholic, my child. You know the rules.

'*Si, si!*' I understand.

Standing back up, I drop on to a knee with gravitas. Then I cross myself solemnly. I mean it more than I've ever meant a genuflection before.

Catholic etiquette:

Never sit in a church's pew without genuflecting.

Do not enter a church without genuflecting.

When in a church, genuflect as often as you might check your mirrors while taking your driving test, just to be on the safe side. Overkill is impossible when it comes to adoring God.

8

Father Massimo nods, satisfied, does his own lacklustre sign of the Cross, then sits too close to me.

Our hips touch.

Silently, we stare at the stained glass ahead.

I'm very bad with silences. I was born with the need to fill them. I sincerely wish I hadn't been, because within seconds I'm nodding up at a stained-glass window and explaining, in simple English, the Fourth Station of the Cross to a man of the cloth.

'Jesus – he's on his way to be crucified. The people spit and shout. They are angry and hate him. He feels sad. He looks for his mother. She can't stop his pain. She can't do a thing to save Jesus. But just to *see* her – he knows she understands, that she cares. He's not alone – that helps Jesus a very lot.'

Father Massimo thinks I'm insane, I can tell.

I address Mother Mary instead. A more sympathetic counsellor, her wet marble eyes don't bother with my face; they scrutinise the cartilaginous pockets of my soul.

I tell her quietly, 'I'm looking for my mum too.'

For the smallest second, I think I've been rescued, because I hear an educated man. His Italo-American accent is exquisite, its cadence hypnotic and wise.

'When people disappear,' the priest says, 'it is better they stay that way.'

Quickly, I turn to face him. He is a snarl of pockmarks, scars and wrinkles, yet I hold his stare. 'Father, it is not.'

'Sometimes it is,' he grumbles.

'She's my mother.'

'So?'

Oedipus issues are extremely bad news in an aggressor.

'She has responsibilities.' I try to explain empathy to him. 'Not just to me – to her son; to our father.'

'You coming here – that won't help your family. The opposite.'

But I don't understand.

When Tommaso alluded to the priest's past, I'd imagined the Eradicator was, these days, a benevolent Rambo. A grand-fatherly renegade. Henry Fonda in *On Golden Pond*. Most of the cast of *Cocoon*.

I watch the pistol teeter on his bony knee. A Colt 45. They were first issued to US Marines in 1986. A hundred serrations dint the steel of this one.

'My search for my mother has hit a dead end. I met a guy in Rome, a friend who said you could help me.'

He squints. 'What guy?'

'His name is Tommaso Bellini.'

The gun clatters to the floor. Instantly, I yank my legs up and on to the pew. But his pistol doesn't spin in circles and shoot repeatedly at my shins. Neither does Father Massimo stoop to retrieve it.

Open-mouthed, he stares at me.

'Rocco's boy?'

I nod quickly.

There's always a small room off the church altar – a holy Green Room where priests nap between services. Father Massimo picks up the gun and wanders towards it.

It's my chance to escape.

This is the plan:

Sprint from this pew to the wooden doors of the stone church – it's a distance of twenty-two metres. On a good day, I'd do that in four seconds. On a day fuelled by abject terror, I'd knock half a second off. Next, I'll run down the hill path, swinging SSW into bracken and olive trees, dodging a route over boulders and goat shit. I'll sustain a fracture or two, but adrenalin will keep me anaesthetised. When, eventually, I tumble free into the village below, I'll steal a bike then cycle full pelt for 500 kilometres, all the way north to Portopiccolo, to find Tommaso bloody Bellini and demand why the fuck he suggested I meet with a sociopath.

I'll have to do all this while outrunning a bullet, of course. The one that's focused like a cruise missile at my head. Because if there's one thing the Eradicator can do, it's murder a moving target. Forty years ago, he recorded a kill from a distance of one and a half kilometres, using a sniper rifle. The bullet would have taken two seconds to hit. When Tommaso told me this story he'd put such a romantic slant on it.

The priest returns from the Green Room with a bottle of Communion wine. He gulps from its neck, patting his lips with a musty sleeve.

'Tell me about Rocco Bellini,' he says. 'Everything. I want the tiny details. Eye colour, hair, height. Are you his wife?'

'No,' I say sternly, because I don't know Rocco from Adam. 'I just said – I only know Tommaso.'

The priest sits on the steps to the altar and says, 'The beginning – we'll start there. Tell me how you met little Tommaso. Then we can discuss why he sent you to me, to your death.'

I talk at length. It's my go-to response and doesn't always do me any favours. In this instance, it's a godsend. While I blether, I retain a bit part on this mortal coil. Naturally, I keep a peripheral eye on handguns, but mostly I expose the unmitigated truth, give the priest the director's cut.

Because all the while I'm talking, I'm breathing. And all the while I'm breathing, I foresee a future – the one in which I hunt Tommaso Bellini down and ask him if this was a stitch-up.

Stag

Rome is best described as an ode to a lot of deep stuff; but most especially to the things man has learnt, and then forgotten, to do with metamorphic rock. There are triumphant acres of the stuff – laterally, vertically and earth-crustily. The sun herself scrutinises it from a new angle every day.

My mother would have explained . . .

It's actually the Pope who changes the light. Clever, huh? Always a new flavour. God can't take His eyes off the balls.

I sigh, because Rome certainly pulls you out of your arse. I've been here two weeks. My aim, to find Mum, while making a little cash along the way. As it happened, a Libyan client of mine suspected that his best friend had fled their homeland to join the Mafia. There was a lot to be intrigued about, so I suggested we hook up.

Our meeting place was to be the Colosseum's main entrance – in the absence of a partner in the shadows watching your back, choose assembly points where armed police patrol.

But Tarik Mohammad hadn't turned up. I gave him an hour, then bought a skip-the-line entrance ticket to use the toilets. Afterwards, I perused a building the size of a nano-quark (astronomically speaking), yet the arena for the deaths of 500,000 people and over a million wild animals.

'Bear, elephant, tiger hunts. Gladiatorial contests, executions . . .' A guide was shouting facts at his huddle of tourists.

'Family entertainment during the Flavian dynasty,' a woman had said – middle-class owner of three well-behaved children-tourists.

I agreed. 'It's the ultimate argument for the invention of the iPad.'

The crowd tittered, good-humouredly. But not the guide. I wasn't on his tour. Thankfully, an Italian guy on the other side of the huddle piped up, took the heat off me. 'That and Candy Crush.'

Twenty of us jostled to hang over a small stretch of railing to gawp into the pit of death below, so I was unable to see his face. Then the tour guide started giving me evils. Money is information, after all, so his gripe was legitimate. It's certainly not British to loiter within a five-metre radius of a person with a flagpole.

So I wriggled a route away from the railing while trying to get a look at the Candy Crush enthusiast. He was attempting to look at me too, but our heads had to dance around craniums, rucksacks and selfie sticks.

We did make eye contact eventually. Just for a second. And it was a very pleasant surprise. Not just because he was the manly type and was also so pretty he had a beauty spot on his cheek. But because my arm hair experienced an instant bout of erection.

I dawdled within earshot of an American tour guide after that, though I did spot the Candy Crush enthusiast three more times. He was always the size of my thumb, on the opposite side of the auditorium, or on a different level, which was frustrating. I wanted a comprehensive look at that face – there had to be something wrong with it.

Now, two weeks later, I can confirm there is not a thing I would change. Though I don't look straight at it. Not currently. I don't have to – I'm in the top two per cent of the population, optimal-peripheral-vision-wise.

We sit on the terrace of Hotel La Barcaccia.

Located at the top of the Spanish Steps, its rooftop bar offers one of Rome's most comprehensive views. You name it, I can point at it – St Peter's Basilica, the Pantheon, Hadrian's Mausoleum . . . the beautiful Candy Crush enthusiast, though that would be rude, what with him sitting less than five metres away, at another table.

For a while I refrain even from glancing in his direction. Instead, I place a graceful arm on the railing. Wait a few minutes before allowing myself a straight-out look at his face.

Yes. He is my favourite view yet.

Late twenties. Roman nose. Equally proportioned nostrils. Piercing eyes – a fusion of strident colour, most belonging to the green spectrum. Lashes – black and dense as tarantula fur. Slim, honest lips. A philtrum the size of a thumb print. The best bit – his smile. It shows the gums around his molars, which makes it warm and no-bullshit. He doesn't crack a grin frivolously, mind you, but when he does it makes my tummy concertina.

Look at me now. We simply occupy the same bar, yet I'm cloaked in goosebumps – which my mother would have said is a biochemical omen.

It reminds us of our primal need to procreate and make your mother some grandchildren!

No, she wouldn't have said that. That's me projecting.

A horrible secret: I no longer remember her voice, though I search for it now, just as I've done over the past two weeks, cocking an ear at Rome's obelisks and domes.

Instead, I hear his voice. He orders two Peronis.

His mother tongue is curt and perfunctory, I notice. Not like his English accent, which is empathetic and practised. His 'A's, for example, are pronounced at the back of his mouth and with an open throat.

Father. Arh.

I heard him speak English again on the second night our paths crossed. That night felt *especially* serendipitous . . .

It was two evenings ago. A Friday. I wandered around Piazza di Spagna, eating a pizza slice and swigging Montepulciano from my water pouch, filling the time before a dubbed episode of *Poirot* and bed.

He and two friends exited the Keats and Shelley Museum. I emitted an actual squeak when I saw him. Then counted his beauty spots – one by his ear, the one beneath his eye. And a third one on the back of his neck – a beautiful neck, as buffed as a yacht's deck.

I followed him up the Spanish Steps. The English chatter was achingly reassuring. I couldn't help but eavesdrop. The worst thing? They discussed Romantic literature, which I know quite a lot about. I had to stop myself butting in.

Then I'd become distracted, fleetingly, stopping mid-step to stare in at a hair salon. Rome does that to you – turns your head and makes you ditch your preceding thought. The space into which I now gawped was marble, igloo-white and vast. Middle-aged women were positioned in a large circle at grooming stations stocked with champagne and truffles. In the middle of them stood a grand piano. At its ivories sat a film-star-type in a tuxedo, playing something by Donizetti.

It was hard to decide if its decadence was harmless or obscene. So I turned my head to the side and mouthed, 'Wow,' at the person on the step above me.

The Candy Crush enthusiast nodded back. 'That is so fucked up,' he said.

I didn't mean to snigger, but I found myself admiring his own cut, the best I'd seen on a boy in a while. Floppily erect on top, a number two at the sides and back, a barbered beard.

Confused, his irises acquired a neon hue. I struggled to hold his gaze.

He and his friends then continued up towards Trinità dei

Monti church, which was on my way too. I stayed six steps behind, transfixed on his gait and gentle swagger. Was taken by surprise when, a few steps from the top, he turned resolutely to face me, allowing him a keen examination of my eyes, lips and neck. My heart knocked at my throat, reminding me who I was. But he didn't recognise me from the gossip magazines; he was recognising me as the girl at the Colosseum. It made me instinctively finger my collar bone.

'Tommaso!' The big, blond man hurried him along.

As though awoken from a trance, he saluted me goodbye, then became embarrassed by the gesture. I rescued his honour, did an enthusiastic scout's salute of my own. That was gratefully received – his smile was so sensational, my core muscles fainted.

While I held myself upright on the railings, he turned on his heels, taking the remaining steps two at a time, swinging a right on to the street above, leaving me in the throes of a crushing loss.

The following morning, I went back to Piazza di Spagna. It was just on the off chance, which is not stalking, because off chances are rarely productive. Anyway, the Roma Commune is a spit from the top. It had been a few days since I'd been there to nag the officials. Again, I demanded why there was no birth certificate for a Bambi Campanella, born on 29 September 1951, nor for any of her family? I reiterated facts. She was not a figment of my imagination. My brother and I have photographs and a trillion recollections.

Saturday was a lonely day. There was no point to me at all.

Tommaso catches me daydreaming at him. Were this a honeytrap, that would be considered a major blooper. You can never appear to have noticed them first – it's not alluring.

Lucky for me, I'm retired from all that.

I style it out. Pretend I'm having an all-consuming daydream. One where your eyes get progressively larger until you snap yourself out of it. Then I frown and say, 'Oh. Hello, again.'

'*Ciao.*' He nods, delighted. '*Again.*'

I am very much not supposed to be giving the old entrapment techniques an airing either. Yet I take a book from my bag – its job, to clarify I am definitely not here to see him.

The paperback I pull free is *The Hitchhiker's Guide to the Galaxy.* An excellent precursor to flirting proper. Boys love it. The reason being, it's both science fiction *and* comedy. I'll be brief . . .

Sci-fi addresses philosophical issues while engaging the mind in an abstract way, i.e. the way in which men deal with emotions best, i.e. not head on. Add a comedic slant and they're hooked, because laughter releases nervous energy in the exact same way as anger and fear – a giggle being a lovely adrenalin rush that peters out before it becomes a fight-or-flight situation.

That's a male-happiness fact.

As is the enjoyment derived from watching a woman light a cigarette like she's Greta Garbo. I blow smoke at Rome. Turn the page. Smile entirely to myself. Refuse to look up from my book for a good four minutes.

By which point, Tommaso has replaced his Ray-Bans with a clunky pair of grandad specs. They make me super-intrigued. As does the book he's pulled from his own bag – *A Pair of Blue Eyes.*

I add it to my reading list immediately. Thomas Hardy loved an ill-fated ending. I'm fascinated as to why a boy would bring him on a stag do.

Oh, yes, another thing I know. He's on a stag do. Always befriend the bellboy. They proffer a priceless commodity at five euros a pop: intelligence. He told me there are three of them in total – the big, blond Englishman, the small, bald Englishman and Tommaso. Though Tommaso has been staying in Rome, on and off, for the last few weeks on business. This evening is their last. Most excitingly, he confided that Tommaso could be currently found in the bar.

'Anything else?' A waitress makes me jump.

Smiling warmly, I confide, 'I'd kill for a lobster Fra Diavolo, but I'm on a diet.'

She couldn't give a monkey's arse so waits, pen poised, looking at Rome as though it's a cacophony of breezeblock.

As curtly as Tommaso, I order a Peroni. I also refuse to say thank you when it arrives, because Peroni tastes like soapy prosecco, yet a rule of seduction is thus – sup whatever the lover-to-be is supping. It helps with the process of subconscious coupling. Assuming the lover-to-be is not completely absorbed in highbrow literature. No matter, indifference is a potent aphrodisiac; it makes me feel deflated for different reasons to normal – and that's a glorious gust of fresh air.

It was this morning that I caught a break.

Rome doesn't sell cigarettes between midday and two on a Sunday. The only place you can get a packet is on Via Frattina. I popped there for some Marlboro Reds. Tommaso's big English friend was in the queue ahead. Strawberry-blond curls, meat on his muscles, a minimal melanin count. When he lumbered back to the Hotel La Barcaccia, he reminded me of an introspective polar bear; one who, in an ideal world, would give very sincere hugs. He didn't see me following him; his sun-bitten nose was buried in his mobile.

He's about to see me now, though . . .

I watch the Polar Bear enter the rooftop bar and sit beside Tommaso. Taking the second beer, he starts to speak conspiratorially to his friend, stopping mid-sentence to look around, because Tommaso isn't listening to him.

My giggle peters out when the Polar Bear spots me.

Without chivalry or a smile, he stares. Forgets to look away when stabbing olives, sucking their stones of flesh, then lighting his cigarette, blowing fat smoke rings.

I quickly cross my legs towards the view and tighten the pashmina around my neck. Which is the opposite of what should happen when you're flirting. The ultimate aim is to slip outer layers off, revealing clothing that's peach-coloured, the shade that best replicates the tone of pubescent labia; it suggests youth and the promise of propagation. Men don't realise it, but they are innately drawn to the connotations of the colour peach.

I re-open my book and gaze at a blur of words, because the Polar Bear might be twigging who I am.

A not-very-secret secret. Three months ago, I was in the newspapers. All of them. The biggest downside: when people recognise me they demand answers regarding the location of my moral compass.

I have a big and very entrenched one. I want to punch them in the jugular. *I was an entrapment specialist, yes. But I was also stitched up.*

Opposite me, a wrought-iron chair scrapes. I look up, warily, half expecting the English guy to be settling in for some finger-pointing.

It's Tommaso, however, who pulls the seat free.

The low sun makes his white jumper as luminous as tin foil. Yet I refuse to slip my sunglasses from head to nose. Placing a hand over my eyes, I watch him sit down in glorious Technicolor. Pushing up his sleeves, he places two hirsute forearms on the bistro table and smiles. I wish he wouldn't.

'May I sit down?' he asks.

'You just did,' I squeak.

'I always get that the wrong way round. Can I buy you a drink to make up for it?'

A bottle of Prosecco and two flutes arrive before I'm able to respond, leaving Tommaso looking very pleased with himself. 'I saw someone do that once,' he confides. 'I've been dying to try it out.'

We watch the Polar Bear tramp out of the bar.

Tommaso shakes his head at his friend. 'He's in trouble.'

'What's he done?'

'He forgot to tell his wife he was going on holiday.'

'That's rude,' I say. 'I hope you forewarned yours.'

He wiggles a naked fourth finger, then fills a glass with the panache of a sommelier.

Watching the bubbles effervesce sends a fast fizz up my vertebral column and into the nape of my neck. That's called Autonomous Sensory Meridian Response. It's when your internal reward system goes into overdrive.

Tommaso waits for me to take a sip of the Prosecco, then stands up, leans across the table and kisses me on both cheeks. Sitting back down and crossing his legs, he says, 'Nice to meet you. I'm Tom.'

I give him my diagnosis. 'You are dyslexic, socially.'

'I'm not,' he says firmly. 'It's you. You confuse me.'

'Already? That's worrying.'

'Exactly.' He pats the table, because I've proved his point. Then he leans forward, to ask quietly. 'You feel it too, right?'

I also lean forwards. 'Feel what?'

He shows me a forearm. It plays host to a swarm of goosebumps.

'Your body hair is very stiff,' I agree.

'It's evidence,' he whispers. 'Of our chemistry.'

Tommaso is one million per cent right. It's called piloerection. In the olden days, when man was eighty per cent hair, getting goosebumps made them appear bigger and scarier to enemies; and stronger and sexier to women. When peacocks do it, it's called nuptial plumage. I hide mine under the table.

'Do you have a name?' he asks, meaningfully.

I mirror his tone. 'Florence. After the urban settlement, not the nurse.'

'Hmmm.' He thinks about this. 'It's long, but ironic. I like it.'

'Close friends call me Flo.'

'Are you staying here at the hotel?'

I shake my head. 'At a guesthouse off Via Sistina. This view is a treat before I leave.' I point at Rome's rooftops and realise a truth. 'It's time to move on.'

His eyes tease me. 'Are you on the run?'

'I'm more like the Littlest Hobo.' I flap a hand, because he wouldn't understand. 'It's a children's programme from the eighties about an altruistic mongrel with wanderlust.' His smile is uninhibited. I admire the pink gum around his back teeth. Then come clean, sort of. 'It's more of a gap month. Next stop, catching up with family.'

'You're Italian?' he asks.

'Half and half.'

'A gap month.' He nods approvingly. 'I'll come too.'

I laugh, then shake my head, because I'm on a very serious mission. 'You have to do a gap month on your own. It's the law.'

He waves a wounded hand. 'I'm too busy, anyway. Though I do have a spare twenty minutes this evening?'

I grin. 'I can give you ten minutes, tops.'

'Done. I'll slot you in.'

We shake hands, though, secretly, I'd like to inhale the inside of his wrist. To stroke a buffed nail. To study his palm – his heart line, girdle of Venus and fate line – because when you're this attracted to someone, you want to know them on very tenuous levels.

'So, what's your plan? It'll have to be snappy,' I say.

'You're very high maintenance,' he tells me. 'It may involve food.'

'In ten minutes?'

Tommaso shows me his piloerection again. 'Or maybe we should just leave our evening to the hands of fate.'

I chink his glass with mine and enjoy a moment of unbridled contentment, because tonight I am going on a date.

Tommaso, on the other hand, becomes business-like. Pulls a vibrating phone from his pocket. Holds it with a straight arm; looks at it from a distance; eventually gives in, putting the fat glasses back on to his nose.

'Candy Crush alert?' I ask. 'In my opinion, phone apps are an under-discussed arm of gambling. They use the same psychological tactic as slot machines, only in a format that's the size of your palm. That's insidious, but clever.'

He ignores me to squint down at a text message, which reminds me of my own responsibilities. I search for my mobile. It's not in my bag. I glance at my watch – it's just gone four.

'I've left my phone in my room,' I tell Tommaso. 'I have to get back for a phone call.'

It's one I have every afternoon. Under no circumstances can I miss it.

I gather my things. Tommaso stands up, preoccupied. 'Yes, no problem. I'll collect you at seven. What's the name of your hotel?'

My guesthouse is a dump. 'How about I meet you on the Spanish Steps? Outside the hair salon.'

As I leave the bar, I check that the Polar Bear is not around, then sneak a backwards peek; my hope, to catch Tommaso admiring the way I walk, because I am rocking the Gliggle, the most amatory walk known to mankind.

But Tommaso stares only at his phone, his brow scrunched.

I don't take it personally. I lone-tango the length of Via Sistina, because enterprise is key in the propagation of love, and I have been the commandant of my own fate.

Operation Kiss Goodnight is firmly off the ground.

My room is on the ground floor, next to a perpetually banging fire exit. The view from my window: a back alley and commercial rubbish bins.

I throw my bag on to the unmade bed. Do a quick

inspection of the room. Check that nothing has moved, that no one has broken in, bugged the place and/or taken a peek at my laptop, hidden beneath the mattress.

Everything is as I left it. That shouldn't disappoint me, but it does a bit.

Things were very different a year ago. I rented a mansion flat in London's West End. There was a pillowcase full of cash, a wardrobe of designer dresses, and cool surveillance equipment; a reliable supply of sleeping tablets and marijuana; a genuine moment of kinship with an A-lister. The absolute cherry on the cake: my brother and I were professional partners, and *very* tight.

Then I got myself in the papers for all the wrong reasons.

Under my pillowcase is a pay-as-you-go. I tug it free, yet there are no missed calls. None whatsoever. That pisses me off.

Yes, my brother is twenty-nine, but I've always looked after him. Well, I did before he fell in love with an undersized osteopath and I became superfluous to his needs. He was never late calling when he was single.

His name flashes up eventually. Thirty-eight minutes late. I let it ring a lot of times before punching a finger at Accept.

'Hello?' I say.

'May I speak to my sister, please?' my brother asks politely.

His voice is deeply Dorset. Our time in London failed to strip him of his habit of over-pronouncing his 'r's and 't's, and I'm pleased for it.

'And who is your sister?' I ask.

'You, Flo.'

'And who shall I say is speaking?'

'Michael Love, your brother.'

'What's the password?'

I haven't given him a password, but he's good for a challenge.

'Pork chop!' he shouts.

'Bingo.' I smile, because what's not to love? There's neither rhyme nor reason – but we go through the password fiasco a lot. Ultimately, it reminds us we have a subliminal connection. That's how I interpret it, anyway.

I stop being antsy, put him on speakerphone, sit at a wobbly dressing table and clean my ears with a baby wipe. 'I've missed you loads today, Michael.'

'I know.'

'You don't.'

'I do.'

I look at the phone beside me. 'You're not in my head.'

'I might as well be. You tell me every day.'

There's no arguing with that. Know what the most wonderful thing ever would be? If just once he told me he missed me back. Which he might have done a year ago, when he wasn't engaged to a dwarf.

'Tell me all your news,' I demand.

'OK. We're playing.'

'We?'

'Trivial Pursuits.'

'What?'

'Me, Dad and Sébastien. And Annie.'

Jealousy is vain and short-sighted. I throw the wipe viciously in the direction of the bin. 'Nobody was having a medical emergency then? You're very late calling. Who's Annie?'

He ignores me to whisper urgently, 'Have you found Mum yet?'

Nearly 2,000 kilometres between us, yet the weight of his disappointment folds me in half. I put a cheek on the dressing table and whisper at the phone. 'No, not yet. But I feel like I'm getting close.'

'How close?'

'Big-time close.'

'How big-time?'

'Like, seven out of ten.'

He gasps. 'That's almost eighty per cent.'

'Which means things are on a trajectory, so there's no need to worry. If she's here, I will find her.' I throw in a sweetener. 'Fingers crossed, I might even bring her to the wedding.'

I will not. I'm a horrible liar.

Two weeks in Italy, and I can't find any background information on her. Never mind an address for Auntie Carina, her sister, who admittedly we never met but who always sent us birthday presents.

My conclusion so far: our mother never existed.

But that's ridiculous. I remember her. So does Michael. She had long nails; their purpose, to tickle us to sleep. She was always preened and glamorously scented; after her passing I spent hours in her wardrobe, enveloped in clothes that smelt of her still, and watching detective shows – the ones from the seventies. That was Mum's favourite pastime. 'The oldies are the goodies,' she'd confide in me, daily. Then I hit eight, Mum died and Dad told us she'd committed suicide. That steals a girl's childhood. You start thinking about last breaths. Everybody else's, but your own especially. Night panics become par for the course.

So, no, I shan't bother Michael with the specifics of my search for her. He'll worry that Mum *is* actually dead, like the rest of the world, like our father, and the police, and the whole British judicial system.

'Next step, Monte San Savino – home of the Campanellas.' I tell Michael my plans, then change the subject. 'How's work?'

'I've got a gig next week.'

'No way?!'

'Way.'

'What's the role?'

'A giraffe for Kia-Ora.'

'On the telly?'

'At Christchurch train station. I'm giving out free drinks. I've got a machine on my back.'

I am not happy. Not one little bit.

Maeve Rivers had promised to keep him in acting work. That had been the deal when I gave her newspaper my exclusive last year. Michael's no Benedict Cumberbatch, but he's too good to play a giraffe.

'Do not get typecast,' I tell my brother.

'I won't.'

'You will. You're six feet two.'

'It's a good job I like giraffes, then.' I can hear the smile on his face. He's being cute. 'They sleep standing up.'

People with Asperger's struggle with humour. But Michael doesn't, not always. The educational psychologists can stick their labels up their arses.

Eagerly, I arm him with giraffe facts. 'If anyone asks, *Giraffa Camelopardalis* is its Latin name.'

'I know,' he says.

'No, you don't. It translates as "fast-walking camel marked like a leopard". And necking is not snogging – it's when they hit necks.'

'And their tongues are half a metre long.'

I frown. 'Forty-two centimetres is usually the top whack.'

'They've adapted to forage in trees.'

I stop him right there. 'Who's been telling you stuff?'

'Me.' He sounds hurt. 'I do my own prep.'

'Really?' I am completely proud.

'The key is preparation.' He even goes on to quote *me*: 'Flo, if I've got six hours to chop down a tree, I'll most likely spend the first four hours making my axe sharp. Give or take.'

Well, it wasn't me who said it first, it was Abraham Lincoln, but I was the one who brought it to Michael's attention. How I long to pinch his cheeks.

Until he blindsides me: 'Dad wants to talk to you.'

'Now?'

'Yes.'

'On the phone?'

I can hear Michael thinking about this. 'Yes.'

I put the mobile to my ear. 'I'm not ready.'

My father refused to help me when I told him I was coming to Italy. He said I was to leave it alone. He forbade me to search for Mum.

But Michael's busy shouting into the distance, 'Dad! Florence wants to talk to you.'

'I don't! No!' My heart beats hard at its walls.

Michael saves the day. 'I'll just get him,' he says, replacing the handset his end, cutting me dead.

I don't wait for him to ring back. I power off my phone, hide it under the Guest Information folder, examine my hair in the mirror and poke volume into its roots.

My new hair still makes me do a double-take. Once a ribbon of chocolate brown, it now entertains a bunch of new shades: honeys, bronzes and caramels. And although I've kept the length, I now own a 1970s fringe.

Michael's fiancé, Sébastien, did it for me. 'I need to disappear in plain view,' I told him. He was once a hairdresser, before retraining to fix spinal injuries, so was thrilled at the opportunity to brush off his scissor holster, then lacked all modesty when complimenting his handiwork.

'You look like Farrah Fawcett, the sexiest Charlie's Angel,' he'd said.

That was factually incorrect. I watched all the reruns with Mum and several times since. Farrah was a luminous sand-pebble blonde, with flicks so big her hair became an entity in its own right. She was also second in the looks department to Jaclyn Smith, who was astonishingly beautiful, and a dead ringer for my mum.

I tug angrily at the fringe. Truth be told, I miss my forehead.

Other things I miss: my dad. Of course, my dad. But we have non-conducive agendas right now.

The next two hours are spent getting ready. Slowly.

It's a sort of therapy. Luxuriating in the thought of someone being close enough to notice the details – yes, very especially, I concentrate on them. Because, were I in London, I'd simply choose an outfit that educes testicular-ache. But this is Roma. It may be October and a pleasant twenty-two degrees C, but Italian townies love a puffer jacket. Flesh, this close to Christmas, is considered desperate.

With this in mind, I plan to wear the following . . .

Joico Luxe Root Lift Volumising Hair Foam. Its scent is sweet and nostalgic, like fruit salad Chewits. A pair of diamond studs, their job to glitter gently, bringing attention to my earlobes and healthy lymph nodes. A lot of make-up, to give me a nude and natural glow. Calf-length, mid-heel boots over my skinny jeans, to remind Tommaso I have legs. An assimilatory navy jacket, spruced up with a scarf. Peach-coloured, of course, because old habits are often the best.

The Spice Angels

I am the protagonist. My entrance must be mesmeric. Once I spot Tommaso waiting handsomely outside the hairdresser's, I ascend the Spanish Steps, oozing allure.

My efforts are wasted, however. Tommaso fails to focus on me until I arrive on his stair.

'Have you tried contact lenses?' I suggest.

'Why's that?' He admires my mouth.

'Because you're blind.'

'I can see you.'

'How many fingers am I holding up?'

'Eighteen.' I think he's going to kiss my mouth; instead he pecks one centimetre either side of its corners. 'You smell edible.'

'Yes,' I say, because so does he. Tom Ford Neroli Portofino. That's a fiver a squirt. I admire his outfit – expensive jeans, brown leather brogues, a navy, wool peacoat. 'Your beard tickles.' I nod.

'So I've been told.'

We then re-descend the steps in silence, because the briefest glance in each other's direction makes us giggle. When we reach the plaza below, I have to be firm.

'Stop it!'

'Stop what?'

'Laughing at me with your eyeballs.'

'It's my natural look.'

I wave him away. 'It's no good. Tell me a sad story or something.'

He obliges, tells one to a passing Chinese woman. 'I've

dumped the boys for this hysterical woman.' Remembering something, he points at my midriff. 'Are you still on a diet?'

That stops me laughing. I hold in a hip. 'Why?'

'I know a place. It does lobster Fra Diavolo.'

'Is it a good one?' I ask, excited.

'Florence, after the urban settlement, not the nurse.' He puts his hands on my shoulders to ensure I am completely still. 'The fresh bucatini is exquisite. You can taste every ingredient in the sauce – San Marzano tomatoes, brandy, kosher salt, the lobster pot, its rope mesh and timber frame . . .'

'Are you a chef or something?'

'Chef, waiter and bottle-washer,' he admits.

That surprises me.

He explains. 'My career path was a done deal. I work at my dad's place.'

Beleaguered, I sigh. 'My dad bought me a bloody post office.'

That makes him laugh. 'At least food is sexy.'

'Thank you,' I say triumphantly.

Tommaso invites me to continue walking.

'So where's the family restaurant?' I ask.

'In the north of Italy. Sistiana Portopiccolo – that's close to Trieste. Visit me, if you're passing through.'

'It's a deal.'

'And where should I come to buy stamps in England – if I want to buy them from you?'

'An unknown village in Dorset.' I point back in time. 'I've done my stretch there, though. I'm going to retrain.'

'To be what?'

'An expert in something.'

Tommaso thinks I mourn missed opportunities. In fact, specialising in just one area would be a huge relief. Out of necessity, the finest PIs are first rate in a lot of disciplines – social anthropology, physical geography, kinesics, martial arts, genealogy, marriage guidance, biochemistry and the international legal system, to name a few. It's a shame I can't tell Tommaso what I really do. Everybody loves a private detective, especially a girl one; it makes you very fascinating. People ask more questions than is socially polite. Then they Google you. Which is nice because, up until a few months ago, they'd have found not a sausage.

'I'm thinking of becoming a criminal psychologist,' I tell him.

'That's cool.'

I nod, because it is. 'What about you, if you could do anything?'

'A writer,' he tells me. 'I've written some short pieces.'

I clap. 'Can I read something?'

'How's your Slovenian?'

'Rusty to non-existent.'

'Then, no,' he says.

'Slovenian?' I double-check.

'Like you, I'm half and half. Now, I have to concentrate on directions.'

I plan to Google 'Slovenian people' as soon as I get back to my room, because I'm clueless as to what makes them physiologically unique. Spying on Tommaso's profile now, he looks squarely Roman. He even holds his map with a good splodge of gladiatorial intensity – a map which, incidentally, I long to snatch from him. My spatial awareness is second to none. At the very least, I'd like to teach him how to orient the map in his hands. He's holding it all wrong. Yet patronising a lover eleven minutes into a first date is not cool.

We arrive unexpectedly on the boulevard that runs alongside the River Tiber.

'Oh,' says Tommaso, confused.

'I love a detour.' I pat his arm, then run across the road to hang over the side of a fat wall and gaze at the Tiber below.

It's alive with light, Hadrian's Mausoleum deconstructing in the water's reflection. We look up and admire the real thing – it's on the opposite bank of the river, just a few hundred metres to our left.

'When I die, I'd like a mausoleum,' I confide.

'I always say exactly that.' He looks at me like I'm the only other one of him. 'Especially when I'm in Paris.'

'They do a good graveyard tour – Jim Morrison, Edith Piaf, Napoleon.'

'The French know how to never let go.'

'And the Italians.' I tip my chin up at Hadrian's architectural ode to himself. 'I'm very Italian in that respect.'

When Tommaso takes my hand, his grip speaks volumes. For this one night, I am his and unfeasibly precious.

Like proper grown-ups on a city break, we continue along the boulevard that skirts the Tiber towards Castel Sant'Angelo, Tommaso having decided we must see it close up. To do so, we cross the Bridge of Angels – a marble crossing flanked by ten giant seraphs on marble parapets, each holding an instrument of the Passion.

Hadrian's ego fact: it knew no bounds. To get to his resting place, you must first replicate Christ's walk along the Via Dolorosa in Jerusalem.

Tommaso tells me who each angel is as we pass.

'That's Sporty Angel,' he says, pointing to one holding a stone column. 'She's very strong.' The next statue has a whip. 'Also known as Scary Angel. And this one we call the Crown-of-Thorns Angel.'

'I don't remember her?'

He nods. 'She was alternative.'

Indeed, tonight she is the majestic backdrop to a trio of buskers. Beneath her feet, they perform a flamenco version of the theme song to *Rocky*, while Tommaso translates the inscription on her plinth.

'"The thorn is fastened upon me".'

And so we find ourselves imagining Jesus's tortuous journey to crucifixion while humming along to the band.

Dada-daa, Dada-daaaa,
Dada-da, Dada daaaa,
Da Da Da Da Da Da-daaah, Daaah Daaah . . .

We don't get to see all the angels, though, or listen to the full rendition of 'Gonna Fly Now', because Tommaso remembers the purpose of our evening. Guides me back the way we came, to cross back over the boulevard and meander through a maze of narrow streets and alleys.

'We're going back to the Spanish Steps,' I try to explain.

But he shakes his head. I'm not sure why, because we are. Nonetheless, I follow him for a good ten minutes more, awarding him a hearty palm-clap when we arrive at our destination.

Piazza Montevecchio.

It's less of a square, more a confluence of alleys. The small restaurant is the piazza's only establishment. The rest of the walls belong to baroque apartment blocks and a church so skinny you couldn't lie flat in it.

Breathtakingly pretty, the secret space is lit only by the candles that flicker on chequered cloths. The restaurant's tables snuggle beneath an iron awning threaded with ivy and fairy lights. It's like an ornamental birdcage. At its door, an old woman mans a shot of grappa, a full ashtray and a receipt spike.

When we first approach, she doesn't recognise Tommaso. But he bends down, whispers soft Italian. Soon enough, she is displaying her naked gums, welcoming us as though we're blood. The woman doesn't speak English, yet I establish the gist of the conversation from her hand gestures.

The last time she saw Tommaso, he was very small. She shows me exactly how tall he was – I deduce he was six at the time. Nowadays, however, he is loftier. She reaches up to show me how tall, though the curvature of the spine means she's a few centimetres out. Twisting his face around, she even shows how handsome he's become.

'*È identico a Rocco. Assomigli a tuo padre!*'

I nod encouragingly, then sneak a hand into my bag. I turn my mobile back on.

Please note. I do not want to talk to my dad. Not in a month of Sundays. But I do want him to chase me. I'm his daughter, it's my birthright.

Four missed calls.

None, however, is from Dad. *All* are from the Poet. Real name, Noah Steensen. Best described as an ex-lover, border-line stalker and the son of my mother's suicide buddy.

I'm so not in the mood.

When the toothless woman disappears inside, Tommaso nods. 'Beautiful, huh?'

I drop the phone back into my bag and wink. 'She's not my type.'

'Well, I happen to like older women.'

On the off chance he is alluding to me, I change the subject. 'And what is the purpose of your visit to Rome?'

'Pleasure. My friend is getting married. Tonight is our last night celebrating his freedom.'

'And I've stolen you away.'

'I told them I'd be quick. Ten minutes, tops,' he winks.

I smile. 'Did you go to uni together?'

'Royal Holloway.'

'Surrey?'

He nods. 'We were known as the Three Stooges. I have no idea why, but we liked it.'

That prompts a twang of envy. Reminds me of the type of friendship that has always given me a wide berth, the type so tight you are universally compared to an iconic threesome. Or a twosome – that would've done me.

Failing that, an iconic onesome.

A waiter arrives. Seventeen. He sports a bum-fluff goatee and a PVC menu.

I should be ashamed that my grasp of Italian is so pitiable. But my mum didn't speak it much; it made her melancholic. When she disappeared, I refused even to listen to it; it left me brimful of self-pity. So I get by using a different language. Non-verbal communication. The young waiter enunciates passionately, pointing at his menu. At a guess, he explains ingredients and cooking methods. And Tommaso appears riveted, asks question after question, while I appreciate his profile. He's achingly well proportioned. I wonder whether he'd look too girly without the beard. That makes me unexpectedly dejected, the fact that I'll never know.

Tomorrow, Tommaso will be returning north.

He confirms the finality of us. 'We only have tonight, so I've ordered the works.'

I nod proactively, because I intend on sharing our evening with nobody else. Not even Noah Steensen, regardless of the promises I made before I left England.

Noah Steensen.

Remembering him makes my shoulders slump. Blindly, I dig a hand at my bag. Power my phone off.

The red wine and the atmosphere go straight to our heads. We jabber incessantly.

'My father came to Rome on business,' he tells me. 'Sometimes he'd bring me too. We'd eat here. Gina would look after me. I was only small.' He shouts over to the old woman. '*Quanti anni avevo quando mi portava?*'

'*Sei, sette.*'

'Seven,' he tells me.

'Is Rocco your dad?'

His nod is a little exhausted.

'I take it you don't want to take over his restaurant?'

'Do you want the post office?'

'Good God, no. And I won't do it.'

His frown is disapproving.

'What?' I demand.

'We have different loyalties.'

I'm offended by that. But rather than argue, I redeem myself. 'Family means everything to me too. That's why I'm here, remember? Looking for someone.'

He tops up my glass, waits for me to continue, because, no, I hadn't said that finding missing people was the purpose of my visit.

'I'm looking for my whole Italian family actually.'

'Wow,' he says. 'Do they know you exist?'

'Yes. Though I never got to meet them.' I take a deep breath. 'My mother died when I was little.'

'That's horrible.' He touches my hand.

'It's fine.'

'Don't be ridiculous. Losing a mother is never fine.'

For thirty seconds, I stow a tear in the corner of my eye. Until Tommaso flicks it free. 'What information do you have about your family in Italy?'

'She had one sister. My mother told me she'd been born in Rome. The family then moved to Monte San Savino when she was three.'

'Your mother's name?'

'Bambi Campanella.' I say this twice. The first time, my voice fails me.

'Her real name?'

'Bambi Love. She married my dad, George Love, from England.'

'No, what was her birth name – when she was here in Italy?'

I repeat it slowly. 'Bambi Campanella. She was one of the

36

original Campanellas that hail from Monte San Savino in Tuscany.'

He breaks it to me gently. 'Bambi just means "little girl".'

'That's not my mother's fault.' I frown. 'And it happened to fucking suit her.'

He puts a finger in the air. I'm apparently to get off my high horse. 'Any middle names?'

'No.'

'Her Confirmation name?'

Tommaso misjudges my silence. 'It's the sealing of the covenant created in Holy Baptism.'

'I know what it is. I'm one too.'

I don't know why I perform a sign of the cross. Yes, I do – to prove my Catholicism. It's also reassuring, being religious. Death is so cruel it has the potential to send you off the rails. So my clan pretends your dead loved ones wait in a parallel dimension. As a further USP, you get to choose an extra name while you're on earth – any one you like, within biblical reason. What fourteen year old would miss the opportunity to reinvent themselves?

Answer: none.

Etymology fact: Mum had not a single religious name – not her first, middle or last. Campanella means 'bluebell', so her name in full translates as 'young female bluebell'.

That is so utterly pretty, I refused to notice it is also quite aloof.

I've been noticing it over the last two weeks, though. When every other official has asked the same question.

My response to Tommaso's question is highly unusual. The secrecy surrounding my stay in Italy has been a matter of necessity. If Mum disappeared for our safety – mine and Michael's – she'd be bat-shit mad. Yet I decide to tell him some truths.

Though, first, I cover my back.

'Swear on the Bible that you won't tell a soul.' It's childish, I hear it, but I need to trust him.

'I'll give you something better, my word – Tommaso Bellini's word.' The palm he places on his breast is grave. I believe him implicitly.

The following revelation feels like an exorcism.

'I don't believe she's dead.'

His eyes grow wide. 'Go on.'

This I say very quietly: 'I got a birthday card. No name. But it was in her writing.'

'Have you told anyone?'

'My dad. He said it wasn't her writing. He's lying. My mum's car was found in a clearing close to our home. There was a dead man in the passenger seat. But no sign of my mother.'

'Your mother had definitely been in the car?' asks Tommaso.

'Definitely.'

'How do you know?'

This is how I know.

When I close my eyes, I see her car-seat cushion on the driver's seat – it was brown with mustard swirls.

Drawing imaginary circles on the chequered table cloth, I give Tom more concrete proof.

'She put little posters on the car windows – so the person who found the car didn't open the doors and get poisoned too.' I look up from my swirls. 'It was her writing. The same as on the card.'

'When was this?'

'1988.'

It feels like twenty minutes ago. Vividly, I see that dented brown cushion, the home-made warning notices, a slumped Caucasian male, his fat face using the dashboard as a pillow.

The reality.

I was eight and didn't see a thing – not the car, not the clearing, not the subsequent media footage. Dad kept us cosseted. Neurotically so. Still, he refuses to talk about it. And as a result, my memories, dreams and imaginings have become jumbled, yet so robust I forget sometimes that I wasn't there. In my head I stood as close as the Murder Investigation Team.

'The dead man?'

Roughly, I rub my mustard-coloured circles away. 'My dad's brother. He had a penchant for the pre-pubescent.'

'Whoa.' Tommaso shows me a palm. 'Your uncle?'

I look at him defiantly. 'If Mum hadn't killed him, I would have done.'

Drawing the air into his lungs slowly, he sums up like a brief the facts as presented so far.

'*Bambi of the Bluebells* murdered a paedophile, then pretended to be dead too, returning secretly to Italy to be reunited with the other Campanellas of Monte San Savino in Tuscany.'

'And to repent.' I say it weakly, because she didn't even have a Confirmation name.

Tommaso shakes his head sadly. 'That's very shipshape.'

'It's not. It's very complicated indeed. Somebody helped her. My dad's too keen for me to leave it alone. No sane man gives up on his wife almost immediately. Not when there was no body. The human condition is to dangle from the most tenuous threads of hope.'

Tommaso places a protective hand on mine.

'Did the police know it was your uncle?'

'They thought it was someone else.'

'He was *definitely* the dead man?'

'Yes,' I say firmly.

'How do you know?'

This is how I know Uncle Fergus was *definitely* the dead man in the car.

In 1988, he stopped existing. He did not apply for a credit card, rent or own a home or pay taxes. He has a roll call of

County Court Judgements pending from the same period of time – a period during which my mum and Noah's entire family disappeared.

Yet the dead man was publicly named as Eric Steensen: Noah's father. In reality, Eric had skipped off to a new life, was alive and kicking up until this time last year.

Tom breaks it to me gently. 'It sounds like a cover-up.'

No shit, Sherlock. I look at him, disappointed. Yet the fact remains: I'm only just starting to believe it myself.

'I can't find *any* information on her or her family. Not in England, and now not in Italy. I've tried the White Pages, the Land Registry, the electoral rolls – you name it. She told me she was born in Rome, but there's no paperwork. I don't know where to go next.'

'To Monte San Savino,' Tommaso urges me. 'The commune there can carry out checks. Your family will have registered their move there.'

'And if there's no record of her there? What then?'

'Hire a private detective?'

'No,' I tell him flatly.

'Or maybe, you do nothing.'

I frown. 'Would you do nothing?'

'I'd listen to my father. He is protecting his family. You should pay yours more respect.'

I look him straight in the eye. 'Are you scared of yours or something?'

He removes his hand from mine. Turns to help the waiter squeeze five dishes on to our table. Comes to a firm conclusion. 'If there are no records in Monte San Savino, Florence, I would suggest that your mother's name, as presented to you, was fake.'

My expression suggests he's absurd. The PI in me comes to another conclusion – it's the only option that makes sense.

*

Tommaso insists on feeding me mouthfuls of fried ravioli, ricotta crostini, artichoke and tomato panzanella, Parma ham, gorgonzola, and sage and pumpkin risotto.

I've eaten nothing all day, so forget to talk. I groan instead. Use my eyeballs to communicate flavour sensations. Three more courses follow. By the time our espressos arrive, we are bloated and merry enough to rest our ankles in a comfortable tangle.

Tommaso nods at me purposefully, but says nothing.

'What?' I gently kick his shin.

He leans forwards. 'I know someone. Someone who knows things.'

'What things?'

Tommaso recites his own name. 'Tommaso Carlo Massimo Bellini. Tommaso after my paternal grandfather. Carlo after my maternal grandfather. Massimo after my godfather. And Bellini after my father.'

'You sound like Russell Crowe in *Gladiator*.'

He puts a finger on my nose. I am to shut up. Obediently, I suck my lips in.

'Massimo is a secret name. You'll not find it on my birth certificate.'

I'm a little lost, so Tommaso sits back, folds his arms and tells me a story.

'Fifty years ago, it was normal for priests to cooperate with the local strongmen. The Mafiosi provided rough justice and protection for the townsfolk in return for their subservience. Some boys would become priests; others, Mafiosi. Sometimes they became both.' He shrugs. 'This was the way of the world back then.'

'That's heavy,' I say.

'Yes, it is. Then you had Father Massimo. He was a wild card. He encouraged children in from the streets. Swapped their toy guns for footballs. Helped them with their homework.

Taught them the Catechism. Showed them there was a world apart from murder and fear. His impact was extraordinary. Dangerously positive. The mafia bosses couldn't allow it any longer.'

'What happened to him?' I demand.

'There was a gunfight. Twenty meatheads turned up. It was to be a message to other priests, should Father Massimo's philosophy take off. Trouble is, they hadn't bargained for my godfather being such a practised shot. The Eradicator, they called him after the shoot-out. He took out three blockheads from his parapet. And a sniper from the church's spire. Rumour has it, it took two seconds for the bullet to hit.'

I bang the table, because I like the sound of the Eradicator very much. Then I worry that Tommaso's got the wrong end of the stick. 'I don't need a hit-man, Tommaso.'

This makes him laugh. 'He's long retired. Though there's a price on his head. Mafia grudges never die. Who do you think it is that protects his arse now?'

'The police,' I state.

He doesn't say yes or no. Just tells me, 'Massimo will have unique lines of inquiry.'

I am beyond excited. I also want to tell him off for being so trusting. But mostly to thank him solemnly for sharing the story of his godfather with me. There's no greater gift than having somebody's most personal data bestowed upon you.

'One day, Florence, I will take you,' he whispers.

I can't hide my disappointment, because that sounds non-committal. To prove his intentions, he reminds me of things. 'My middle name is confidential. There are three people in the world who are privy to that information.'

His secret is safe. 'There are four people now. But why tell *me*?'

He shrugs. 'You give me goosebumps.' To prove it, he awards me his arm. I rub against the pelt. He watches my

42

face as I do it. Then pulls the arm away impatiently, because his phone vibrates in his pocket.

'Excuse me, I have to take this.' He sighs, standing up. Before answering it, he issues a warning: 'Truths don't always make you happy, Florence Love.'

'The truth is the only thing I seem able to get my head around,' I say back, but Tommaso is already leaving the birdcage, talking industriously into his handset.

I watch the back of his neck. Its mahogany sheen. Its symmetrical nape and hairline. The beauty spots – I feel especially possessive of them. When he wanders out of view, I even find myself doing a secret sign of the cross; just in case there is a God and He had anything to do with me meeting Tommaso Bellini.

Tommaso doesn't return.

I hunt for him. Jog around the squares, the surrounding roads and alleys. I return to speak gesticulatory Italian with the toothless woman. She's seen neither hide nor hair of him since he wandered away to take his call. I offer her payment for our food, but she looks appalled, so I pat her firmly on the back then carry out a sweep of adjacent streets.

It's futile. There's only one of me.

While I search, I make excuses for him. His eyesight is poor. He's hopeless with a map. He's well oiled. Maybe he'll eventually return, embarrassed, to the roof bar. Organise a nightcap by way of apology. Followed by that kiss goodnight, just as I've mapped out in my mind.

That puts a spring in my step.

But the bellboy at the Barruchia shakes his head resolutely. Tommaso has not returned – none of the three men has.

I leave my telephone number at reception, along with a note asking that Tommaso drop me a text, just so I know that everything's OK, then pigeon-step the length of Via

Sistina. Switch my phone on. Watch its inactive home screen; press the on/off button, just in case it's forgotten to flash and warble during incoming calls.

Watched-pot fact: it don't boil.

With each small step I take back towards my hotel, my disappointment balloons. Bona fide chemistry doesn't happen every day. Not to me. Rarely these days does the old Autonomous Sensory Meridian Response kick in. We grew nuptial plumage and shared family secrets. The vibe was textbook. As was the cherry on the cake . . .

The Eradicator. What a delicious ember of hope the vigilante priest offered.

When my phone rings, I yelp. Relief, however, is quickly replaced by irritation.

'The Poet', reads the display, the name evoking all the wrong aromas – damp motorcycle leathers, London, redtops and humiliation.

'Noah,' I say quickly.

A born-again Scot, he coats nothing in sugar. 'This is not regular contact.'

'I'm busy scouring Rome.'

'You said you'd call in.'

'We're talking now.' I look behind me. But Tommaso doesn't run apologetically towards me. 'How's your wife?'

Noah avoids pleasantries. For him, speech is a mechanism to be used sparingly and for dramatic effect. 'I feel like a spare part. I've had two calls. One a week is not enough. Where the bloody hell are you?'

In the same city as Tommaso Bellini. But only for a few hours more. Then he'll be lost to me, for ever.

Reminder to oneself: when it comes to the propagation of love, enterprise is key.

'I'm actually on an assignment.' I turn on my heels and head back towards the Hotel Barruchia.

'What assignment?' demands Noah.

'One where I can't chat about the minutiae.'

He thinks it concerns the search for my mum. 'When can you talk?'

'Later. No, tomorrow.' Noah's staunch about arrangements. I'm not in a reliable mood.

'OK,' he says reluctantly. 'Just remember I need to know stuff as urgently as you.'

This I refute entirely, but now is not the time. So I take a deep breath.

'I've been formulating a plan. Your mum and dad's house – search the loft, the cellar, behind the wardrobes, under the floorboards, the shed. We're looking for something, anything that helps us build a picture of them before your family did a midnight bunk. You concentrate on the domestic investigation, OK?'

'I'll phone in as and when I find any information.'

Noah's not a PI or a potential lover. He needs a bit of patronising. 'Now, you're clogging up my line.'

'Very good.' Noah's purpose restored, he hangs up.

I hang around the Hotel Barruchia until 4 a.m., when the bin men arrive to unsettle me with their visceral Latin banter, clashing steel and rude lights.

Back in my room, I watch my phone until 8 a.m., then return to Tommaso's hotel. The bellboy is off duty, but the receptionist tells me things free of charge: the three men have paid up and checked out.

'But I left him a note.' I point at the letter caddies behind her.

She wipes an efficient finger around the one belonging to Room 17. It's proof that Tommaso has my number.

That makes the walk back to my hotel conclusive. There's not a thing left for me in Rome.

Operation Bambi Love

I've sunk a bottle of house white and am playing cards with myself – Scopa, an Italian game. It's easy to learn but difficult to master: my very favourite kind. This deck, however, doesn't come with an instruction leaflet or an English-speaking bartender, so I'm working out the brass tacks for myself.

I place six cards on the bar. Three for me. And three for me.

It's my go first.

The Queen of Hearts. I like the look of her. All desperate to wriggle free of her bustier and live a little. Unfortunately, she has been born with a very defensive face. She also has a pudding-bowl haircut, a medieval crown and a conjoined twin attached to her waist.

Oh, truth be told, I'm a little drunk.

Two days in Tuscany, and I've yet to venture outside.

My plane landed on Monday evening. Too impatient, I saw nothing of Florence, caught a train to Arezzo, then a bus to Monte San Savino. I didn't see anything of Tuscany either; its moon trapped behind swollen clouds. The view from the bus window lent only a shadowy promise of hills and spruce.

Hand in hand, the rain and I arrived in Monte San Savino. I found a room at the closest guesthouse; its unfamiliarity left me feeling overwhelmingly dislocated. So instead of exploring the town in which my mother had spent her formative years, I wrapped myself in an eiderdown and watched BBC News on the room's small flatscreen.

For most of the next day, I slept, waking instinctively at 4 p.m. in anticipation of Michael's call.

He didn't ring.

Leaving me to stare at the chestnut ceiling beams and laurel-stencilled cornices. Pretty, yet jaded, my room is taller than it is wide, with long, dusty, golden curtains and an en suite the colour of coffee beans. The view from the window is of rolling acres of hills, carpeted in scratchy spruce trees and vineyards. All that photosynthesis reminds you what a biological spectator you are.

I feel completely flat.

This is the second day my brother has forgotten to call. He's definitely alive. I've sent him three WhatsApp messages, each now showing two blue ticks. *Received*. And he's been on Facebook.

So I'm punishing him. By not looking for our mum. By not even looking at Tuscany, which is just outside. By staying in a wine cellar and getting rat-arsed.

In my defence, I read a leaflet . . .

Monte San Savino. A town and commune in the province of Arezzo. Arezzo is located on the Essa stream in the Valdichiana, and several of its villages occupy higher hills. Its total population is just shy of 9,000, which is tiny. If you can't find a relative in a populace that small, you're not worth the paper your Diploma in Private Investigation is written on.

I stare at my phone. Other people who haven't phoned: Noah.

Yes, it was my job to phone him, but historically, he does the chasing.

'*Tout de suite*.' I wiggle my empty glass in the direction of the barman and look down at the Queen of Hearts. Her frown is quizzical.

So you want to know about Noah? I nod.

She *so* does.

My defences are inebriated. I tell her things in the privacy of my own head.

He was my first love, I was eight and really good at kissing. I'd practised a lot – on my knee, on a pillow and then the windowsill. By the time I did it for real, I could do a head-sway and everything. You know, how they used to snog on the telly in the eighties.

She's not convinced. I reassure her . . .

It was very dramatic. I made sure of it. He was older than me – nine. Of course, I'd been keen to impress. We didn't see one another again after the kiss. Not until recently. Life got in the way.

You can say that again. The Queen of Hearts has a dry sense of humour. The easy ambience between us gives me loose lips.

That was a corker of a discovery – working out that Noah's father wasn't the dead man in Mum's car. That it was my uncle. Heavy shit, huh?

The bartender fills my wine glass and I secretly give the playing card a confused smile, because how was I to know that Noah's parents and my parents had been friends?

His mum and dad, and my mum and dad.

Here's a weird truth: my dad made out he didn't know Eric Steensen at all. The sum of his knowledge was: the dead guy in Mum's car was a businessman from Sandbanks. Like her, he'd suffered with nerves. They were suicide buddies. For a long while I assumed they'd met online. For much longer, I was terrified they'd been lovers.

What was it that Tommaso said to me? *That's very ship-shape.*

I bang the bar agitatedly, because why the fuck has Tommaso not even dropped me a text? I confided in him. Shared a lot of personal stuff.

Reasons would-be lovers don't drop you a text:

1. They're not that into you.

2. They're dead.

3. You confided in them too soon. Shared far too much personal stuff.

4. Their best friend has told them what you once did for a living.

I whimper. The barman gives me a look. The *I think it's time for bed* look. But I haven't finished my game; neither have I started it.

It's my go, so I turn over a second card. One large, apathetic coin.

Firmly, it reminds me of Tommaso, and Noah, and my brother. And my dad. And the barman, who actually dusts around my cards. Still I try to make the fucker like me; insist on helping him tidy – by sweeping the cards together; shuffling, then spilling them over the floor, leaving them where they drop. Apart from the Queen of Hearts – I rescue her, slip the playing card into my back pocket. She's had too sheltered a life and I need a protégée. *Hold tight, sister*, I warn her in the elevator. *You're in for a hell of a ride.*

Day three.

I have a humdinger of a hangover. My shower lasts forty-seven minutes. The lift to the breakfast room is too jolty. It makes my brain crash into its skull.

The breakfast room is also the wine-cellar bar, only with a rectangular table on which sit cups, cutlery, fruit and a lot of protein products. I go for a Lipton's and scrambled eggs, eggs being chockful of amino acids. Cysteine mops up toxins. Taurine boosts liver function. I gulp the caffeine in one, immediately prepare another one, because I have a full working day ahead.

The Chianti's warmer than their tea, I tell the Queen of Hearts, whose main job now is to be a bookmark/confidante. I remove her from my notebook. Place her next to the sugar sachets. Am about to re-examine my findings so far, when I'm interrupted by a ringtone.

'Michael Love,' the screen tells me.

'I was beginning to think you'd emigrated!' I squeak.

'I still live at home,' he confirms.

'Excellent.' His literalness is like a morphine shot. I forgive him everything. 'What you been up to?'

'Out and about in Whitton.'

'That's on the Christchurch ring road.'

'I do know. It was Darcie's birthday.'

'Darcie?'

'Yes. We did this weird tour of the naval base, like me and Seb were kids. They reminisced a lot, then took us to dinner at the Ship.'

I stop stirring my tea. 'Michael, who's Darcie?'

'Dad and Darcie went to school together.' He puts his hand over the mouthpiece, does an accidental Darth Vader. 'I think her and Dad are . . . you *know*?'

That makes me motionless. 'No, I do not.'

'Seb says they're in the early throes.'

'Of what?'

'Being, you know . . .'

'No.'

'*Companions.*'

My roar is small and involuntary. Because this is the definition of *companions* – when old people are having sex but pretend they're not.

'I've never fucking heard of her.'

'She exists.'

'Are you absolutely sure?'

'I've seen her.'

'I mean, are they definitely, you *know*?'

'I'm not putting a camera in his bedroom,' he complains.

'Good.'

'I know what you're like.'

'There are lines,' I frown. 'Now I need you to be objective. Did they kiss hello and goodbye?'

'Yes,' he states.

That makes my heart hammer at my oesophagus. 'How?'

'It was a French kiss.'

I whisper, horrified, 'With *tongues*?'

'No. On both cheeks.'

Kissing fact: cheek-kissing is the worst kind. Because my dad doesn't kiss women on one cheek, let alone two. It's too reminiscent of Bambi, and Italy, and of me – he only ever kisses *me* on both cheeks now; it's his unspoken commitment to my mother.

I rant out loud, 'But if Mum's alive, Dad's still married to her – that's bigamy.'

'Marriage is a way off yet,' Michael says, maturely.

'Adultery isn't.'

'Why would you say that?'

'Because French kissing is against the Bible when you're still married to the mother of your children. Dad needs reminding about that. Can you remind him? He'll be imprisoned for a term not exceeding seven years, Michael. Christ, I have to find Mum.'

My brother is as quiet as a house brick. An educated guess: he's thinking about his father as a sexual being. It's vital I change the subject.

'How *is* Seb?'

He sighs. 'OK. But he's getting on my nerves.'

'He smothers you,' I agree.

'And he doesn't always know best. Not always.'

Michael doesn't have to convince me. 'Do you remember what I told you when you asked me to be bridesmaid?'

He quotes me verbatim. '"A marriage certificate is just a piece of paper that makes it tricky when you separate – which we will one day, because time is a cruel magician."'

I nod. 'Marriage is an exhausting walk in Disappointment Park. I should know. Twice, Michael – *twice*, I did my darnedest.'

'And failed.'

I have no inclination to be defensive. My father has got a companion. Admittedly I've not physically seen him in two months, but why would he exclude me from such a momentous occasion – the one where his children get to meet his girlfriend? In my entire living memory, he has never had one of those.

The answer: he did wait – until I was 2,000 kilometres away.

I tell Michael to phone back later at the normal time, hang up, then study the first page of my notepad – a forensic account of my Italian investigation to date. I'd not written a single word in it until last night when, drunk and livid, I summarised my findings so far:

The square route of jack.

Looking now, I see I did a drunken bubble-dot above the 'j' and spelt 'root' wrong.

New-day fact: this is one, and it has presented me with a brand-new priority.

Tearing out the first page, I discard it on my breakfast plate. On a fresh sheet of paper, I write in capital letters that are slanted soberly to the right:

OPERATION BAMBI LOVE

Back in my room, I pack a bag for a day in the field. Cash, a collapsible sunhat, Scandinavian-style specs, my spy-sunglasses, Dictaphone, water from the mini-bar – twice the price, but never go into an investigation dehydrated. Christ, my eyes throb. I down two Ibuprofen before digging out my most important tool – a pair of North Face walking shoes.

Private investigation is best accomplished via the soles of the feet. Colin (my first and only PI boss) told me that, despite his insistence on being exclusively sedentary. Distance definitely makes the heart grow fonder – I smile, despite Colin being a total tool, and neaten my laces.

Always opt for hiking-lacing – it distributes pressure evenly while keeping the knots on the inside prevents snagging on undergrowth – that is essential during getaways.

Finally, I examine the front cover of my notebook – a laminated topographical map of the Mezzogiorno. Fingering Tuscany, I decide to speak to each and every one of its residents, the intention being this . . .

When I find Bambi, she and Dad are getting back together. End of.

Nun

Genealogy in Italy is a ball-ache.

You must present yourself in person at whatever office it is to explain your motives for wanting a stranger's personal data. The bureaucrats need to see the whites of your eyes. If given the benefit of the doubt, it's essential you fill out their forms in perfect foreign. The whole experience makes you feel very guilty indeed. Especially when the small details you do have are an educated punt, gathered via a lost mother's stories. Desperately, I hope not to have muddled or embellished them over the years.

The official double-checks my form.

'Bambi? *Nome conferma?*'

'No confirmation name.' I shake my head.

One thing I do know for sure: at the very least, she *will* have had a confirmation name, because Bambi was an unswerving Papist. She spoke of Adam, Eve, Noah and Moses with such fond familiarity, you'd be mistaken for thinking she'd been to school with them. My brother, Michael, was apparently the double of the baby Jesus. I was a dead ringer for the Virgin Mary.

Piccolina, she said, *you're exactly the right hue.*

My mother was right – twice I played the Mother of God in the school nativity.

Even *I*, an enthusiastic agnostic, have a confirmation name. Maria. After Saint Maria Goretti. An eleven-year-old girl who defended her honour so well, her attacker gored her to death with a screwdriver instead. Not only did she die a virgin, but she forgave her murderer entirely before passing away, enabling Maria to become the patron saint of chastity.

My dad chose it. In the absence of the Facts of Life talk, I was given a big dose of fatherly projection. Most girls get to choose their confirmation name. Dad guilt-tripped me into mine.

It would have been your mother's favourite, he told me. No argument.

Sometimes the bullshit's too suffocating.

The reality. I'm requesting details of a woman whose name I do not know. And if Mum's name was an alias, then Nonna and Nonno might have been too.

My remaining hope? That Bambi held on to her surname, because without the Campanellas, Operation Bambi Love is indefinitely closed.

The commune official files my form, then waves at a desk calendar – with a following wind, I'll have my answer this side of the apocalypse.

That's too long.

Outside, I sit on a bench in the public gardens and imagine Bambi and her sister running around the paths, over the symmetrical squares of grass, obediently avoiding its neat herbaceous borders. My grandmother ran a tight ship, I think. Very proudly, they will have registered their move here, what with Bambi's father having missed the town of his own childhood so desperately. The fast pace of policing in Rome was an unbridled culture shock. He'd been raring to come home.

The story goes like this.

Had God not sent a sign and asked Pope Pius VIII to cross my mother's forehead as a baby, my grandparents' marriage would not have endured. The last straw was the fact that my grandfather missed his daughter's birth, despite a solemn promise to the contrary. My grandmother would conceive, carry and push her first baby free on one condition

– that her husband stood outside the room and listened to her suffering. Histrionics are in my genes.

Yet my grandfather had been called away to deal with a shepherd leading several hundred sheep down the Via del Corso during the Treaty of Rome.

'Those first years were a crazy time in the whole history of the world, but mostly in the history of your *nonna* and *nonno*,' Bambi had confided in me. 'But in the end, he got his wish. We all returned home and, guess what? We were happy again.'

That was until Bambi hit fifteen. Then Nonno got killed on the job. She didn't cry or go into details when speaking of her father's death, which was unusual for my mum. I get it. Sometimes stuff hurts too much.

I squint back at the office – symmetrical as a Rubik's cube, a haughty coat of arms on its front. Somewhere inside that building could be information vital to my case. I don't contemplate a burglary for long – its staff have batons and a Latin temperament. The sensible thing is to chivvy myself along.

Next stop, the Biblioteca Città di Arezzo – the region's main library. Its website boasts of an extensive archives section. And in any town in any country, dead policemen are a local hack's wet dream. The newspapers would have been all over the story of my brave, murdered Nonno.

It turns out, they weren't.

The librarian – a young, raven-haired, B-list-celebrity-type – helped me search. I was honest enough, told her exactly how the story went. She accepted the challenge with alacrity and determination. Her English was as efficient as her ability to pull up information.

'We will search the local papers, magazines, community pamphlets and Google,' she stated.

Were I still the boss of my own PI company, I would have employed her instantly. Moving the computer's mouse efficiently, her lips ajar in concentration, I felt a little redundant, so admired the gap between her teeth – the excess gristle in between them, the size of a clitoris. That's called a diastema and is the result of a labial frenulum issue. In some circles it's considered extremely lucky.

Indeed, we quickly discovered that two policemen had died on the job in Monte San Savino and its immediate peripheries between 1965 and 1967. The first, a nineteen year old, had drowned saving the mayor's dog. The second, a grandad, eight months' shy of retirement, was beaten to death by a man with revenge issues. Neither man was the correct age, or surnamed Campanella.

'Are you sure your grandfather died in Monte San Savino?' asks the librarian.

'That's how the story went,' I say.

Never mind, there's a final avenue; I assume she phones a colleague. Though I can't be sure, the librarian now abrogates me from her inquiry. Power struggles have no place in private investigation – I sit back, listen to her no-bullshit Italian; it's twice as fast as her English, yet her lack of movement and steely glare give me few clues. It's impressive. As is the regimental rise and fall of her breasts.

Then I look at her lips, because she just said, '*the Eradicator*.'

'*No, no, no – le date non coincidono . . . No, non ha nulla a che fare con lo Sradicatore.*'

'Sorry,' I interrupt. 'Did you say *the Eradicator*?'

She doesn't put a hand over the mouthpiece. 'Police from other constabularies were called in to help with the situation. But the dates don't match. The Eradicator incident happened in the seventies.'

'That happened around here?' My mentioning Monte San Savino must have been what prompted Tommaso to tell me about his godfather. Had he not disappeared so suddenly, I would have *definitely* wangled a meeting. 'What do you know about him?' I ask.

The librarian smiles with one eyebrow. 'Some thought him devil; others thought him angel. It depends who scares you the most. God or the Mafia.'

Her melodrama is extremely erotic; more so when I don't have to tell her what to do next. Hanging up, she moves on with her next challenge – providing me with a number of newspaper reports.

She translates them for me, twice. The story tallies with the information Tommaso supplied, though I'm provided with extra details as to Father Massimo's prowess with a rifle; his training and background were a source of great speculation. Opinions oscillated – a self-styled vigilante, undercover cop, messenger from God, psychopath – nobody seemed to come to a firm conclusion.

The Eradicator disappeared soon after, making him the stuff of legend.

And although I remain furious with Tommaso for deserting me in Rome without so much as an explanatory text, I am extremely grateful we met. His memory provokes a spontaneous outbreak of goosebumps. I remember his molars. And those irises that actually glittered when he smiled. It could have been the face of an angel sent by a higher force. Nudging me in the right direction, only to disappear into the ether once his mission was complete.

That's beautiful. And cold. Which is why I don't trust God. He doesn't operate like me.

I refocus, concentrate on the black-and-white photograph of Tommaso's godfather.

'He's not what I expected,' I tell the librarian.

Blond and tanned, like a young Robert Redford, Father Massimo poses charismatically amidst an adoring huddle of nuns. Beneath the picture are printed the words: '*Padre Massimo Satori, al centro, con suor Bernadette, suor Agnese e suor Teresa del Convento di Monte San Savino.*'

'They look like an ecclesiastical pop trio.' I smile.

'A terrible waste.' She nods.

'Can I have copies?'

'Fifty cents a sheet.'

'Deal.' We shake hands, so gently it tricks me into a love-shiver.

And while the librarian prints up the newspaper report, I take the notebook from my rucksack. Update my findings so far. Leave a few pages to stick the newspaper cuttings in.

Then I tell the Queen of Hearts things with my eyes: *When the goalposts change, always sprint left of field.* Because this afternoon will now be spent looking for nuns.

Gossip is the chief reason humans started to speak. It serves the same societal function as primate grooming, only in a more time-efficient way and with less bias on hygiene. And of all the categories of human gossiper, Holy Sisters are the best. They're not allowed to bear false witness. That is the law.

Convento di Monte San Savino.

The Indonesian-looking nun who'd jerked open the oak door was similar in age to me, and enthused at the prospect of conversation.

'Welcome! You're from England. Let me guess, London? I'm too nosy. Ignore me. Welcome! The charge is forty euros each night – that includes a bed, food and time for spiritual contemplation.'

I'd stopped her there. 'I'm on a different kind of mission.' And so we'd sat on a bench in the convent's entrance hall. 'I'm looking for three dear friends of my grandmother's.'

'Who is your grandmother?' she'd asked, wide-eyed.

'Nonna's passed.' I'd shaken my head. 'I doubt her friends,

the sisters, are still with us. Nonetheless, she made me promise to try and thank them personally, if I could. So here I am.'

'Thank them for what?'

Catholic guilt hindered my ability to fabricate beyond what was absolutely necessary. 'For the profound impact they had on my grandmother. Their names were Sister Bernadette, Sister Therese and Sister Agnes.'

Still she waited for elucidation.

'They were a beacon of hope and love to our family in a time of personal tragedy.'

The nun gave up in the end. Performed a disappointed sign of the cross. 'Sister Therese and Sister Agnes are with the Lord.' A little more quietly, she had added, 'But not Sister Bernadette. Bernadette left the sisterhood many years ago. Convent life is not for everybody.'

I had reminded her of my Nonna's dying wish: 'It's essential I thank her.'

And so the nun had leant towards me. 'The last thing I heard, she lives with a cousin in Signatra. He owns a bar. That's as much as I know.'

It was as much as I needed.

Signatra teeters on a blustery peak just a few kilometres north of Arezzo and a hundred years left of Greenwich Meantime. The taxi drops me at a donkey bridge. I must cross it on foot and ascend a cobbled track, passing medieval houses constructed from local stone; were it not for the clean edges and varnished doors, you'd be forgiven for thinking they were the beautiful by-product of a rockslide.

I head towards a towering spire and what I assume will be the town's centre. It takes a good twenty minutes. The hub is dominated by a church square crammed with market stalls, and a restaurant, its al fresco terrace a litter of uncoordinated tablecloths. I've no need to check its blackboard: the dish of the day is mutton. My taste receptors leak. My tongue relishes the imagined flavour of roasted bone marrow.

When I see an old woman wearing jeans, I smile. It's like spotting a wristwatch in a period drama. She makes me feel less conspicuous. I ask her for directions.

'*Il bar, signora?*'

'*Laggiù.*' She points a few hundred metres further up the road.

I find Sister Bernadette immediately, perched on a stool at the bar. Her white hair is short, spiky and sparse. Her tiny frame is swamped by mismatched cardigans. Ever so noisily, she sips from a saucer. I feel immediately protective of her, especially when I sit beside her and discover that she's swapped one habit for another.

'*Buongiorno*, Sister Bernadette. Another drink?'

'*Meme male!* There you are.' She puts her saucer down with a clatter, then grins. There are too many teeth in her head; each has a life of its own. 'You are very late,' she tells me, her English half suffocated by a thick Italian accent.

'Am I, Sister?'

'Yes, you are.'

'Forgive me.' I look around. An elderly barman is in the kitchen washing up; otherwise, we're alone. An old television – stuffed between liquor bottles and a coffee machine – blares. The programme is *Affari Tuoi*, the Italian equivalent of *Deal or No Deal*.

'You have money?' Bernadette asks me.

When I call to the bartender, he first checks that Bernadette is OK. I assume the man is her cousin. '*Tutto bene, Bernadette? Conosci questa ragazza?*'

'She is my friend.' Bernadette fobs him off. 'We went to school together.'

The old man looks at me, deadpan.

I smile. 'We did, actually.'

Vindicated, Bernadette takes my hand. Holds it like I'm her mother. Socially, this should be awkward; she has no intention of letting go. Nonetheless, I cradle her cold and bony knuckles in mine.

The barman likes me, is grateful for a new sitter. He pours my wine, leaves Bernadette a bottle of grappa, then shuffles back into the kitchen.

I gaze into the eyes of a woman who once had a full complement of marbles and sass, because to divorce the Church takes enormous balls. I don't know the woman, but I absolutely mean it when I say, 'It is *lovely* to see you, Sister.'

'Then you should visit more. I have no visitors since 1997.'

Dementia fact: it's fucking brutal. The only means of circumnavigation: lies. The afflicted live in the moment. My rule, never let them know there's anything wrong. Forcing them back into a world from which their brains are disconnecting is indefensibly cruel.

'I came last week, Sister.'

'Last week?'

'Yes.' I manipulate my contraction furrows to portray complete sincerity, which is allowed when the intention is good.

'I am silly and old.'

'We is what we is,' I say. 'Now, how are you feeling this week?'

'Ah, you know. I keep busy. Until my time comes.' She doesn't glance up at her maker or cross her chest. She smiles at the host of Italian *Deal or No Deal*. I do, too. He has very expressive eyebrows.

'How is the boy?' She remembers someone from her past.

'He's great.' I nod. 'Absolutely fine.'

'Bravo.' Her eyes are milky turquoise, her pupils lost somewhere beneath.

'And how's Father Massimo? I was thinking of visiting him while I'm here.'

Bernadette's spare hand cups my mouth. Her palm smells like sweaty bottom. 'Not so loud,' she says.

I mumble, 'Is he OK?'

Releasing my mouth, Bernadette pours some grappa into her saucer. 'He won't see me. He promised me to keep in touch. But that was one thousand years ago.'

'But you and Massimo were such old friends?'

'Best friends,' she tells the television.

For a gratuitous moment, I wonder if they were lovers. 'Maybe I could talk to him for you?'

She looks me up and down. 'Why?'

I try to neaten her hair. Impatiently, she flicks my hands away. So I retrieve my notepad, remove the newspaper photograph of Father Massimo and the three nuns. Put it on the bar in front of us.

'Look at you.' I smile. 'Did you have hair under that habit?'

'A mile of it,' she says, her pupils back in the room, standing black and true. 'It was like the lava from the volcano.'

'You were a redhead?'

'That was a long time ago, when I was alive.' She pats Massimo's face with a bent finger. 'This was Assumption Day.'

'You're all so good looking.'

She cocks her head. 'Then the shootings. He had to disappear.'

'Where is Father Massimo now?'

I don't like the look she gives me next. Like she's crash-landed in a moment of lucidity. As if it were a matter of urgency, she retrieves a purse from the pocket of her cardigan. Pulls a slip of paper from its flap. Pushes it into my hand.

'I trust you, yes?' she says.

'Completely.' I unfold the slip and smile. 'Sister, this is a shopping list.'

'I stock up.' She juts her chin in the direction of the kitchen. 'He steals my food.'

'But what about Massimo?' I whisper back.

'Yes. If you see him, you tell him.'

'Tell him what?'

'I meet him on the mountain. But I'm old now, so he must bring a cart.'

'Word for word, I will tell him that,' I swear. 'But, Sister, I need his address.'

'I told you. You find him on the mountain.'

'Bernadette.' Ensuring she looks at me, I talk directly to her pupils. 'That is very non-specific. Do you have a post-code?'

I'm not expecting the next voice. Its owner's mouth is too close to my ear. 'Mountains have no postcode.'

Swinging my head around, I'm surprised to find a boy squinting down at me. Fifteen, at a guess. All nose and limbs. He's as memorable as a cricket stump.

'*Buongiorno.*' I frown at him.

'She not know Massimo.'

I may not speak Italian, but I can tell the barman arrives to reprimand the boy. '*Ma che maniere? Che fai, arrivando così di soppiatto.*'

'*Sta chiedendo di Massimo a zia Bernadette.*'

'*Massimo?*' The barman scrutinises me.

'*Sì, voleva il suo codice postale.*'

I shake Bernadette's hand. 'I'll be off now.'

'Come tomorrow.' She nods. 'Bring my food.'

'Definitely.' I put ten euros on the bar and leave.

This is how I know the boy follows me out:

1. The door doesn't close behind me.

2. Now and then the wind sends a zesty waft of pubescence.

3. His left trainer has a loose sole. It scrapes the dusty cobbles – that is a noise that severely jangles my nerves.

Noises-that-jangle-the-nerves fact: they have their roots in prehistoric predation. Listening to nails on a chalkboard, for example, brings to mind a macaque monkey's alarm call. Squeaking polystyrene resembles the noise our molars make should we accidentally crunch on anything harder than tooth enamel – a pebble, for example. Teeth don't heal, hence our heightened alarm system. And although I've yet to establish what lazy footsteps replicate, without fail, they make my neuropaths badly misfire.

The church square.

I mosey around the stalls, coveting the olives, feta, sieved passata, while keeping the boy within my peripheral vision. Then I enlist a basic counter-surveillance manoeuvre – swing three consecutive lefts. Back on the square, I hide behind a tree, spy on the boy re-entering the piazza.

Gormless, he checks left then right.

Ensuring I have easy access to my atomiser (Eau de Tabasco Sauce), I emerge from the tree and stomp towards him.

'OK, what?' I demand.

That stymies him. He mumbles, embarrassed, 'Mountains have no postcode.'

'I got that bit.' My nod is impatient. 'Now you're following me. What's that about?'

He looks appalled at the suggestion, because a few locals have stopped to listen. Shuffling away, he acts like I'm the unreasonable one, and heads back in the direction of the bar.

Exploiting a minor is an ethical grey area. Among less principled PIs, it remains common practice. I have a non-negotiable rule: steer clear, always. The single caveat is that if you do give it the big I-am, whatever your age, be prepared to get it back in spades.

I catch the boy up. 'It's OK, I understand now. You know where Massimo Satori lives?' I hold his arm. Obediently, he stands still. 'Well, do you or don't you?'

His nod is almost imperceptible.

'Good.' I pat his shoulder. 'Now we can talk business. How much for the address? You want money, right?'

The boy is an idiot. 'Five hundred and I take you.'

'Sorry, did you just admit that you know Massimo?'

He frowns.

'*And* that you'd sail him to the wind for a few hundred euros? For fuck's sake, I could be anyone.'

The boy takes a step back.

'No worries, you've told me now. That makes you officially fucked. We might as well go all out.'

'I tell lie.'

'I was here. You said, "Five hundred euros and I take you." Yes?'

'No.'

'How do you know him?'

'I no know Massimo.'

I pull a twenty-euro note from my pocket. Wiggle it at his nose. 'No more questions, I promise. Just tell me this – *how* do you know him? Then I am gone. For ever. Cross my heart.'

'I deliver the wine.' He snatches the cash free, jogs away.

I'm not the fastest runner, but I have a dogged stamina. 'Is he near?' I trot beside him. 'Do you walk to his home?' I use two fingers to show him how you walk.

He shakes his head. 'Vespa.'

I grab a hold of his arm again. Exasperated, he stops. 'There, you did it again. Too chatty for your own health. You've literally given me your whole life story.'

'Go away,' he begs.

'No,' I say, with certainty.

'Who are you?' he mumbles.

'A sort of historian. Now, this is what is going to happen next. The taxi ride here cost me thirty euros. I'll give you fifty to take me back into Arezzo. I won't tell a soul we met – you have my word – assuming you do one thing, and give me Father Massimo's current address.'

'Mountains no have postcodes.'

'Better!' I clap. 'Now let's hop on the scooter in plain view of everyone. Just in case you're a rapist.'

That makes his eyes too wide.

'Don't worry, amigo. I'm not expecting you to actually take me to Massimo. That would be ridiculously dangerous for you and Sister Bernadette. Never offer to do that for anyone again, do you hear me?'

Using my iPhone, I take a mugshot of the boy, forward it to my brother.

'Safety first,' I explain, then reassure him with regard to my investigative abilities. 'I've been known to work wonders with the first line of an address.'

Total Buffoon

Father Massimo is sitting on the altar step. Pushing himself stiffly from a sitting position to a standing one, he shakes out his limbs and rubs his coccyx.

I remain seated on the pew. I have told him everything I intend to. Naturally, I exclude the fact I was once a private investigator; nobody trusts one of them, especially under these circumstances. My insinuation throughout is that I'm extremely resourceful.

Neither did I mention that the snitch was the boy who delivers his communion wine – loyalty to your contact is an unbendable rule.

'A drunk told me how to find you.'

'His name?'

'We didn't swap numbers. To be honest, I thought he was having me on. Nonetheless, I bought him several drinks for the privilege and, this morning, got a bus to Ciggiana. Then I hiked a trail into the foothills of the inner Northern Apennines via the north-east of town.'

I do, however, very much mention the ex-nun. I made her a firm promise.

'A Sister Bernadette was there, too, but she had nothing to add. I'm sad to report that she's very befuddled now. Though she was strict on one thing – that I pass on a message, should I bump into you. She said she'll meet you in the mountains. But you'll need a cart, because she's an old woman now.'

For a moment, he stares at me, gormless, his shoulders slack. Then he pulls my rucksack from the floor, opens it, removes my notebook.

'Most churches have a road leading to them.' I watch him intently.

He doesn't look up. Reads my notes. Stares at the newspaper article. 'This isn't a church. It's private.'

'As is my journal.'

The good news: I've not updated my case notes since my trip to the library; the bad: I feel entirely violated. And embarrassed, because I've stuck the newspaper in with a plaster, and made notes on the photograph of the nuns.

'The Andrews Sisters?' he double-checks.

I shrug and tell my feet, 'They were an American close-harmony trio of the swing and boogie-woogie eras.'

'I know who they were.'

I nod at the photograph. 'You've changed a lot.'

Massimo employs a lot of energy to generate his next look. It says, *You are a total buffoon.*

Suddenly, I spot the Queen of Hearts. She's grabbed the opportunity to flutter free. Spiralling to the floor, she and her twin wave their maces, forewarning me of the inevitable. But Massimo is already emptying my bag on to the flag-stones.

Something I'm certain of: *nothing* in that rucksack is going to work in my favour.

'Churches also have an open-door policy,' I mutter.

He picks up my spy glasses. 'What are these?'

'They're for extreme sports.'

'You brought a video camera with you?'

'I do base jumping, mostly.' Sometimes, I wish I had an off switch. 'And movie piracy. Video cameras are less blatant than a handheld camcorder—'

The Eradicator knows his spyware. 'Who are you?'

I shrug, because, on so many levels, I haven't a fucking clue. Exhausted, I look at the chapel floor. At my playing card, sprawled dead. Her twin, I notice, glowers over at the stone statue of the Virgin Mary. As always, the Queen of Hearts looks at me, sort of, with one eye.

'I am Florence Love, after the city, not the nurse,' I remind her.

Yet that eye belies an awful truth about death – she's forgotten me already.

Massimo disables my spy glasses with a single stamp. The Dictaphone comes to the same swift end, as does my mobile phone. Putting the notepad in his cassock pocket, the priest then clears his lungs of phlegm. At the very least, I expect him to spit at me.

Instead, he slaps the side of my head with a lacklustre palm and mutters, 'How is she? Bernadette? Not in her head. In herself.'

I'm quite tachycardic, so I tell it as it is. 'She could drink me under the table.'

He smirks. 'On your feet. Walk with me.'

The mid-afternoon sun hits my eyes like a flurry of darts. Retinal light-detection takes a moment to adjust. When it does, I see that we are crossing a cobblestone courtyard.

It's been lovingly attended to.

On three sides are walls of slung ivy. The pots at our feet contain nasturtiums and sun roses – electric oranges and hot reds. Lavender and lemon trees live in terracotta urns. There's a drinking fountain made of broken cobalt tiles. Opposite us, an outbuilding – it looks to have once been a stable block – now sports an awning, glass walls and oak shutters.

I follow Massimo inside. Squint again at the rude change in light. And at first I make out little more than a blond man's back – he's wearing a white shirt and sitting at a desk facing the wall. Above his head hangs a crucifix the size of a machine gun.

Father Massimo nudges me towards the man.

'Massimo.' The priest speaks loudly. 'A friend of Rocco's boy is here to see you.'

I stifle a gasp. Look, confused, at the man I'd assumed was Tommaso's godfather. Lie to the real Massimo's back: 'Tommaso was supposed to tell you I was coming.'

'Well, he didn't.' The real Massimo takes an age to get to his feet and inch the desk's heavy chair around to face me. When eventually he sits back down, his arms and legs are splayed as though he's just completed a zumba class.

And I want to give the old man a hug. Two decades older than the bald priest, he sports Liberace-yellow hair and an impressive bouffant.

With gusto, I smile, to show him I come in peace, then wrestle with a very strong need to giggle. I'm not helped by Tommaso's godfather grinning back at me, all sugar-white dentures and liver-spot tan, a chuckle collecting in the corners of his mouth too.

My gut instinct: we've clicked biochemically.

I bob respectfully. 'Your godson told me all about you.'

'Little Tommaso?' he says. 'I do hope not. That wouldn't be good for anybody's health.'

'Of course, not *everything*,' I say. 'Nothing at all, to be honest with you.'

When I spot an episcopal ring on Massimo's finger, I genuflect immediately, because that ring means he is quite somebody, I think. I'm not up to speed with episcopal rings – it's a sign of office, I know that much. If I get out of here alive, I'll research the topic as a matter of urgency.

Massimo points at me. 'What are you doing down there on your knees?'

'Genuflecting.'

'I'm not a priest. Not any more.'

'Oh.' I stand back up. 'What are you then?'

'Halfway to hell.'

That is an excellent comeback. I certainly intend to use it in the future. Pointing at his bald, deranged sidekick, I say, 'He's definitely headed downstairs.'

Massimo nods. 'I have been telling him this for years.'

'He put an actual gun in my mouth.'

Massimo's voice becomes shrill. 'You did what?'

The priest shrugs. 'We have need of vigilance.'

I tell them facts: 'There's vigilant, and there's the United Nation Convention against Torture and Other Cruel, Inhuman or Degrading Treatment or Punishment.'

Not that they listen. Doggedly, they bicker between themselves.

'What was I to do? I didn't know who she was.'

'She's just a girl.' Feminism fact: this is very sexist of the real Massimo. Nonetheless, I nod heartily.

'Believe me, the *girl* can look after herself.'

Again I nod, the bald priest saw me in full flow . . .

I let myself into a locked church. When a rabid priest bounded towards me, my instinct was to enlist karate hands and a *yoko geri* foot hover. 'Shorinji Kempo is a Buddhist-inspired martial art,' I warned him. 'It hurts a lot.' Just not as much as a gunshot wound – the priest outmanoeuvred me by packing my mouth full of steel.

Massimo fumes at the priest. 'What did I do to deserve you?'

'You want to discuss this now?'

They behave like lovers. No: nemeses incarcerated in a marriage of someone else's convenience. I watch while they nettle one another. Massimo does it deliberately: lets me into secrets.

'Rocco, Tommaso's father, was like a son to me. I looked after him for a while – after his father died. He called me Marilyn Monroe.' He pats his hair. 'I have a name for him these days too. Henry the Eighth.'

'Rocco this, Rocco that . . .' mutters the priest.

'That's quite funny, eh? He's on wife number five!'

The priest interrupts. 'She has surveillance equipment.'

'I'm on a genealogical mission,' I explain to Massimo. 'He stamped on my phone and pocketed my most private diary.'

The priest removes my case notes from his cassock, hands them to Massimo. Curiously, he takes my pad, studies it briefly, then delivers instructions: 'Father Benedict, please go and pray for forgiveness or whatever it is you do all day.'

Benedict seethes, but does as he's told. 'You're very patronising,' he moans, then slams the door behind him.

But it's Father Massimo Satori that likes the last word. 'Whatever you do, however, do *not* wash. God forbid, you take a fucking wash!'

Massimo wiggles a finger at the floor, indicates that I'm to sit. There's no chair so I position myself cross-legged at his feet, while he recovers a splayed orange from his desk. Its juice squirts on his shirt, and on my notebook. Christ, its aroma makes the sides of my tongue ache, reminds me how thirsty I am. And emotionally banjaxed – less than an hour ago I was preparing for my own execution.

Yet Massimo forgets to offer me even a scrap of sustenance – he's more interested in Operation Bambi Love.

When he's finished reading, he leans back in his chair and waves the notebook at me. 'You've been watching too many spy films . . . I don't know your name.'

'Florence Love.' I touch my chest. 'A friend of Tommaso Bellini's.'

He shows me his palm. I'm to be silent. Again, he reads the notebook, only with more squinty eyes.

And, for a bit, I look at Jesus. Whittled from olive wood, the large crucifix behind Massimo's head has a savage beauty. Which is why the domestic kind are smaller and situated above a door, so children don't have to look at them directly.

A rood cross, like this one, can be horrific viewing for the pure of heart. Thorns, rusty nails, nipples and ribs, a suggestion of male genitalia beneath a cloth drenched in blood and gall-infused vinegar.

When I was a child, my mother tried to reassure me: 'Gazing at the cross gives us nice feelings, Piccolina. Ones of hope, love and trust.'

Today I can confirm it serves only as a reminder that men still get murdered for being left of field. That's extremely depressing. It's little wonder exhaustion lands on my head like a heavy towel. I wrestle with my need to give into it. Especially, I cannot lie in the recovery position on the marble tiles, a cheek against their cold shell, enjoying a recuperative nap under a gentle mist of Tarocco blood orange at the feet of a kindly Liberace-doppelgänger who's halfway to hell . . .

Massimo makes me jump when he says, loudly, 'Let's get to the nitty-gritty.'

'Yes, signor.' My nod is vigorous.

'I don't know him.'

'Who?'

'That Rocco person.'

I frown. 'You do.'

'No.'

'You loved him like a son.'

'No.'

'You call him Henry the Eighth. He called you Marilyn Monroe.'

'Ah, rumours. You hear about people. Rocco Bellini is a name from the north – but I've not had the pleasure. I'm sorry, you've been sent to Ciggiana with false hope.'

What is he saying? I shuffle closer and tell him earnestly:

'Signor, I'm not sure what the set-up is here; rest assured, I have no interest in it. But I solemnly know that your godson,

Tommaso, sent me with good intentions in his heart. And with the firm belief you'd help me look for my mother.'

Massimo watches the door and says loudly, 'Help you with what?'

'You've read my diary – I'm looking for my mother, Bambi Campanella. Latterly, Bambi Love.'

'No,' he says conclusively. Then leans forwards and whispers, I assume in case the bald priest is eavesdropping. 'Does Lucia know about you?'

'Rocco's wife?'

He nods. 'Number five.'

'I doubt that very much,' I whisper back. 'Because Rocco and I are not lovers. I've never met him. I just know Tommaso – sort of.'

'A one-night relationship?'

'No.' I frown.

Then he places a tender palm on my face. I become as tranquil as a hypnotized chicken. Speaking softly and fast, his words are accompanied by tones of citrus, digestive biscuit and garlic.

'I won't find your mother. It will unravel lives. People disappear for a reason. Rocco and I both know this. Even if I could give you answers, you will owe a lot of people. Me, and Rocco.'

'But I don't know Rocco.'

'And Benedict.' He motions outside the room. 'Owing Benedict is not something to recommend.'

'I don't care. I've no choices left.'

He looks at me as if I'm a child. 'You have so many there isn't time to explore them all.'

'I don't understand.'

Still holding my face, he speaks more quietly. 'Forget Bambi Campanella, or Bambi Love, or whatever name she gave herself. Look at those around her instead. You'll find your answers there.'

'That's exactly what I'm doing. My grandparents were from Monte San Savino. My aunt still lives here.'

Letting go of my face, he flicks through my notes again then, without looking up, asks, 'Your grandfather, the policeman, when was he killed?'

'My mother was fifteen. So, it was 1966, or thereabouts.'

Massimo and I stare at each other for quite a while. It surprises me when his shoulders slump, as if I'm Mata Hari and he's the biggest fool known to man.

'Campanella, you say?'

I nod. 'Bambi was proud of the family name.'

We both know that doesn't stand for much. Yet Massimo sighs, and says, 'You stay here.'

The silent anticipation makes me feel safe and drowsy. I assume the recovery position and rest my eyes.

I don't know how long I doze for – a minute or an hour – but when I lift my head from the floor tiles, my joints are stiff, my temples pulse, my tongue is as good as desiccated.

There are some objects in front of me on the floor. I focus on the broken phone, glasses, Dictaphone. A glass of water. I sit up, grab it, gulp it while I look at Massimo.

He's back in his chair, my notebook sitting on his lap like a missal.

Massimo tells me straight: 'Your mother has no connection to Monte San Savino.'

I ask him, very slowly, 'You are totally sure?'

'If she or her family, or any Campanella, had lived here – especially a murdered policeman – I would know.'

I rub my face. Gruffly, free my wits of their accidental siesta. 'Where is she, then?'

'Somewhere else.'

'In Italy?'

'I would suggest not.'

He would *suggest not*? 'Do you know, or don't you?'

'I know about such things.'

But I need to know *how* he knows? Where did he just go? Who did he speak to? I explain my predicament. 'Massimo, I wasn't asleep for long enough for you to search everywhere – not in every single region and every single commune.'

Firmly, he tells me this: 'You're looking in the wrong country. Concentrate on those closer to home.'

I shake my head. 'My dad won't talk.'

'Not family, never family. Other people – friends, work colleagues . . .'

'She was shy, mostly. She didn't go to work.'

'The post boy. Her hairdresser. The women she talked to at church.'

Massimo has hit upon something there – the only times my mum and dad went out was to attend mass or a church do. That, at least, is what my memory has decided was the case.

'All those who crossed her path, however briefly – look into them.'

'It was almost thirty years ago.' I shake my head.

'Then your timing is perfect. Stories fall apart when you factor in the passage of time.'

The only people I can think of to talk to are dead.

One specifically. Eric Steensen.

The police said he was the gassed man in Mum's Datsun Sunny. Yet six months ago, I discovered a corker of a fact. It wasn't him. Eric Steensen had, in fact, been alive and well and living in Scotland until a time so recent I can smell it. Eric died in a car crash, leaving behind two children. A daughter called Hannah, who I don't recall. And a son called Noah with whom I'd shared a kiss.

We discovered further common ground too, Noah and I. That as children we'd been subject to a grown man's advances: Uncle Fergus, my dad's brother, had a penchant for the offspring of family and friends. One day, my dad caught him buttering me up for a kiss.

Neither I nor Michael saw our uncle again.

'Tell me this,' I ask quietly. 'Was she a Campanella? In your opinion?'

He shakes his head sadly.

There's a noise outside the door.

'What now?' Massimo shouts.

Father Benedict speaks through the door frame. 'I'm just checking.'

'Checking what?'

'That everything's OK.'

'For fuck's sake!' Massimo looks at me with exasperated eyes. Reads my mind. Shrugs and gives me as much information as he's prepared to: 'Polar opposites sometimes get washed up on the same desert island.'

It's all he needs to say. I don't pretend to know the finer points but I understand the sentiment: exceptional situations provide middle ground for the diametrically opposed. In my job, the middle ground is your office.

'Now, get yourself out of this place, out of Italy,' he implores. 'Go back home – build her backstory in England.'

He senses that I'm about to ask another question, which I am, because I have a million pertinent ones.

'*Quei giuramenti, quei profumi, quei baci infiniti, rinasceranno,*' he declares, then translates: 'Those promises, those perfumes, those kisses, they will arrive again.'

That reminds me. I deliver his news with the *gravitas* it deserves: 'Signor, I made a firm promise to a special woman. Bernadette. She asked that I tell you that she'll meet you on the mountain. But she's old now, so you must bring a cart.'

He blinks too many times.

'That's all she said. *Nothing* else. We were passing ships in the night. You're safe.'

He nods slowly, then waves me away. Somewhere, anywhere. 'I wish you and Tommaso Bellini every happiness in your future together. Whoever the Bellinis may be.'

'I promised to do her shopping.'

His eyes speak volumes. His irises, their crypts, they're as crowded as mine. I know there and then that he and Bernadette had been lovers.

'She likes to stock up,' he concedes.

'Apparently so.' I smile.

Slowly, he nods. 'This is how things will go. You will tell no one that we met. Not my godson. Especially not Rocco. No one in Italy, and no one in England. For many people's safety, most especially your own, today *never* happened.'

'Understood.'

He looks at me for a long time.

I relent. Give him the checkmate of oaths: 'On my mother's life.'

Smoothing the creases from his chinos, he sighs, assuaged. 'Good. Now, get the fuck out of the country.'

Obediently, I pull myself to my feet. Put the broken equipment in my bag, gingerly slip my notebook from his lap, am about to walk to the door, when he grabs my wrist. His adieu is as imperial as a monsignor's. Regardless of his one-way ticket to hell, I genuflect. I'm sad to say goodbye.

Outside.

The sun's brilliance, a sharp wind, the air clean and invigorating.

Father Benedict lingers around the water fountain. I give him a wide berth. Make a circuitous dash for the side gate, the one back to England, Noah Steensen and a few home truths.

Part II

Part II

Retired Entrapment Specialists 101 – Tip #2:
Never go home

PIs were once children suffocated by the close-knit scrutiny of the people around them. My personal experience: a village tribe in Dorset, the entire population of which attended my baptism, confirmation and both weddings. The PI-to-be escapes, finally, but becomes infected with the same diehard nosiness.

• A positive. On retirement, your people will welcome you home with an attentive smile, donning your infamy so greedily you'd think it was their own.

• A not-so-positive. You're a cheap talking point whose misadventures are too juicy not to share. Over and over and over. Your people have forgotten you're a human being, first, a slick entrapper of men, second.

It's prudent to find a new place to call home.

1. The woods, perhaps. (For legal advice, visit UKHippy.com)

2. A faceless newbuild in Milton Keynes, where you can open an eBay business.

3. Alternatively, there's a swift suicide-by-sea.

A caveat: you can nip home *only* if it's a matter of life and death. Be ready, however, for a stay tinged with shame – your tribe especially love your most humiliating bits.

Kathy Bates

October 2014 – Controlled airspace, The Solent, UK

The plane circles Bournemouth Airport. I press my nose against the cold, plastic window. Sigh heavily at the leaden sea from which sea stacks and promontories crane their necks, their putty-white faces exposed to both sun and spiteful breeze. I know how harsh it is down there from experience, having walked the Jurassic coastal trail enough times – with Husband Number Two.

The plane leans gently to its right.

Bournemouth, Poole then Sandbanks come into view. Buttery crescents of beach. Monopoly houses. Swimming pools, neon in the sharp autumn sun. Slipways, jetties and boathouses. Billionaires' yachts bobbing like flotsam.

Three Sandbanks Facts:

1. According to the National Council for Metal Detecting, it's an excellent spot for the detection of metal.

2. The Great Recession (2007/8) had a significant impact on the property market – the average house price on Sandbanks dropped to just twenty-squillion pounds.

3. Eric Steensen lived there. Before he'd pretended to die from carbon-monoxide poisoning but actually emigrated to Scotland.

I force myself to scrutinise the view, because I suffer disconcertment around heights.

We leave the coast behind. Rocks give way to a lowland heathland. Weevil-sized sheep and ponies keep the vegetation shorn. I know this because I've seen them do it; Husband Number Two liked a heathland ramble too.

Further inland still.

The chalky grassland below concertinas to form the Purbeck Ridge – this is my bit of Dorset – six miles north of Christchurch.

Mine and Michael's.

Thinking of my brother makes my chest prickle excitedly. I do a secret palm clap. At least I'll be seeing him soon.

He and I grew up in a stone cottage made two centuries before from the rock on which it sits. Looking down, I can smell our childhood. Manure, homey as a fart; lime-stone walls that leak the scent of petrol when it rains; the spitting open fire; out-of-print hardback books; a pine dresser. The aromas mingled to provide a potpourri inextricably linked with evenings in front of *Black Adder*, *Moonlighting* and *Cheers*.

But mostly of Mum.

Suddenly, the plane changes direction. I double-check my seatbelt, practise buckling and re-buckling. *Always* do this when flying. Some passengers have a total mental block about how to do it – their charred remains are found pinned in their seats in the crash-landed plane, their skinless knuckle bones still clasping their two-point lap-belt.

Seatbelt fact: they hinder evacuation. It's important to practise.

Also, should you be involved in an aviation disaster, ensure that your knee and elbow joints are totally relaxed – it reduces the impact thirty-six-fold.

Cruising back towards Bournemouth, we begin our

descent. The plane's undercarriage squeals open. My heart joins in, too.

We are going to die.

Assiduously, I watch for bird strike, scrutinise the speed and direction of the clouds, should we be attempting a tail-wind landing. Check the plane's electrics, now exposed under the circulation control wing, because I'm travelling with a budget airline; their pilots are not long out of the simulator: they need all the help they can get.

Budget airlines are also tight with petrol. Far too quickly, we land, with a walloping hop, skip and jump, then freewheel to the Arrivals building. Yet my elation at having survived another plane journey is short-lived. With each minute that passes, my gut becomes weightier.

I haven't spoken to my dad in weeks.

The last time I did, he used a new voice. One with a cautionary and unnerving timbre. He used words like these:

'Florence, listen to me very carefully indeed. You're dabbling in events that are extremely dangerous. You must not get involved. Do not look for your mum. I cannot help you or talk to you about this again; I WILL NOT help you or talk to you about this again.'

I disobeyed him.

And now the prodigal daughter returns to ask her father if he ever actually knew his wife at all. Was he aware that she wasn't called Bambi Campanella? That she didn't come from Monte San Savino, maybe not even from Italy? That her entire past was a badly thought-out work of fiction?

In truth, I'm not sure it's worth even broaching the subject. Usually, I'm fantastic at body language, but I won't know whether to believe a single thing he utters; loved ones suck the dispassion from a situation, when kinesics requires absolute objectivity.

Baggage Reclaim.

My suitcase is already on its way round when I arrive to collect it. It bobs, all alone. But I don't jog to catch it up. I let it disappear for a final lap while I take a few deep breaths. Then I hoick the case from the belt like it's a body bag, and enter the United Kingdom through the Nothing to Declare door.

Arrivals.

My entrance back in to the UK is a flop. Family and friends have not secretly liaised to provide the welcome of a lifetime. Everybody has forgotten to arrange a lift home for me. Most especially, Michael is nowhere to be seen.

Admittedly, it was only this morning that I left a message on the answerphone. My brother wasn't picking up his mobile, so I gave in, rang Dad – because I was using a phone box and couldn't remember any other number, apart from the emergency services. I was relieved to get the machine. I also thought leaving a message was a safe bet – my father *always* picks up his messages; the machine's little red flashing light makes him rub his hands together like he's about to open a bottle of red.

Yet it's 15.09, and neither Dad nor Michael is here.

So I stroll past a bunch of strangers who have a good look at me. For them, I'm a sideshow before the main event. I push my chin into my neck. When a camera flashes, I look too quickly for the culprit. Once upon a time, the British press hounded me – that leaves a girl jumpy. I give myself a mental poke, remind myself of the truth:

You, Florence Love, are last season's chip paper.

When I pass a small girl with a posy of flowers, it all becomes too much. My need to weep is overwhelming – sometimes, you yearn for a gerbera and car ride home.

This is a perfect example of: be careful what you wish for.

'Woohoo, Flo! Over here!'

Christ's face. I style out a shudder and do my best stage smile. It's the brother-in-law to be.

As I approach him, he claps loud and fast. I wish he wouldn't, everybody's looking at us – but mostly at Sébastien Tremblay, who is quite the enigma.

While he's squashing an ear against my breast, I'll give you the lowdown . . .

My future brother-in-law doesn't have hair, per se – it's better described as a painting of a crew cut, onyx-black. His complexion is flour-white. He has the height and figure of an eight-year-old girl. His voice is a genderless Canadian drawl. Today he's come dressed as a stagehand – skinny black jeans and black turtleneck.

He takes a step back to admire me. 'You are so tanned.'

I present him with a forearm, because it's true, I am. Were I to classify my hue with a hexadecimal code, it would be #BC7642, also known as Coconut Shell.

Top-secret fact: sometimes I really make myself laugh.

'Have you shrunk?' I'm on fire.

He shows me his shoes. 'Not wearing heels.'

He is, however, wearing black patent winkle pickers, which is perhaps why I don't trust him entirely.

Tests show that it takes less than one tenth of a second to discern whether a person is trustworthy or not, with bad footwear being a major deal breaker. Take me as a barometer.

Currently, I'm wearing Converse All-Stars. Agreeable people wear shoes that are practical and affordable. Whereas expensive or glitzy shoes, or ones that are a bit outré, are deemed to give off a less friendly vibe.

Nota bene: that doesn't make individuality wrong. There's just a time and a place.

'I am loving the hair,' he tells me, sprucing it up, like I'm his muse. 'You look like Jennifer Aniston.'

I shake my head. He's wrong. She's too old.

'Have you been using sun protection?'

I touch my crow's feet. 'Factor thirty.'

That's a lie. I never use cream; I have a touch of the Mediterranean, or so I'd thought.

'Good,' he says. 'You don't want wrinkles.'

Sébastien doesn't have any. He's also incapable of over-doing any facial expression whatsoever. Which is another reason I can't trust him. Botoxed from the ankles up, Sébastien is unable to mirror other people's facial expressions. This is antisocial and alienating. The only thing that separates him from a poor soul with Moebius syndrome is that his sixth and seventh cranial nerves are entirely healthy and he can move his eyeballs laterally.

Unfortunately, the syndrome doesn't affect Sébastien's ability to speak. The man once had a stutter. It was his one redeeming feature. Yet he was cured by the love of a good man – my brother. I listen to him explain our business in full to a plump woman to his left.

'Flo's timing is perfect,' he says. 'Her dress arrived yesterday. It's stunning, just stunning. Ivory. Chantilly lace. Vintage, but no high neck or shoulder pads.'

'I'm not the one getting married,' I explain.

'You're not the bridesmaid either,' he tells me. 'Not any more.'

Ouch.

I won't lie. I never wanted to be a bridesmaid. I was totally hoping their relationship would fizzle out. But that hasn't happened, so I expect to play a starring role in my brother's big day.

'Are you shitting me?' I ask.

'Yes,' he admits. 'Michael wants you to be his best man instead!'

The plump woman covertly looks me up and down – I know this because of my astonishing peripheral vision. I turn, stare her square in the eye and put a hand on my hip.

She's plucky, I'll give her that. She refuses to look away, holds my gaze and smiles – a smile that enlists so much effort I can see her nerve branches strain. My cheeks ache just looking at her.

'The best man, eh?' she says. 'That'll be a talking point.'

'Why?' I wonder.

'It's very modern.'

'It's also very poignant.'

'Yes, I'm aware.' The woman looks at her feet.

What is she aware of, exactly? I glower at Sébastien. 'Shouldn't the request to be a best man come from the groom?' I demand.

Sébastien nods apologetically. 'I was too excited to wait.'

That's another reason I don't trust him, not completely. He's a Capricorn. Capricorns are rubbish at keeping a secret. Not the big secrets – generally, they're OK with them – it's the little ones you have to worry about.

'Where is Michael?' I ask.

'Back at the cottage, getting things ready for your arrival.'

The woman stares at me again. 'He'll be making me sushi,' I tell her.

'I love sushi.' She nods.

From this point on, I decide not to engage her in further conversation. She has a good dash of the Kathy Bates, in a bad way.

'What about Dad – is he at the cottage too?' I ask.

'The Royal Bournemouth.' Sébastien nods sadly.

'The hospital?' I gasp, then look away quickly – there'll be answers in his eyes. I'm not ready for elucidation.

Parental death fact: it happens after you've left a rotten taste in their mouth. Dads are worst. They're achingly fragile when it comes to wilful daughters; often, they die of disenchantment.

'It's not George,' Sébastien says. 'It's Darcie.'

Thank God. I exhale. 'His companion?'

'She suffers from diverticulitis.'

That's when poo gets stuck in the pockets of your colon and goes off. It's debilitating, but not fatal. Why would he not be here to welcome me home?

'Take me there now,' I demand.

The plump woman interrupts. 'You must be so excited?'

Is she sane? 'About *what*?' I ask.

'The wedding.'

I whisper-roar at Sébastien, 'They're getting married?'

'Our wedding,' he explains.

'Good,' I tell him. 'Because them getting married would be bigamy.'

'Bigamy?' frowns Bates.

'You *are* aware this is a private conversation?'

'Oh, I'm sorry.' She does that smile again. This time, a few nerves bypass her eyes. It's fascinating viewing: mind over muscle. We become locked in a stare-out, one I've no intention of losing, until Sébastien hugs me hard, once again squashing his ear against my breast.

'I have to pee.' He looks up expectantly. But I have absolutely nothing to add. I had a piss on the plane.

So, without waiting for Sébastien to disappear to the loo, I head to the short-term parking lot and look for his car.

Sébastien drives a Ford F-Series Twelfth Generation. A monster of a pickup truck, it's parked badly, in a disabled bay. The blue badge on it belongs to Dad, which is extremely illegal – not that you'd question Sébastien's need for parking dispensation. Nonetheless, it surprises me, Dad knowingly defrauding the welfare system; he's usually ethical to a fault.

I look inside the vehicle. It's as expected. Plumped-up driving cushions left at an attractive angle on the seats. Hypoallergenic air freshener. A dustbuster in the footwell. Like my brother, Sébastien is a neat freak. The domesticated have discovered how to trick the brain into some semblance of order, and I envy that.

Sébastien makes me jump. 'I was looking for you.'

'Here I am.'

'And it's wonderful,' he tells me. 'Flo, we need to talk.'

'About what?'

'Lots. Michael, for one. He's been a complete worry-guts.'

'Is he OK?'

'Fine. It's wedding stuff, mostly, he's anxious about. Look, we need to talk about Annie.'

This is the second time I've heard Annie mentioned. Michael was playing Trivial Pursuits with her this time last week.

'That's better,' says a breathless woman behind us. 'Where did you get to, Seb?'

Kathy Bates.

I frown. 'He got to here.'

She ignores me. Issues Sébastien with instructions. To unlock the car, put my suitcase in the boot, help her into the front seat like she's a paraplegic. She's not – she's the wrong side of forty and rotund.

I admit I'm a stickler for etiquette. But I'm the guest. And the matriarch of the family, now Auntie Carina Campanella doesn't exist. Of course, I'm spitting feathers when I find myself buckled into the back *and* completely out of the loop.

I stew until we're on the B3073. Then I tell Sébastien straight, 'Might have been nice to have had an intro.'

'I know,' he agrees. 'We were all too busy chatting.'

He avoids looking at me in the mirror. Or talking. Squints, all consumed, at the road ahead as if he's just got his P-plates.

'We've been friends for a while now,' says Annie, without turning round. 'How long's it been, Seb?'

Seb doesn't know. 'Just a few weeks. Annie couldn't wait to meet you.' Sébastien steals a look at me in the mirror.

Whereas he looks apologetic, my stare is cold, my laugh short, because Annie is the name of the character Kathy Bates plays in *Misery*. Annie Wilkes. She pushes the car seat back as far as it will go.

'I've heard so much about you,' she says.

'Really?' I dig my feet into her seat like it's a leg press. 'I've heard nothing about you.'

'Flo, I am loving your hair,' says Sébastien.

'So you said.' I give up on the leg room, unbuckle, move to the middle of the back seat, lean forward so my head is between theirs.

'So, my dad has taken a lover?'

Sébastien says it ever so quietly: 'Darcie is Annie's mum.'

That's a conversation stopper.

For a good three minutes, all three of us watch the Christchurch Road.

The reason for my silence is that I'm bamboozled. Sébastien's silence comes from a place of spinelessness. Annie's silence screams, 'Touché, bitch.'

If I sit back in my seat, that would suggest defeat. Instead I turn my head to the left and send Annie cruel thoughts. Because if she had half a brain cell, she'd be channelling her self-loathing in a more affable way; one that's sympathetic to her audience, her current audience being me, the only daughter of her mother's lover.

'How old's your mum?' I ask.

Annie flicks me a look. 'Sixty-eight.'

'Is she on the Atkins diet?'

'No, why?'

'Her diet must have been low in fibre. Was she constipated?'

'Flo is a genuine hoot,' Sébastien tells Annie earnestly.

'Was she constipated?' I repeat it, because I want a profile on this Darcie woman. A profile that doesn't provide answers to any of the important questions. Like, when did this debacle start? What does my dad's flirting face even look like? Is there the smallest chance that Annie out of *Misery* and I will become step-sisters?

Finally, Annie turns her head to tell me, 'Mum's a hospitality minister at St Stephen's.'

'She makes cakes?'

'She serves the Eucharist, too.'

This is terrible. Dad loves simple carbohydrates. He also likes laywomen ministers, but usually only as friends.

'I'm not into God,' I tell her flatly. 'You can't do broad brushstrokes when it comes to creation.'

'Ah,' she sighs. '"Do not be unequally yoked with unbelievers."' Her breath, I notice, smells of celery; that's indicative of a urinary-tract infection.

I sit back in the seat. 'Leviticus said, "No haircuts". But I guess we're skipping that one.'

'Oh, I'm all for an open mind, Florence. Just not the type of open-mindedness that makes your brain drop out.'

She actually just misquoted Dawkins at me. 'Have you even read *The God Delusion*?'

'Yes.' She so lies.

'And you understood it?'

'Yes.'

'What's chapter one called?'

'You have a very aggressive tone.'

'"A Deeply Religious Non-believer".'

Sébastien's laugh is desperately appeasing. 'You two are funny.'

'I am,' I tell him firmly. 'Can you take me home, please?'

'What about your dad?'

'I need to see my brother as soon as possible.'

Sébastien nods. 'I'll phone ahead.'

'He's not the royal family. Just drop me in the village, I'll walk up the lane.'

Annie mumbles to Sébastien, 'I haven't seen Micky since Friday.'

'Blood relatives only,' says Sébastien seriously.

'It's getting dark. She shouldn't be walking on her own.'

I am perilously close to violence. 'Just drop me in the village. I need air.'

Leaving my suitcase in the boot, I alight at the green. Sit on a bench while Sébastien does a six-point turn, Annie in full conversational flow beside him.

Once they've gone, I centre myself for a minute or two. Stare at grass. Look at the bench's plaque. I've read it a hundred times.

Harriet Humphries (1960–1996) I have loved thee with an everlasting love. Your husband, Aaron.

That's so unbelievably romantic it brings a single sob to my throat. Because if Dad was so sure Mum was dead, why no bench? He's a bench kind of guy.

I'll tell you why – her name wouldn't have been worth the bench it was written on. Not now he's got himself a *companion*.

I chivvy myself along, do a few tricep dips; use the bench as an indicator of my fitness. In my twenties, I could do fifty. Today I manage just twenty-three. I walk it out around the green, glancing now and then across the street at the village post office. Technically, *my* post office.

Dad bought it for me as a gift. I didn't want it; it's been a total bind. But given what happened to my mother, the point of it was exactly that. To hinder wanderlust and keep me moored.

For a few years, I humoured him, learnt the ropes, because my first divorce had left its toll, plundered me of spark. I'd experienced something metaphysical with another human being, but he'd found someone better. I'm not sure there's anything more wicked than having your moment top-trumped while you still inhabit it.

I power-walk to Cowslip Cottage. The route takes me through a stretch of woods and an open field.

I love the dark when you're in a place you know like the back of your hand. It makes you feel at an advantage. This evening, however, everything feels skew-whiff. Bates was on the money when she said I should consider safety. As soon as I get home, I'll make myself some pepper spray, Annie bloody Wilkes being number one on my hit list.

The faster I walk, the more determined I become. Yes, I feel totally out of the loop. But that is *only* because I took my eye off the ball.

Home

The Motte – that's what Dad calls our hillock, the one upon which our little stone castle sits. The nearest neighbour is 380 metres away, back down the lane, though we can't see their house and they can't see ours. We're separated by a thin strip of woodland, stone walls, a cattle grate and the freehold. For the first eight years of life, that house proffered solitude and safety. Then Mum left and I felt like a hostage.

It's only Michael inside, but every light is on. He doesn't like twilight, or the dark, or ghosts, or anything with oversized eyes – the uncanny, in general, tips him over an edge. Still, I can't help myself.

Tiptoeing through the flowerbeds, I avoid the gravel, press myself close against the wall of the cottage and arrive at the kitchen window, a nervous tickle in my bowel.

Peering in through the wooden sash, I spot Michael in the corner. He has his back to me and is placing sushi on a plate – green cones that spew seaweed and raw fish.

I knew it, I smile. The certainty of him.

Once upon a time, I mentioned I liked temaki, and he's not stopped making it since. I grew bored of it years ago but, while I inhabit this earth, Michael will *never* know that.

My little brother has been muscly since adolescence, but his shoulders look especially broad tonight. I imagine he's been caning it at the gym in preparation for his big day. The plain white T-shirt embraces his teres major and minor, his lats and traps. His long neck is as noble as an American

Saddlebred's. It's the type of back you hope complements the face.

My brother turns, walks towards the window, a bowl in his hand.

His front matches up all right. His skin is a bright West Country brown. Sun-kissed hair, chin-length, with a surfer's wave. His colouring and build is the same as our dad's, though his facial features are more Mum's – the symmetrical nose, pillowy lips, the round and vulnerable eyes – the eyes especially are down to Bambi, her dominant mien being one of perpetual bewilderment.

Michael is washing the bowl in the sink when, finally, he catches sight of me. My smile is as gigantic as I can make it. His scream could shatter bullet-proof glass.

Quickly, I make things right – kiss the window repeatedly.

He can't kiss his side because the sink's in the way, but he is able to violently throw open the sash and screech, 'Why would you fucking do that?'

'I didn't mean to scare you.'

'I thought you were Mum.'

At once, I feel ashamed. 'Oh, God, no. I'm not. I'm Flo.' Because Michael might have Bambi's snooker-ball eyes, but I have everything else of hers – and she was my age once, the age he remembers her best.

'I can see it's you *now*.' He's close to tears.

And I shout strictly, 'Stop it!' His weeping is like kryptonite to me – my stomach fails completely; the air bolts free of my lungs. 'Wait there!' I say.

I head south-west for fifteen metres, through a gap in the fence and into the back garden, across Dad's lawn and through the back door. Once in the kitchen, I snatch a cone of sushi and take the biggest bite.

'That is the best temaki I have ever had.'

'You haven't swallowed it yet.'

'Have now. And it's sublime.'

'I did try hard.' He sighs. 'Sébastien bought the salmon from a shop that specialises in fish.'

'A fishmonger's.'

'Yes.' He is utterly depressed. 'I don't like your hair.'

'Why not?'

'I liked your old hair better.'

'Me too. But it was for my own safety. I couldn't be recognised.'

He nods. 'You did mess up.'

'Actually, you were the one who botched it.'

'That's true.'

Indisputable fact: it is not true. I was set up, and that was entirely my fault.

The client was working on behalf of the Dutch Minister for Security and Justice – an ex-target, who fitted me up. Non-racist fact: never entrap the Dutch – they are gratingly cool when it comes to revenge.

I argue weakly, 'You have to admit, you did think there was something dodgy about the client.'

'I did.' Michael is his own worst enemy.

'And at no point did you share those concerns with me.'

'I did not. I was being measured.'

'Which is brilliant. Just don't be measured without telling me first. This is private investigation, Michael, not human resources.'

'You fell in love with the target.'

I put a very final finger in the air. 'Let bygones be bygones. A bygone is something that's been and gone.'

'I know what a bygone is.'

'You don't.'

As fed up as I've ever seen him, he asks, 'Is Mum a bygone or not?'

And I hold his forearms tight. 'She is and she isn't. I just haven't found her yet. But I'm here now.'

Still he forgets to hug me and ask how I am; to tell me he loves me and that it doesn't matter if I haven't brought Mum home; the main thing is I'm back safe and sound; and that I'm never to go away again, not for more than a week, ten days, tops.

I put an ear to his heart and bear-hug his waist.

'I can't breathe,' he says.

'You can. I'm just impeding it a bit.'

'No, I actually can't, Flo.'

'You can.'

But the truth of the matter is, his heart beats too fast. A resting heart rate over 110 beats per minute is considered tachycardic; Michael's currently dances to a drum-and-bass beat. I look up at his face, it's a gainsboro grey.

Pulling him on to a chair, I hold his face still.

'Copy me, Michael.' He follows my every move. Slowly, we inhale and exhale together. 'It'll stop us getting carbon-monoxide overload,' I tell him. 'Because I'm mirroring your breathing now, and if you don't slow down we'll both pass out.'

'I do know.'

And he does. We've been through this enough times.

Michael is prone to emotional overload. Most especially, guilt fills him to the brim like quickly poured lemonade. He has to burp the lot out before his head can settle from the fizz overdose. It's a lot of the reason I love him so much – everyday bullshit sits so uncomfortably with him.

It takes a good ten minutes, but eventually my brother is calm.

'I'm sorry I didn't meet you at the airport,' he finally admits.

'That's OK. You were preparing for my arrival.'

'No.' He looks at his belly. 'I wasn't. That was an excuse.'

'I thought so.' I try to make light of it. Remind him of happier times. 'When I was eleven, I'd get the bus to Christchurch, do you remember? You'd be waiting for me on the green. You'd walk me home. It made you feel grown-up – making sure I was safe.'

'I missed you. It was our thing.'

How I wish we had audio-surveillance in the kitchen. What he just said is proof of our connection. In an ideal world, I'd listen to it on a loop.

I missed you. I missed you. I missed you . . .

'The trouble is, Flo, I just wasn't ready.'

'For what?'

'To meet Mum yet. You said it would be a surprise. I didn't want a surprise.'

My shoulders wither, because it's such a valid comment. Michael has spent his entire life thinking she was dead – up until a few months ago. I told him about the birthday card, told him it was Mum's writing, whatever Dad said.

'Christ, Michael, I'd never have done that to you, just turn up with her. *Never.*'

But how would I know where his head was at? I was gallivanting around Italy. I tip his chin up so he can see how serious my eyes are.

'She's not here. She won't be here – not for your wedding, or for a while, or ever. I didn't find her. I have avenues, but I'm putting them to one side. I'm here for you now. Forget Mum.'

I see it. The utter relief in his eyes. And I feel wounded. Why don't we need the same thing? Of course I know why, but still, *why*?

Michael takes things literally. Utterly placated, he stands up and polishes kitchen surfaces. While so doing, he congratulates me on my melatonin content: 'You're brown as a nut.'

'I'm coconut shell.'

'And you've put on weight.'

I tuck my stomach into my jeans. 'It's muscle.'

'Seven pounds of it.'

There's no point in arguing. Michael's phenomenal at stuff like that. As retribution, I rabbit-punch him in the kidneys, until he stops me to say, all-mature, 'So, Dad's got a woman.'

I sigh. Let my hands dangle. 'It's too weird. How does it make you feel?'

'Too weird.'

'Is he happy, though?'

'He steals my aftershave and he's cut down on his drinking.' He whispers, 'I've been monitoring him.'

'Good work. I hate her.'

'Who, Darcie?'

'Kathy Bates.'

He puts every fingertip to his chest. 'She's one of the finest character actresses that ever lived.'

'Yes, she is.'

'She won an Oscar.'

I start again. 'What do you make of Annie, Darcie's daughter?'

'She's tidy.'

'Everything I'm not.'

'Yes,' he says. 'Sébastien says you're misunderstood.'

There's a compliment in there, but I take great umbrage. 'He'd know all about that. He's definitely shrunk.'

'Do you think?' Michael's not listening. 'She's here a lot, Flo.'

'Kathy Bates?'

'No, Annie.'

'Well, *I'm* here now.'

'Thank the gods,' he tells me dramatically, his eyes threatening to escape their sockets. And I feel like Queen Daenerys of House Targaryen – my brother and I now fight for a common cause, the dethronement of Annie whatever her last name is.

'Had any acting work lately, apart from the giraffe stuff?' I make small talk.

'Not much.' He looks sorry about it. But he shouldn't be.

Michael has trained hard to act normal, so hard he's making a living at it, securing regular work as an extra and the odd line in a commercial. That is utterly admirable.

'Leave it with me,' I promise. 'I'll talk to Maeve. Get you a few gigs. We have to stick together from now on. Get it?'

'Got it.' He nods. 'Are you back for good?'

'For the meantime.'

'How much of the meantime?'

'A lot of it, just for a bit.'

'Good. I think I need to talk to you.'

Hands down, this is the most indispensable I've felt in months. 'Talk.' I nod wisely.

'I'm in between a rock and a hard place.'

'We've all been there. Let's start with the rock?'

'Sébastien.'

'And the hard place?'

'Marriage.'

It's wrong, but I want to whoop. 'What has he done to you?'

'You're such the cynicism type.' Michael looks disappointed in me – it ruins the moment. 'I don't think I'm ready for the commitment. He annoys me sometimes. It's normal.'

'Is that what Sébastien says, "*It's normal*"?'

'No, Annie says it. She's here a lot.'

'You said.' I squint. 'What's with Sébastien and her? He's like her gimp.'

'He used to be my gimp,' explains Michael.

'And mine.' I nod, because when we lived in London he'd do my shopping, wash my smalls and check the larder for out-of-date soup.

'Watch Annie, will you?' I tell Michael. 'She's the type who'd chain you to the bed and hammer your feet into right angles.'

Michael gasps.

I point. 'I'm home now. You can stop worrying about everything. I think it's high time we just concentrated on you and this wedding.'

He rubs his hair, relieved. 'Yes, because I might still want to marry Sébastien.'

'Within reason, you will do whatever you want to do.'

'No more talking about Mum, though,' he tells me firmly.

'No more talking about Mum,' I say, ever so sadly.

I can think about her, though.

Personally, I blame Mum for my untidiness. Her OCD made me lazy. From a young age, she taught me about microscopic pathogens, showed me how best to wage war on them, and I decided there was no point in us both making our lives a misery – too many cooks, and all that.

Were Bambi still in residence today, my bedroom would have seen a fumigator within seconds of my leaving home. But she isn't here, leaving Michael to reap what I sowed. And he's done a fabulous job tidying it up – because five years ago, when I bid farewell to the Motte and said hello to a flat in the eaves of a mansion block in London, I left this room looking like a crime scene. I'd been in a rush, was running late for my new life in London. Michael joined me in the capital a few months later. But not before tidying up.

Everything's back in its place now – my bedroom is a tribute to the eighties.

Wallpaper, curtains and bedspread showcase a rash of tiny pink flowers. There's a little white dressing table with cabriole legs and a three-panel mirror, a modernistic black ash unit on which sits a huge portable TV, and a radio alarm clock, its digits a traffic-light red and utterly unconducive to sleep.

And on the back of the door, a film poster – *An Officer and a Gentleman*. It was the only place I was allowed to put Blu-tac, plus Mum loved Richard Gere too – we were both a bit mesmerised by his overbite.

An old, familiar noise makes me motionless – as a child, I'd imagine it was a masked maniac who was staggering in the front garden below, dragging a metal rod across corrugated iron, playing his shield like a satanic accordion. It wasn't a maniac. It was the cattle grate, an excellent if antiquated alarm system. I wait for the inevitable crunch and dispersal of gravel, the blare of the security light. Then I jump on to the bed, kneel at the window.

Sébastien alights on the driver's side, opens the passenger door. Annie insists on first taking his hand before hopping free of the truck. It doesn't take a genius: she has something over him. When Sébastien panders to me, he does so with a voice that suggests I'm incorrigible but sweet. He's wrong. Nonetheless, there's fondness in his voice. With Annie, his voice is different, nervously deferent, which means she's either genuinely royal or has Seb's balls in a vice-like grip.

As they pass beneath me towards the front door, I notice she has a bald patch. In an ideal world, I'd aim something at it. A peanut or a dart. Or the portable telly, because within seconds her voice fills the house, downstairs and up, her bossy phonetics feeding off the cottage's acoustics.

I push the bedroom door shut and lie on the floor, my ear against the carpet. The gap between the floorboards and the plasterboard funnels the discussion below. I'm able to gather the main gist – Darcie's large intestine is fucked.

'There are worse things than diverticulitis,' I tell the carpet. 'It's just a bit excruciating.'

Outside, the security light turns off, my room is suddenly dark. Yet I remain face down. It's quite comfortable here. The carpet is musty and familiar. My photoreceptor cells have begun to fill with rhodopsin, the low-light-sensitive pigment that tells your brain it's bedtime. I become entirely limp and make firm plans: to close my eyes for one minute and not a second longer.

The next thing I hear is a voice from above – gentle, male, as familiar as my own.

'Florrie, sweetheart. Let's get you more comfortable.'

The light that streams in from the hallway is a familiar pink. I squint up at my dad, allow him to manoeuvre me to the single bed. I'm fully clothed, yet he tucks me in tightly.

The duvet's fabric is soft with wear and smells exotic – sandalwood and tuberose. When he kisses my head, I get a heady whiff of Paco Rabanne.

'Welcome home, Piccolina,' he whispers.

And even though everything smells different, I'm utterly relieved to see him smile, a one-hundred-per-cent genuine one. I wish I could wake up properly and grin back, only bigger, but each of my eyelashes is as heavy as a panel pin. They drag my lids down. I manage only the odd peep before giving in, closing my eyes, snuggling into his hip.

'She's not in Italy,' I tell him straight.

'No, Florrie.'

'Did you know?'

His tone is abysmally sad. 'I don't know a thing any more.' I don't have the energy to open my eyes and tell him his wife had a pretend name. He puts a line under the matter, anyway. 'It stops now, for Michael's sake. He's got too much on. There've been a lot of changes.'

'Your companion, you mean?'

He fidgets like a teenager. 'You've not left him for this long before.'

'I have.'

'Not when you've gone abroad.'

'He's not my child.'

'I do know.'

I do know.

'We get that from her. *I do know.*'

'Your mother was very defensive.' He's smiling, I can hear it.

I smile too. 'In a nice way.'

'Yes,' he agrees.

This is momentous. Dad and I haven't spoken like this since I hit fourteen. Too often, I bombarded him with questions about her, left him rabbit-eyed and battening down the Truth Portals. Frightened to alter the new dynamic, I keep my eyes shut.

But he changes the subject back to Michael.

'I know you need things saying out loud and your brother's not that way inclined, but he's missed you.'

'He told me out loud tonight.' The fact that Michael was talking retrospectively is utterly irrelevant.

'Then there's the wedding – that's getting on top of him.'

Disappointed, I open an eye. 'So that's that? We go back to how we were before. Us all pretending the past is tied up and shipshape? Don't you want to know what I found out in Italy?'

He takes a deep breath. 'It's our turn now – yours, mine and Michael's. I haven't seen you since the beginning of August. Christmas is coming up. Can't we just *be* for a bit?'

I close my eye. Turn away from him. Push my nose into the pillow. 'I'm done looking for her, anyway. Michael's not in the right place for life's nuances.'

'Not at the moment,' says Dad.

I'm unsure how long our silence lasts, but it makes me jump when Dad asks, 'How long are you back for this time?'

'A while,' I mumble.

'Then I need you to promise we'll forget everything for a bit.'

'I just did.'

'Promise me, Florence.'

I open both eyes. My father's face is backlit, his features in shadow. His hair is shorter, I notice; its silhouette suggests a Caesar cut.

'Always listen to your father. He is protecting his family. You should pay him more respect,' Tommaso had said.

I take my dad's hand.

'OK. I'm under your roof. Your rules. I won't talk about her or do any searching or stuff. It'll be like Bambi is a figment of our imaginations. As well as an administrative blip. Globally.'

The hall light shines at me. He knows what I'm implying – whereas I can't see him, can't judge the rapidity of his blinks or analyse his micro-expressions, so haven't a clue what he thinks in return.

I flop back on to the pillow and close my eyes.

'She was endearing, though,' I tell him.

'Oh, yes.' His voice cracks, and I'm pleased. I'd begun to wonder if he'd loved her at all. That maybe I'd invented the bit of my childhood where Mum and Dad were soulmates.

Dad strokes my hair for a long time.

Prostitute

Usually, I'm a diehard insomniac, but I let it slip last night. In my defence, I've travelled nearly 2,000 kilometres and am physically and mentally harried. I certainly haven't had the time to play fluffer to my sleep fixation. I wish I was being facetious, but too often insomnia is the person's own fault.

I've read the journals, visited sleep therapists, interrogated other poor sleepers, and my opinion is this: the sleep deprived are sane, mainly. They do, however, display above average signs of internalisation, neurosis and perfectionism. I've tried everything – herbal remedies, cognitive behavioural therapy, Ayurveda and self-hypnosis. Leaving me to conclude quite firmly that, unless someone gives me a personality transplant, my circadian rhythm is fucked.

I say all this because, for a girl with my disposition, it's unbelievably invigorating not to remember the night time or even your dreams, just to be awoken by the smell of sausages and a brand-new day.

My first morning home.

Groggy, I find my old button-up dressing gown. It's tight, but as line fresh as my sheets. I sniff its cuff and take in the view from my window – Dorset is sunny, the hills are a bright mustard, the distant sea a familiar prison-bar grey.

A mobile rings. I don't have a working one. Nonetheless, there's one on the bedside table, an old iPhone 4. I pick it up and recognise the flashing number immediately. It's the landline: Dad's calling me from downstairs.

'Hello?' I say.

'Good morning, Florrie,' he sings. 'Breakfast is served.'

It's nice knowing that your dad's happy you're home; of course, I half skip into the kitchen, wave the scratched phone at him and say, 'Can I have this?'

'All yours.'

'Is it your old one?'

He butters toast. 'Darcie's. She suggested it might tide you over, until you get yourself a niftier handset. It's a pay-as-you-go.'

'That's thoughtful.' I sit at the kitchen table.

Dad places a man-size fry-up in front of me. I ignore it to look at him.

The last time I saw him his face was as grey as his unkempt hair. His sweater needed darning. The clothes he wore might as well have been hanging on a valet stand, a very tall and slightly depressed one. These days, he's fuller in the face and body and wears trousers and an ironed shirt. His skin tone seems to have reacquired a more youthful yellow. As has his hair – the Caesar cut has a hint of bottle-blond.

'Is Darcie OK?' I ask.

His response is grateful. 'They're discharging her in a few days.'

'You know you're all making such a fuss. A liquid diet and antibiotics and she'll be fine.'

He squints at me. 'Any other philanthropic advice?'

'Paracetamol. Not the non-steroidal anti-inflammatory ones, though.'

'You'll love her,' he says.

If I had the energy, I'd punch him in the face, because how can he move on, just like that. 'Do *you* love her?' I ask.

He nods gravely. 'As a friend.'

Truth Portals . . .

We have them over the body. Examples include the soles of the feet, kneecaps, heart, the holes in your head and most places with a sphincter. Fibbers shut them off when they withhold facts; suck their lips thin or cup their testes. Dad does nothing other than spoon mushrooms on top of my breakfast.

'It's great to have you home.' He grins.

And I grin too. Because it *is* great to be home now I know he and Darcie aren't having sex.

'Any idea how long you're back for?'

'I've no plans. Definitely for a bit.'

'Good. Then you need to think about work.'

'Bloody hell, Dad.'

'It would be good for Michael too.'

There's no disagreeing with him there. Four months ago, we were the dream team. Just not in the way Dad would have liked – he went mad when he discovered I'd had Michael working as gumboot.

'So, what's the deal?' I sigh. 'You're understaffed at the post office, right?'

He sits opposite me. Eats. 'The opposite.'

'Really?'

'Which means you can do whatever you want.'

I put my cutlery down. 'I want to be a criminal psychologist.'

My dad looks genuinely interested, and I'm surprised. Normally, he'd have a look of unease, fully aware that I might actually give it go. He doesn't worry that I won't succeed. It's the possibility I will that concerns him; I might never come home again.

'A criminal psychologist studies the thoughts and intentions of criminals,' I tell him. 'It's a subfield of anthropology. I did a unit in criminal anthropology when I was at Chichester.'

'Did you?'

'I did.' He's even showing an interest in my qualifications, of which I have a few. 'You know how much I love mental health.'

Nope, his headshake tells me. *I had no idea.*

'I'll get to meet psychopaths. Sociopathy is fascinating. I've actually tested myself.'

He stops eating. 'And are you one?'

'Nope.' I stab my fried egg. 'Full to the brim with empathy, apparently. I will have to retrain, though.'

'To be a psychopath?'

Dad-jokes are the best. I spit breakfast back at my plate. 'A criminal psychologist.'

'Well, look into all the possibilities, by all means. Until then, I have a friend. He said he can put some work your way.'

Maybe our ten weeks apart has reset the default button. I like my new dad. He's less ineffectual. He's pretending to trust my judgement. He's also completely insane, having forgotten a very pertinent issue.

'Not too long ago, I had a very recognisable face,' I remind him. 'Anonymity is key when you're in entrapment.'

'I'm not talking entrapment.' He scowls. 'I'm talking regular cases.'

'Lost kittens?'

'Tenants with arrears.'

'Debt collecting?'

'Oh, I don't know. Trevor Hannigan said that he needed someone. He runs Hannigan and Dean Solicitors in Christchurch.'

'I don't like lawyers,' I sigh. 'We turn to them instead of our own conscience. Do I know him?'

'He comes into the post office. Monobrow.'

I point my knife. 'In Tajikistan, the monobrow is considered very sexy in men and women. Does Darcie have one?'

He's pretending to think but doing a secret smile; I can see it in his earlobes. 'If she does, she plucks.'

'For the best. In men, it signifies virility. I usually avoid ambulance chasers, but as Hannigan's a friend of yours.' I pick up a sausage with my fingers. 'Can I take Michael?'

'I was hoping you would,' says Dad.

'Really?' I squeak.

'I'll let Trevor know you're coming.'

'Good. But it's just to tide me over for a bit. Then I'm off to Scandinavia to study serial killers.'

He does an actual laugh and I feel like we're invincible.

I am totally going to kill my dad.

I won't work in the post office, so he's trying to get me to deliver someone else's letters instead. Admittedly, these are important ones – Bankruptcy Petitions, Section Notices, Orders to Attend Court, N39s, N79s, N61s. Possession Orders, Non-molestation Orders, Summonses, Injunctions, etc. But it is not my cup of tea and, worst of all, it's entirely insulting.

Scrapheap fact: PIs who can't private investigate process serve.

Nonetheless, I convey deep concern for Hannigan's staffing issues, because beside me I can hear Michael's brain struggling not to send words to his mouth; like 'epilator' and 'Veet', as Hannigan suffers a teeny touch from Werewolf Syndrome. His unibrow packs quite a punch. With luck, he'll think Michael's looking concerned at his need for reliable staff. That being the reason we're here.

The guy that used to do Trevor Hannigan's process serving was a liar. He pretended to serve legal papers when he hadn't. As a result, he's in prison for fraud.

Turning to Michael, I explain process serving in a nutshell.

'Mr X has been subpoenaed to give evidence in court. The letter must be delivered to him personally so that, if he doesn't turn up, they can send Mr X straight to jail. The PI's job is simply to hand deliver the unhappy tidings, then to swear on a bible of our choice that Mr X has received the letter.'

Hannigan interrupts me to humour Michael, which is extremely kind, but his pitching's all wrong. 'But what if Mr X, say, runs round in a circle and refuses to accept the letter?'

Michael fact: he is not retarded. I wonder what my dad says to people about his son.

'You tap his arm with it, drop it and run,' I tell Hannigan firmly. Turn back to my brother. 'It's like tag rugby or It.'

'Quite simple, really.' The solicitor smiles encouragingly at Michael.

Intellectual disability fact: Michael doesn't have one. Asperger's is part of normal human variation. That's society's prejudice put right.

'Trevor, when people know an unwelcome letter is coming, they avoid PI-looking types at all costs. They go missing. Other people pretend to be them. You need a process server worth their salt. One that doesn't come at a tenner an hour.'

Hannigan scoffs. 'I should be so lucky.'

'You want a job doing properly, you should honour the requisite skill monetarily.' I hate misers. 'That's polite.'

'Absolutely.' He's not listening.

'I assume you have a copy of *The British Process Servers Guide*?'

Hannigan's office is chaotic. 'It's here somewhere.' He taps an empty square inch of desk but makes no attempt to look for the book.

I tell Michael, 'There's one in Dad's garage. It includes the Woolf Reforms, explanations of rules and procedures and examples of affidavits and statements of service for all process in the UK.'

My brother's eyes tell me: *I am bored shitless.*

My eyes tell him back: *I am bored shitless too. Don't worry. I've no intention of taking this job.*

Then Trevor Hannigan tells me I can't have the position, anyway.

'Miss Love, personally, I don't recognise you from Adam. But I'm not sure infamy is a useful quality when serving court papers.'

Michael folds his arms defensively.

'You're right.' I stand up. 'My dad led me to believe you had suitable work. I'm sorry to have wasted your time.' I shake his hand sincerely.

In the car park, Michael is beside himself. 'He had an actual moustache on his forehead. It was like a hair-ruler. Oh, what's her name had one?' he points.

'Frida Kahlo.' I look for my keys.

Michael has a half-decent voice: "*Non, rien de rien. Non, je ne regrette rien.*"

'That's Edith Piaf.'

'I do know. Hannigan looked like Hitler.'

'Hitler didn't have a unibrow.'

'Magnum PI.'

I punch him in the shoulder because he didn't have a unibrow either, but I love *Magnum PI*. Mum made me watch it when I was little. Then I made Michael watch them, quite recently, actually.

'Florence!' Trevor jogs up behind us. 'I wonder if I might speak with you alone.'

Usually on a case, my response would be: *where I go, Michael goes too*. Being thirty-nine on the autistic spectrum makes him phenomenal at the things regular people are shit at. Guessing your ring size, for example. Or your bowling shoe size. Or your deep-vein-thrombosis socks size. When Michael meets a person they appear to him as an annotated PowerPoint diagram. That's very useful on a case.

Unfortunately, my brother's past the point of taking this particular client seriously. Plus, I see something in the lawyer's eyes – the need to catch a break. That's such a carrot to a girl like me.

'Wait for me in the car,' I tell Michael, earnestly.

I follow Hannigan back into the office, closing the door behind me.

He heads straight for the window, yanks up the sash.

'We got off on the wrong foot,' he states. 'Would you mind if we start again?'

'I thought it went quite well.' I smile.

When he offers me a cigarette, I take one. Research has found that non-smokers can be dangerously controlled and self-absorbed. Whereas me and Trevor bypass the bullshit and hang out of the window like schoolkids. He even blows on the end of his cigarette as if stoking up a joint. I wish it were one – *Two's up*, I'd say.

Exhaling, he remembers to light mine too. 'I didn't want you to do my process serving.'

'Thank God. When you started to talk about your last guy . . .'

'I actually have a personal matter that needs attending to.'

I hide my excitement. 'My speciality.'

'It's a bit sensitive.'

'It always is.'

'I'm not sure you can even help me.'

'How about I be the judge of that?' I'm tempted to give him a cheeky shoulder barge, but that would be too intimate, given the circumstances.

'Very well.' He taps his cigarette. A breeze blows the ash back at his facial hair. 'I have a friend.'

I stop him right there. 'No, you don't, Trevor. This isn't *EastEnders*.'

His smile is apologetic. 'It concerns a member of my

family. My sister, Fiona, heard about you. We knew your dad, of course.'

Specifically, Fiona would have read about me. *Heat*, the *Sun*, *TMZ*, you name it, the grainy stills of Scat Delaney and I were in it. I shudder. Imagine Fiona and Trevor gossiping about me and my family because, in their world, we're connected – what with their dad knowing my dad once.

Infamy fact: it's fostered by the most dubious of connections.

'How *is* George?' Trevor remembers to ask.

'Oh, lovely.' It throws me off track, encourages me to digress. 'How long have you known my dad?'

'For ever. But not at all, really. He and my father worked at the sorting office in Lymington. They were kids, just out of school. Doubles partners too.'

'Tennis?'

He nods. 'County players. I haven't seen George in years.'

I frown; Trevor might as well accuse Dad of being an acrobat with the Cirque du Soleil. 'But you use his post office in Laurelbridge?'

'My dad mentioned he worked there years back. I popped by to ask after you.'

'I had no idea my dad even lived in Lymington.'

Trevor becomes impatient. 'Well, he did.'

I remember what Massimo said: 'Stories fall apart when you factor in the passage of time.'

'Did you know Mum too?'

'Dad and George lost touch before he married.'

'Where does your dad live now?'

'Heaven.' He throws the cigarette on to the grass below. 'Sorry, is this relevant?'

Not to his case, no. 'Everything is relevant,' I tell him, discarding my cigarette too, switching to professional mode, frowning like a Macmillan nurse, because people are broken by the time they speak to a PI – it's rude not to show compassion.

When we sit down, I lean across the desk and speak frankly. 'If I can help you, I will. If I can't, this conversation will remain confidential. I do, however, need the nitty-gritty.'

'Of course.'

'So, what is the nitty-gritty?'

'Fiona, my sister, wants a divorce.'

'What's the husband done?'

'Nothing. They bicker a lot. She wants out.'

'That's it?'

'He's an academic,' he explains.

'There are worse things. Have you suggested marriage guidance?'

'You should have been a comedian.'

And you should have been a carpenter. Or a peripatetic teacher, I don't say, because surely therapy's a less dramatic option during a relationship crisis.

'So –' Trevor pats his thighs proactively – 'Fiona needs you to entrap her husband.'

I'm still unclear as to what the academic's done wrong. 'Can you be a little more specific?'

'Of course.' He leans forward. 'We need the full works. Photos, audio, lots of compromising positions. It has to stand up in court. I take it you do the full works?'

Whoa there. 'The full works?'

'Intercourse, cunnilingus, fellatio – one or all of the above.'

A key point he's not grasped: I am not an actual prostitute. Never have I and never would I do *the full works*. The worst thing that's ever happened to me during an entrapment is a dry hump and an attempted tit-up, both of which I've put to an immediate halt.

My instinct is to give Hannigan a Glasgow kiss, then cry. To him, I look the *type*. The rude bastard even visited my father's workplace to ask if his daughter would fuck a man on film.

My eyes taper. 'I kiss for five seconds with tongues. That's it.'

He shakes his head. 'That won't work. We need to don a lawyer's head. Daniel won't divorce her, not now Fiona's wealthy – our father left us solvent. If Daniel's unfaithful, however, he'll have no rights, neither legally or financially. The prenup is watertight. I wrote it myself. We need to make Fiona's case incontrovertible. Low-level fidelity insinuates hope on the part of the respondent, leaving the petitioner looking like an idealist. Therefore, in this case, the five-second kiss is inadequate for my require-ments.'

I stand up. 'I think I have had all the nitty-gritty I need.'

'Is that it?' says Hannigan.

'I'm afraid it is. I'm not sure infamy is a useful quality when duping somebody into the full works.' I make my way to the door.

'No, no.' He stands up too, reassures me. 'Daniel won't recognise you.'

I turn around. 'Is he registered blind?'

'He's a physicist. He's holed up in his study seven days a week writing equations. He doesn't know who the prime minister is. Pop stars, like Scat Delaney, are definitely not on his radar.'

There, Hannigan dropped a clanger. I *love* physicists. They make everything possible. What sane person would want to mess with their emotional mojo?

I squint. 'Do they suck you free of compassion at law school, or were you born an arse?'

'I'm sorry?'

'There are two types of entrapment, Hannigan. Your type and my type. My type is about putting minds at rest and righting wrongs. Your type is so calculating it borders on sociopathic. And, by the way, the most sexually charged encounters *never* culminate in sex.'

At last, Hannigan has nothing to say. I watch a wash of pink penetrate his face. I don't know who the hell his dad is, but I put a pitiless nail in the coffin of our association: 'Your father would be turning in his grave.'

Furious, I return to the car park. Michael is doing research on his phone. Flopping into the car, I put my belt on, then scream into the back of my hand.

Michael ignores my meltdown.

'George Bush,' he tells me.

I turn to the right. 'What about him?'

'He had a monobrow.' Michael likes to rinse a joke of its joy. 'Brad Pitt had one too, but he had electrolysis. And Groundskeeper Willie from *The Simpsons*. Though he never had electrolysis. Why are you screaming?'

'Because Hannigan asked me to shag his brother-in-law.'

'In a bad way?'

'In an extremely cruel way. The guy's a bloody physicist.'

He doesn't know if this is a good or a bad thing. 'Do you want me to beat him up?'

'Hannigan, definitely one day.' I flick his cheek. 'I've been thinking.'

'Oh no,' says Michael.

'Why don't we get the business up and running again? You and me. We were a pretty neat combo.'

He nods. 'I carried you.'

He did not. 'We'll do the same as we did in London, only here in Dorset. I can rejig the website. You can be the front guy, but in the background. I'll have to stay in the shadows too. No more entrapment.'

'Can Sébastien work for us too?'

'Nope.'

'Good. I want it to be like the olden days.'

I agree with him entirely. In the olden days, it was just me and him.

'I will need two weeks off, though,' he says. 'Sébastien would be disappointed if I don't turn up.'

'To what?'

'The wedding.'

'You're not taking his name?'

'I have my own name.'

'Yes, you do.'

'Annie thinks I should.'

'Mr and Mr Tremblay is *never* going to happen.' I remember to humour him. 'I should try my best-man's outfit on tonight. We could have a dry run.'

'I'm not in the right frame of mind.'

'Then we need to address that,' I state. 'I'm taking you for lunch. How long's it been since we had some you-and-me time?'

'Years.'

'It'll be a practice hen party.'

'Yay.' That bucks him up.

'You'll have to pay, though.'

'Deal.' He starts the car. 'Where are you taking me?'

'Lymington.' I bang the dash. 'And put your foot down. We're already late to that table.'

Jesus

Lymington, Hampshire

Now we're here, I can testify it is quaint and touristy and cobbled. Situated on the southern edge of the New Forest, the town sits on a harbour and is rich in maritime history. From the nineteenth century particularly, it was heralded for its shipbuilding, salt-making and smuggling.

I *love* smuggling. Enid Blyton's *Five Go to Smuggler's Top* is in my top thirty children's books. As a child, I read it fifty-two times. Michael had a soft spot for piracy too. Captain Pugwash, especially – he'd memorise all the Pugwashisms, would say things like, 'lolloping landlubbers' and 'kipper me capstans'.

The clincher: Lymington has a whole network of tunnels that lead from beach to tavern. You can go on an *actual* tour.

Yet neither Michael nor I have ever been here. It's just twenty-five kilometres from Laurelbridge, but Dad had not considered it worthy of a daytrip. Neither had he felt it worth mentioning that he'd once lived here, nor that he represented its county at a racquet sport.

Here's the thing.

I came from a family that went to every tourist facility within an eighty-kilometre radius – twice. Every botanical garden, castle, coastal landform and museum. My dad loved an enrichment activity. He'd test us on what we'd learnt when we got home. It was his way of bypassing meaningful conversation. By the age of thirteen, I could have written a *Rough Guide to the South-west*. Unless there was a chapter in it called 'Lymington'.

Other facts about Lymington.

The ferry trip to the Isle of Wight takes just twenty-two minutes. Yet when we holidayed in Ventnor, Dad drove us all the way to Southampton, which is an hour further along the coast – the final sea leg takes twice the time.

Not only is that an unnecessary carbon footprint, it's extremely cruel. I suffered from stage-five motion sickness and Dad had to give me Cyclizine and a sick bag.

Currently, I'm sitting on the marina wall, in a t-shirt because the sun shines a balmy spotlight at this place, despite it being autumn, while Michael kneels by the water's edge. He shares a panini with a shoal of mullet. They're rabid as piranhas. It makes him laugh. I, on the other hand, want to spear, fry and eat them like whitebait, because Michael only had a fiver and he's forgotten I exist.

'Look at them.' He beams.

I sigh. 'Who doesn't love a tuna melt?'

And while he coos over fish, I watch the yachts in the distance, drifting in and out of Lymington Yacht Haven, caravans for the rich. How lovely it must be to sail away around Europe's tourist attractions, avoiding both traffic and riffraff.

I ask Michael, 'If you could jump on a boat this minute and go anywhere in the world, where would you go?'

'Trevescan,' he states.

'That's very specific.'

'Yes. It's the end of the world.'

Technically, it's almost the most westerly point of England. I jump free of the wall, kneel beside him. 'Things must be bad.'

He tells a grey mullet, 'It's a secret and we're not conjoined by the head, so don't ask.'

'Ouch.' I touch my heart. Respect his need for privacy for a good thirty seconds. Then say, 'You know you can tell me anything.'

Michael does that look, the one where he's drunk too

much lemonade. I rub his back. He throws the remaining panini like it's a baseball at a mother and her toddler.

I snatch his hand. 'Michael, what is it?'

He shakes my fingers free, stands up. 'I'm just not sure I love him, Flo. Not any more.'

'What's he done?'

'Nothing. I've just gone off him.'

'That's it?'

Visually speaking, Michael is the blueprint of someone who speaks the unequivocal truth. Palms exposed, open-eyed, shoulders as limp as Stone Age man's – you could take a photo of him and use it in a textbook about trustworthiness. 'Sometimes, it's just as simple as that.'

Where he suffocates in guilt, I want to perform a conga. Gently, I chivvy him from behind, along the walkway, away from tourists who have stopped holidaying to stare.

'Forget about it for the moment,' I say. 'Let's just *be*, like vegetables. You have plenty of time to decide.'

Though if I have anything to do with it, there'll be no family weddings this year, or next. That goes for Dad and Darcie too.

'How much cash you got left?' I clap my hands.

'One-pound-five,' he sighs.

'Good.' I hold out a palm. 'That'll cover dessert.'

First we follow the footpath to Lymington Yacht Haven, which relaxes Michael no end, because the marina is an incredibly symmetrical set-up: 300 motorboats neatly parked in demarcated rectangles of sea. Our coos escalate as we pass sailing dinghies, weekender motorboats and sky-loungers.

A luxury yacht makes us simultaneously screech. Acres of white fibreglass, cherry wood and chrome, the twenty-metre vessel belongs on a film set. It's the type of beast Scat Delaney would have chartered for a holiday. Though that's conjecture

– our relationship stalled long before we got to the week-end-break stage.

Michael pulls me away, more interested in the onshore facilities: the laundry, boat hoists and salt-water baths.

'You *have* to use the urinals,' he tells me, offering me his fingertips to sniff. 'They have complimentary toiletries and everything.'

At the shop, I treat us to a Twix.

Nibbling a finger each, we wander past a restaurant staffed by bronzed waiters in white polo shirts. Michael admires them, as though he's just experiencing the gift of sight, and I feel a pinch of pity for Sébastien. My brother, having voiced his concerns out loud, is already moving on. I envy that, his ability to be so cut and dried.

For a while, I watch the waiters too, because Tommaso Bellini was a chef, waiter and bottle-washer. I told him things I shouldn't have. In my defence, there was a biochemical connection. What man – unless they're a professional conman – would leave a woman who gave him goosebumps in the middle of Rome without settling his bill?

It's funny the things that consume you with nostalgia. I have to wander off for a bit to mourn Tommaso's loss. To stare wistfully at a small yacht while wallowing in the memory of love's starting post. How easy would it be, I wonder, to navigate my way back to Sistiana Portopiccolo from here?

When a man emerges from the boat's deckhouse, I show him my palms, apologise for staring so wantonly at his vessel. But the guy's nice. A dead ringer for Jesus. Topless, thirty-three years old, with an auburn beard. His laughter lines make my solar plexus tingle. The only difference between him and the son of God is his shorts; hotpant-small, they produce quite the camel's toe.

I look rigidly at his face. 'She's a beauty.'

'You know anything about boats?' The rounded vowels, his consonant mutation – I know instantly he's Cornish and kind.

'My mum was a sailor,' I lie.

He puts on a t-shirt, then walks to the boat's edge. Places a bottom cheek on its side. And I see he's an experienced boatman: his body is much younger than his head.

'What she sail?' he asks.

I think about this, because I'm not sure of the type of boat my mother would go for. Glancing at Jesus's motorboat, I check for clues as to its make and type. It's definitely cream with red trimmings, four-berth, but nothing gives me a clue as to its make or type. Though there is the name of a saint etched across its stern, the font a bold and racy scarlet.

I read it. Inhale sharply. Forget to breathe out.

Santa Maria, she's called.

Fatalism is not my bag, but my confirmation name is splashed across the side of a boat owned by a man who looks holy. Yes, a boat called *Bambi Love née Campanella* would have been really conclusive, but in its absence *Santa Maria* feels as palpable a message as there could be.

'My mum sailed away one day and never came back.' I frown hard at the offing, just as I've done countless times before, but this time I imagine her bobbing upon it. 'She's not dead,' I clarify. 'She just moved on. It's very easy to disappear by boat, you know.'

The sailor's beard seems to lift of its own accord. He's smiling somewhere beneath it. His eye-lines definitely concertina.

'I'm not an expert.' I shrug and smile. 'But I bet people-smuggling is rife among the boating community.'

Note: the oath I gave Dad is binding – I cannot and will not talk about Mum. The topic of human trafficking, however, is entirely different.

'Oh, it goes on.' He folds his arms. 'You have to plan it proper. Get in a boat, get picked up in the middle of the sea by another boat . . .'

I finish his sentence. 'Wear a bikini; have a fake passport in your beach bag; hop out at a busy coastline – just another tourist coming back from a daytrip.'

'That's one way.' He nods.

'But you'd need to have contacts, right?'

'Yep.'

'I imagine there's paperwork to circumnavigate.'

He humours me. 'Or you can do a cruise. Two hundred passengers have gone missing from cruise ships over the last twenty years. They get off at a port, forget to get back on. Eventually, they drop out of the system. "Suicide by sea" – that's what the insurance companies call them. It only gets tricky if the coppers are looking for you.'

He thinks my lost mother is a front, that I'm looking to do a Lord Lucan. I don't put him right, just nod, because he's on-point concerning the police – they weren't and aren't looking for Bambi. Nor Dad – he did an especially conscientious job of sweeping her under the carpet.

The conversation comes to an end when Michael approaches. I bob at the sailor reverentially, then pat his vessel.

'*Santa Maria*. It's a nice name. She was the patron saint of purity.'

'That'll be about right. My mum chose it.'

Mine, too, I don't gasp, because he already thinks I'm a fibber. I walk away, doing a quick finger wave. He responds with a farewell salute that gives me a flushing sensation above the navel that is the *exact* feeling you get during transcendental meditation, but only if you've practised for aeons.

On the way back into town, I clarify a few things with Michael.

'We've been to a lot of ports over the years, eh?'

'Weymouth, Portland, Exmouth, Southampton, Plymouth . . .'

'Never Lymington, though.'

'Never.'

'I wonder why?'

'Dad probably didn't know it was here,' he says seriously. That's worth double-checking.

The tennis club is off the high street. We bypass it on the way to the car. I ask Michael for his phone – it's safer than using Darcie's – and tell him to wait outside while I whip in to use the loo. Ignoring the Ladies sign and the barman, I march straight to the teak Champion's Board on the back wall of the clubhouse, because *never* have I seen Dad pick up a bat of any kind, nor become remotely enervated at the start of Wimbledon. I become enervated. I bloody *love* Wimbledon.

The board, however, tells a different story.

George Love won the West Hampshire doubles tournament three years running. His partner was Bob Hannigan. The dates were 1975, 1976 and 1977. Dad must have moved away in 1978 when he married Mum; their marriage certificate stated that they tied the knot in Christchurch. And their wedding night was the first spent in their marital home – Mum told me how Dad had carried her over the Motte's threshold and got her veil caught on a nail.

A little hysterical, I use Michael's phone to take snaps of every wooden board in the place. Then I drag my brother to the post office.

'In the future, I may need to send a letter,' I explain as we wait in the queue. 'Especially now we're getting the business up and running again.' In truth, I'm here to smell the air, and Dad's scent is everywhere. Then again, post offices all smell the same, both comforting and depressing, like a great-grandparent's sitting room.

Paternal-grandparent fact: mine lived in Swanage. That's where Dad and Uncle Fergus grew up. 'Dorset born and bred,' my father likes to brag.

Cashier number four, please.

Halfway to the counter, I remember we're out of cash, so push Michael back out of the post office and in the direction of the car.

'I've been to better practice hen parties,' Michael complains.

He hasn't. 'You live in the moment and are currently bored. If Dad asks, we've taken the Hannigan case.'

'Ooh, have we?'

'No, Michael. But it'll stop him worrying about, you know, stuff.'

'Dad does worry about stuff.'

'You said it. In the meantime, I'll get us some business.'

'That'll take weeks.'

'Give me twenty-four hours and I'll have us a job.'

And I will. But Michael skitters behind me, finding things to whinge about. Leaving me to concentrate on marching to the car, embedding my hypotheses so far . . .

This town was kept off our childhood radar for a reason.

The good news: that provides me with a new lead.

My guess, Mum and Dad met in Lymington. Maybe she arrived in England by boat, with a new name – Bambi Campanella. Or perhaps they made it up together. Whichever, disappearing from administrative radars is impossible without a lot of help. Help with clout. My father might be aware of what happened, but he's not involved in the intricacies – his helplessness is palpable. Half clueless, George Love was left behind to pick up the pieces.

The bad news: the possibilities with regard to my mother's original and current location are infinite. No paperwork anywhere – not here or in Italy. All that ocean. Not even a name.

My mother remains as lost as space-junk.

Concentrate on those closer to home, Massimo had said. 'Not family, never family. Other people – friends, work colleagues . . .'

Noah Steensen's parents were friends – secret ones, who disappeared on exactly the same night. It's time to find out how my childhood lover is coming along with the domestic investigation.

Nuclear Bunker

Cross-legged, I sit on my single bed and Google Tommaso Bellini. Because, despite his late-night flit, the Candy Crush enthusiast has set up camp in my head. First, I get to grips with his local history.

Sistiana Portopiccolo, the town from which he hails, is in the foothills of the Alps, just a few kilometres south of the Slovenian border. Admiring the area's publicity photographs makes me feel totally hard done by. Tommaso's usual stomping ground – a six-star coastal development popular among the Italian glitterati – is exquisite.

Über-cool eco-pads nestle in a hillside that overlooks the Adriatic Sea. Sumptuous yachts bob within the pebble-walls of a marina. There are discreet designer shops, impeccable eateries, infinity pools, acres of glass, marble, walnut and chrome. At night, halogen lighting invades every nook – from a distance, Portopiccolo twinkles as though Bulgari-encrusted.

Not only had Tommaso given me goosebumps, he was a total catch, making Operation Kiss Goodnight an unregimented flop. As a professional entrapment specialist, my success rate was through the roof. But that was because I had an audience to impress, i.e. the client. Plus, the men were, by and large, quite ugly.

I must try harder . . .

An online check of the Italian business register makes me whistle. Tommaso's father, Rocco, owns most of Portopiccolo. A local newspaper goes as far as to describe him as an 'aesthetic philanthropist'. Tommaso, on the other hand, avoids attention entirely – no Facebook page or Twitter account, not using his regular name, anyway. He's as enigmatic as a sign from God.

Though I do discover that a Tommaso Bellini plays squash for an amateur team in Trieste. That gets me thinking about racquet sports.

I type 'Lymington Lawn Tennis Club' into the search bar and press Enter.

The webpage is under construction.

Tennis-coaching fact: when playing at my father's level, you need to have had a lot of it. You'll also have a narcissistic streak – that's endemic among the sporty, the need to teach your own children everything you know, to saddle them with unrealistic expectations, and to re-mortgage your home so that they might achieve the accolades that eluded you.

Yet George Love, Hampshire champion of lawn tennis, never expected a thing of me. He was more than content for me to underachieve. I am incorrigibly eager. Michael is naturally athletic, with excellent rhythm. Dad's ever so dictatorial. We should have been the next Djokovics or Williamses.

I feel cheated.

A leveller: everybody buggered off, leaving my father to hold together a mouldering façade. Unexpectedly, I feel the weight he must have carried – and it's a lot, because my own shoulders flag.

Sébastien kicks open my bedroom door, his face hidden behind a tower of books.

'Careful with those,' I remind him. 'By the window. Keep them in the same order. That's all the "A"s, right?'

Books safely deposited, Sébastien puts both hands on his hips. 'Adams through to Auster. Anything else while I'm at it?'

I nod. 'Tell Michael the old PI website is tweaked and back up.'

'How exciting,' says Sébastien.

For a while, we stare at one another. 'Anyway, I'd love to chat . . .'

'Flo, can I ask you something?' He looks pained.

I put my laptop to one side and point at the bottom of my bed.

He perches on the end and asks, 'Have you ever thought about having children?'

'Yes, I have.'

'What if you don't meet the right guy?'

'I've thought about the physiology of having children, Sébastien. I didn't say I wanted any.'

'But if you did? Meet the right guy?'

I fold my arms. 'What's your point?'

'I would like them. But only with someone I love.' I watch him half wince, as if expecting a flurry of slaps.

'No,' I tell him gently.

'I'm very decided on it.'

'Well, stop being very decided. Michael hates change. He especially hates children. They confuse him.'

'We could get him over that, though. You and me? I'm not talking straight away, but we could pave the way a little. Sow the seed.'

'Michael doesn't like kids. And I don't want him to have any either.'

He misunderstands me: 'I've been on forums – the risk of passing on his disposition is really low.'

I say this through gritted teeth. 'If the world was populated with Michaels, there'd be no war or messiness or grey areas. Marriage and procreation should never be a slave to genetics.'

He nods obsequiously. 'It's about evolving.'

'And children do not help you evolve. They're thoughtless and complicated and extremely fucking cruel. Has Michael *ever* told you he wanted kids?'

'Never.'

Case closed. I open the laptop and pretend to type busily. As soon as I have the chance, I will be reminding Michael of all the reasons he doesn't want a child. Not because it's all about me, but because it's very, *very* much all about him. You should never procreate with someone you've gone off. But my brother's too eager to please, he can momentarily be persuaded. You've only to look at their engagement and the speed at which Sébastien's wedding plans are going. I'll mention it to Dad too – he'll be keener than me to put a stop to Sébastien's dream of a modern family.

On cue, my mobile rings.

'The girls are going to be here in an hour,' Dad tells me. 'Just a heads-up.'

I've been getting the heads-up at twenty-minute intervals. About our relaxed supper with Darcie and Annie. Know what I want to do more than anything? Take my father into the garden and ask him to demonstrate his top spin and slice, to mime a volley, talk me through the differences between his first and second serve. But I'm banned from raking up anything prior to Tuesday just gone.

'What are we eating?' I ask.

'Shepherd's pie.'

I look at the books Sébastien placed on the floor. 'Good. That won't clog up an intestine. Dessert?'

'Tiramisu.'

'Ditto.'

'Busy on the Hannigan case?' he asks.

'You're doing it again, Pater. I told you earlier, I can't tell you a thing.'

'If you're going to be shady, I'll just ask Michael.' I can hear him smiling.

'No, you will not.' I notice a book – the one I've been waiting for. 'Go do some seasoning. I'll be down in an hour. And remind Michael he doesn't want children.'

'Why?'

'Sébastien's getting broody.'

Quickly, I hang up. Dangle off the bed. Pick up the novel.

PS I Love You by Cecelia Ahern. Chick lit at its most cruel, this book always feels like a nod from my mum.

Its cover is smooth and cool to the palm, but inhale its paper and you'll be left feeling flat. Chick-lit books smell different to the old classics. It's not their fault: they contain fewer organic compounds – not enough vanillin, benzaldehyde and 2-ethylhexanol. Traditional tones of vanilla, almonds and flowers are overshadowed by modern-day adhesives and inks – they give contemporary commercial literature a top note of bleach.

Tipping the novel upside down, I fan its pages – a business card falls free.

Note to oneself: learn the telephone number of everyone you ever meet off by heart. I can't believe I've not insisted on doing that before. I decide to subcontract the task to Michael, after we've had the babies chat.

First, I make a call.

Noah is an absolute stalwart. The type who'll sit by his handset for half a year. Today, he answers his phone within one ring.

'It's Florence,' I tell him immediately.

A born-again Scot, he coats nothing in sugar. 'You took your bloody time.'

'You said you'll call me?'

'I tried on Friday.'

'Friday, I was being held prisoner at gunpoint and my phone got destroyed.' I have the best excuse ever. 'I'm back in Dorset now, though.'

'You were held at gunpoint?'

'I know!' I change the subject, 'So, my dad's got a companion.'

Noah's too preoccupied. 'I have information. Where are you now?'

'You're the stalker.' I jump straight on to the bed and look out of my window. Noah, however, is not in the drive. Neither does he loiter by the cattle grate or wander tormented up the wooded lane. That leaves me disappointed – when I was in London he loved to make an unsolicited visit.

'Whose phone are you using?' he asks.

'Dad's. Well, Darcie's. She's the companion.'

'Get rid of it.'

'Why?'

'It's dangerous.'

I pull the phone from my ear. Ask it from a distance, 'What about email?'

'Better face to face,' his little voice says. 'The Shed of Death. Twenty minutes.'

I put the phone back to my ear. 'You *are* here.'

He's not in the mood. The line goes dead. And I high-five thin air, because although I feel nothing towards him whatsoever, it is hugely satisfying when someone's behaviour verges on the obsessive – that gives us single women an invigorating dose of attention.

There is an old pair of Adidas Superstars in the wardrobe. I slip them on then exit via the loft window. It's best to avoid Dad. He'll ask questions. My aim: to have been and gone in sixty minutes flat.

Back in time for *the girls*.

Breaking out of my bedroom is a manoeuvre I'd perfected by the age of ten. Shimmying down the stone wall, jumping the final couple of metres on to the grass, avoiding the chomp of gravel. I never went down into the village, though – I wasn't the type inundated with friends. I'd circumnavigate the stone wall, sneak into the garden and back into the kitchen. It totally freaked Michael out. I told him I had magic powers, that I was a reincarnation of the Great Lafayette.

It's two and a half kilometres back in to Laurelbridge. At St Stephen's, I follow its side path into the cemetery and make a circuitous route through the headstones, careful to avoid the beer bellies of soil.

The Shed of Death.

A nuclear bunker, built during the Cold War as a provisions store should the village fall victim to an atomic bomb. Michael and I would tiptoe down its concrete steps, huddle in a cool space that was eye-level with dead people. I'd tell him stories about zombies and the Apocalypse. One night the older kids locked us in, then sat outside singing nursery rhymes in a sinister key. In the end, the church committee took the door off. Not because of me and Michael. Because Laurelbridge's teenage pregnancy rate was sneaking above the regional average.

Nowadays, the grave digger keeps his secateurs, shovel and marble wax in there. I'm having a good nose around when I hear the thud of feet. Too quickly, I stand up, twatting my occiput on the ceiling.

'Awrite, hen,' Noah shouts in.

My aim is to join him above ground, yet he's halfway down the steps, his broad shoulders blocking the light. Moving to one side, I allow him entry, instantly catching his air of doom.

Noah Steensen is a textbook Virgo. He wears his anguish on his sleeve and is inclined towards ritualistic grooming behaviour, so he looks identical to the last time we saw one another. White-blond hair, shoulder length, worn in a bunch – my hunch, he trims it himself. Stubble, between one and a half and two millimetres and of the sand-colour palette. Teeth – perfect, were they adult-sized. Nonetheless, the illusion of having milk teeth does give him a vulnerable air.

Also in his favour: he's very good looking from a distance.

Tall, built like a winger and with the chin-lift of a paladin. Close up, however, he's not all that. Freckled taupe, his nostrils are too girthy. I can see his nasopharynx, the nasopharynx being a difficult part of the anatomy to keep on top of, especially on days like today, when the sun shines so vigorously at it.

Noah holds out a hand.

I shake it firmly, then rub the back of my head. 'You look the same.'

He doesn't return the compliment. He thinks I'm too full of myself as it is, so censors all chivalry. I make up for it, invite him to sit opposite me on one of the wooden benches.

Our knees touch, and I remember the last time we were here. It was up there as one of the most perfect moments of my life. Eight and in love. Back then, his nostrils weren't an issue. The cartilaginous framework of the nose doesn't ossify until adolescence.

Twenty-five years later.

Careworn and stripped of innocence, we boast three lost parents between us. It's still unexpected, how comfortably we let our knees lean against each other's.

'This place has shrunk,' he says.

'Tell me about it. I remember ten of us squeezing in here.' That's not true. It was only ever Michael and I. Then Noah and me. 'What are you doing in Laurelbridge?' I ask.

'Carrying out a recce of my old patch. Like you said.'

I lean forward. 'I've got the girls coming round. I have ten minutes, tops. Why is Darcie's phone dangerous?'

'Well, that depends on how involved your dad is.'

'A lot, I think. But not at all – if you get my drift.'

He leans forward too. 'Hen, that's clear as shite.'

I've suddenly no idea where to start. I rub my face. 'OK, so my mum was called Bambi Campanella, right?'

'Right.'

'Wrong. That was never her name. She'd run away once before.'

'From where?'

I shrug. 'Nothing she said about her past was true.'

'What about your family in Italy?'

'Lies.' I tell my knees. 'I really looked.'

'She was definitely Italian, though.'

I squint at him. 'She never taught me any. Not really, not if you think about it.'

Noah is a far more reliable witness. 'She had an accent, Florence.'

'Yes, she did.'

And it *was* Italian. I know this because, after she died, I heard her in every Itie I ever met. The elongated double consonants, the inconsistent outcomes, the phonetics would leave me ruined. Reminded me that my mother's lungs, vocal chords, tongue, palate and lips existed nowhere other than in my memory. By twelve, I'd stopped remembering her voice entirely.

I suck in a tear. Noah has to see it, yet he doesn't hold me. He folds his arms and gives me hypothetical answers.

'Maybe she could be more truthful here than she was in her old life. Maybe you were the only one who knew the real her.'

But I don't want a hypothetical discussion. I want to have a minute's silence.

Noah tries to get me back on track. 'Tell me more.'

I shake my head. The boating and tennis angles seem suddenly tenuous, which is the problem when you're a creative thinker – other people usually piss on your parade.

'You first,' I insist.

He quickly undoes his belt.

Usually in these situations, it's prudent to finger your atomiser and plan an escape route. But I'm a little transfixed.

As Noah struggles with the buttons of his fly, he looks up apologetically. *It's fine*, I nod. Which it is, sort of, until he digs five fingers and a palm inside his pants.

I quickly clarify: 'You're not having a nervous breakdown, are you?'

'And there she blows.' He removes his hand and points. 'Always undermining me.'

With serious eyes, I tell him, 'I undermine everyone.'

But the truth is, Noah's especially precious. Take our first kiss. His recollections involve me being a game-playing minx who threw him to the kerb as soon as I had had my way. Mine was that I got to kiss the Boy in the *Miami Vice* jacket. I'd only kissed a windowsill before then. I was proud as Punch. That's very unsettling, when a shared memory is so disparately interpreted. It's like Schrödinger's cat, just the complete opposite of it: the truth is there, but only if you're not looking for it.

Noah is less existential than me; a hand back in his jocks, I watch him pull free a sandwich bag, which he throws at my lap. 'I cleared out my parents' place in Scotland. Found that in the loft.'

Using a finger and thumb, I remove a folded leaflet.

'It's the company my father worked for when we lived here. His business card's there too.'

First, I examine the pamphlet. Tilt it towards the light.

ACME – IT solutions for corporations for a renewable future. Our expertise includes the design of computer systems compatible with wind-power projects.

I skim-read the leaflet. It's full of terminology but says nothing of the specific services provided, though it does have pictures of wind farms – an offshore one, an onshore one and one in the desert.

'It's like a poorly executed GCSE project.' I frown. 'Do you know what ACME actually stands for?'

'It means "zenith" in Greek.' When I shake my head, he takes another punt. 'It gets you top listing in the Yellow Pages.'

'It's from the *Road Runner* cartoons. Wile E. Coyote bought his dynamite from them.'

His smile is reluctant. 'Exploding tennis balls too.'

'And iron anvils. ACME is an acronym – A Company that Makes Everything. Their products always went wrong.' I look at the business card. 'Your dad was a technical consultant? Is the office still there?'

'It's in Weymouth.' He nods. 'Above a doctor's surgery. Video entry system. The company secretary's the same, mind.'

'You did a Companies House check?' I ask, impressed.

He nods again. 'She's also the receptionist. Tina. I spoke to her on the phone. Pretended to be a customer.'

'How did that go?'

'She took my details. Guess what they sent me?'

'Not this leaflet?'

'The same one.'

Last I heard, he was a motorcycle courier. I'd no idea he was so calculating. Excited, I hit him with the leaflet.

'IT and renewable energy are at the cutting edge. What are they really doing there?' I peek outside – up the stairs – check nobody's in the graveyard above. 'You've been discreet with your inquiries?'

As evidence, Noah points at his groin, and I applaud his security measures. When he puts a hand back into his pants, it feels like Christmas. I want to hurry him along, to help him out – he's stashed *another* truth down there. I practically snatch the cellophane packet from his hand.

Inside is an orange plastic cone the size of my thumb. My gran had one – a slide viewer with a chain you could attach to your keyring or belt loop. Back in the day, they were the ultimate stocking filler. Hers contained a picture of Mum and Dad on their wedding day.

I hold Noah's up to the light. Look through the lens.

Inside is an official portrait. Black and white. A middle-aged woman with a neat bun holds a handbag like the Chancellor of the Exchequer. Beside her, her son, I assume. Nineteen years old, in a black suit, tie, helmet and truncheon. The certificate in his hand says something to the effect of: *I am a bone fide rozzer.*

'Recognise my dad?' I hear Noah say.

'I think I definitely do,' I lie, because I have no memory of Eric Steensen whatsoever. Either I was so egocentric he didn't enter my psyche, or he, like Lymington, was kept off my radar.

I can't look away from the photo. 'This makes so much sense.'

Noah disagrees. 'He never told us he'd been a cop. Neither did Gran. I think his old pals helped him disappear. He got into trouble with the business – the force bailed him out.'

I take the slide viewer from my eye because something clunks into place. 'Or maybe they weren't old pals at all – your dad and the police.'

Noah misunderstands. 'You mean, Dad left under a cloud?'

'Quite the opposite.' Repeatedly, I pat Noah's knees. 'There's only one reason a person hides the fact they've ever been a policeman. Because they still are one.' I stare blindly at Noah.

The first rule of undercover policing: you can never speak about undercover policing.

The Brady Bunch

Dad is several sheets to the wind so flings shepherd's pie at plates like he's playing lacrosse. That's the excellent thing about my dad: he's in no position to comment on my alcohol consumption. I walk straight into the kitchen via the back door, pour myself a Rioja and finish it in four gulps.

'Where have you been?' he whispers.

'The garage.' I refill the glass. 'I've been looking for a book.' As evidence, I throw it on the table.

Undercover: The True Story of Britain's Secret Police.

Its jacket comprises of a picture of *V for Vendetta* and a tagline that sums up Eric Steensen's exact job role: 'They steal identities, they break the law, they sleep with the enemy.'

Dad definitely isn't fuzz; his observational skills are shite. He glances at the book but fails to see it. Instead, he hands me two plates. 'Take these and be nice.'

En route to the dining room, I go over Fergus's death.

It was neat and efficient – carbon-monoxide poisoning. All those implicated disappeared and the case was nippily sewn up. Of course, Eric was a cop – but why was he also selling computer systems compatible with eighties wind turbines above a doctor's surgery in Weymouth?

'Da-dah!' Dad comes up behind me, presents me to the table as though I'm a magician's assistant. 'For those who don't know, this is our Florrie.'

I do a curtsey and finger wave.

Annie and Darcie finger wave back, as do Michael and Sébastien. Annie, I note, showcases a blouse, its pattern life-sized hydrangeas. It makes my smile entirely genuine. Her smile isn't – head tilts are the physiological manifestation of indecision and/or weighty enmity.

I hand *the girls* their plates then concentrate on Darcie.

Small, angular, a white, chin-length bob. In truth, I'm completely taken aback. I'd anticipated meeting my mother's doppelgänger; a sixty-something Jacqueline Bisset or Gina Lollobrigida. Leaning across the condiments, I give Darcie a warm handshake, but it's like strangling a baguette.

'Your hair's so straight,' I tell her. 'Who's your hairdresser?'

'Bradley's in Winkton,' she mouths, delighted.

Her voice is totally petite; I'm forced to tip an ear at her. My mum would have said, *Piccolina, she sounds like a singing mouse from Bagpuss.* And she'd be right. We'd mimic those cloth mice all the time. Warble in a harmonious falsetto, while tidying, 'We will fix it, we will stitch it . . .'

That makes me feel unexpectedly empty.

I sit beside Michael and take a gulp of his beer. 'It's six kilometres away on the Ringwood to Christchurch road.'

'What is?' he asks.

'Winkton.' I point at Annie's blouse. 'You're a fan of hydrangeas?'

She cups her breasts. 'You like?'

I have a firm belief when it comes to white lies: they are insidious. They undermine trust, compromise your moral code and inhibit the chance of self-improvement. *I have to admit, I think it is fucking vile*, is what I should say.

Instead, I nod. 'It is absolutely flowery. So, what do you do?'

'I manage your post office.'

'Since – *what*?'

'Six weeks ago. I took Suzy-Ann's position. She died.'

I fling a palm at my chest. 'Suzy-Ann died?'

Who just drops that in the conversation? Suzy-Ann was a young and vibrant woman who'd worked at the post office since she was a child. When I saw her last, she'd got engaged to a chef at the Harvester. They were saving up for a Winnebago.

'How did she die?'

'A brain haemorrhage,' says Dad quietly. 'I'm sorry, Florrie. It was very sudden. You had a lot going on at the time . . .'

'You should have told me.' I put down my knife, feeling devastated. I didn't like Suzy-Ann – she was a snaggle-toothed orca of a gossip – but I knew her better than any other person around this table did.

'So, here I am now,' concludes Annie, tucking into her food.

I tell her squarely. 'That is awful.'

She nods at Dad and Darcie. 'Sometimes things happen for a reason.'

'Try on your best-man's outfit later,' suggests Dad quickly.

Annie stabs a pea. 'It dates back to the Domesday Book.'

'It does not,' Michael argues weakly.

'Winkton, I mean. It was actually called Weringtone back then. We get lots of Americans.'

'I don't like Americans,' says Michael. 'They're very affected.'

'That's racist,' whispers Sébastien.

Michael shrugs. 'They smile too much.'

I give my brother the lowdown. 'The Yanks were stationed there during the war.'

'But that was, like, two hundred years ago.'

'And after the Napoleonic War, you had the Second World War.'

Annie is Winkton's number-one Fan. 'It dates back to 1675.'

I, on the other hand, am a stickler for fact. 'It's 1673.'

Wiping my mouth on a napkin, I turn to see if Dad is watching what an effort I'm making, because the woman is an insufferable attention seeker.

He's not.

He's doing adolescent eyes at Darcie. *Are you all right?* eyes.

Don't worry, we'll have some time on our own later eyes. It makes me feel dislocated and used – like I'm here to facilitate a façade, the one in which I give them permission to fall in love and be happy. How selfish of him.

Annie whispers, 'I introduced them.'

'Why?' I whisper back. 'Your mum's ever so monosyllabic.'

She squints. 'Only because George likes to monopolise a conversation. When he comes into the post office, I have to shoo him away. Full of natter.'

I squint back at her. 'Loquaciousness runs in the family.'

'You're certainly all special.' She turns to Michael, ruffles his hair like he's the village idiot. 'The Americans weren't in the Napoleonic War. Was history not your strong point, lovey?'

'I got a "C",' he tells us proudly. 'I learnt everything off by heart.'

'Applying the facts appropriately, that's the most important bit,' she warns.

I breathe in a lot. It stops me arm-sweeping the table free of accoutrements and disembowelling her with my teeth. On my final exhalation, I sink a glass of wine instead and look her up and down.

Annie likes a bit of Bakelite, I note – the bottom half of her engagement finger is monopolised by a butterscotch cocktail ring.

I point at the plastic jewellery. 'Are you engaged?'

She polishes the ring on her skirt. 'I'm in between lovers.'

Michael does a retch.

'Any kids?'

'Not yet,' she tells Sébastien.

That makes me squint.

Michael chooses to give out marital advice. 'It's just a piece of paper that makes it difficult to go your separate ways. Don't ever get married,' he tells us all. 'I'm getting terrible cold feet.'

'Sébastien worships you,' Annie says sharply. 'It breaks his heart when you speak like that.'

Obediently, Michael shuts up and rubs at a stain on the tablecloth. The pity I feel for him is like being tasered. Then I see it again – Annie glancing at Sébastien, brief and conspiratorial.

Fuck me. Does she intend on being first in the queue for any turkey-baster action? Though nobody would want a mini-Seb. Not when you have access to the spermatozoa of a genuine physical specimen.

Sperm-theft fact: Michael's will be stolen over a lot of dead bodies, none of them mine, because if anybody is going to have my brother's child, it's me.

'Annie.' I stand up noisily. 'Help me with the champagne?'

'I'll do it.' Michael's halfway to his feet – he wants out.

I put a palm on his shoulder. 'No, sweetheart. Just us girls. You all know each other already – I feel left out.'

And because Dad has started to stress-blink, I give both him and Darcie a very encouraging wink. A *you can count on me* wink. An *Annie and I will be best friends in a jiffy* wink. There would be no benefit in apprising them of my actual plan. The one where I avenge Michael.

I don't give a fig that she doesn't like Dad. I'm used to women not warming to me. But Bates just crossed an unpardonable line – the one where she belittles my little brother. And for that reason, I'll be communicating entirely via the power of Shorinji Kempo. Otherwise known as Shaolin Temple Fist Law.

I'll give Annie this: she misses a gene. Specifically, the Stathmin gene; its role is to stabilise fear.

As proactively as me, she follows me into the kitchen and out through its back door. We march to the furthest corner of the cottage's garden, stopping beneath my old tree house, the spot where Michael and I used to practise our assassination skills.

As children, fighting was permitted regardless of jeopardy levels, as long as it occurred at a speed of a thousand frames per second. That's how *The Six Million Dollar Man* got on the telly before the watershed, Dad explained; anything bionic had to occur at a funereal pace.

Michael and I would fight in slow motion for hours.

Annie and I eye one another up. She assumes a spread-eagled, hands-on-hips stance. I assume *migi chudan gamae*, an offensive stance suggestive of imminent combat. This is how you do it:

Soft knees, shoulder width apart, front foot turned in at ten degrees, rear foot turned out at forty-five, one fist horizontal, the other pointing directly at your enemy's skull. Then you focus inwards, while apprising your attacker of the rubrics.

'Shorinji Kempo is not a sport, Annie. Sports have rules. Self-defence, however, requires none. Buddhism won't let me attack you first, of course. Lucky for me you struck the first blow.'

Annie frowns. 'How's that?'

Another rubric: self-defence does not require you to explain the ins and outs of a duck's arse. 'It was a psychological blow,' I say, then punch her twice.

When I say 'punch' . . .

I check Dad's not looking through the window, then touch the side of her head with a cupped palm. Really hard.

She clasps her ear as though I've belted her with a brick. I'm relieved when, instead of screaming for the police, she does a whisper-screech. 'What is your problem?'

'*My* problem? You don't like Dad. I get that – for some baffling reason, he has designs on your mum. You don't like me – no explanation needed there, the feeling is entirely mutual. But Michael?' I point at the cottage. 'I fought people like you every day of his life at school.'

She snorts. 'Now she cares. I'm the one who's been here while you've been gallivanting abroad, remember?'

That does it. I snap. Touch her cheek again, hard.

'Stop it!' She stamps a foot. 'I'm looking out for my mother. Why aren't you looking out for yours?'

My eyes bulge murderously; still she refuses to shut up. 'Darcie is a good woman. She doesn't deserve it.' The Bible-thumper quotes Deuteronomy at me: 'He shall not acquire many wives for himself, lest his heart turn away . . .'

Annie drops her arms and sighs, exhausted. 'Level with me here. Do you actually want them to marry? Because they will. They're the sort.'

I lose a little wrath. She's right.

'Look, George is the only man Mum has known apart from my dad. She's too naïve for your family's baggage.'

There's movement in the kitchen. I squint back indoors. Tell her flatly, 'All families have baggage.'

Her headshake is mulish. 'Not your type. Let's work together. We despise each other. We can pool that hatred and put it towards a common cause. Fingers crossed, we'll be out of one another's hair in no time.'

'There's nothing to find out,' I state, because as long as I live, she'll know nothing about my family.

'Then why is George so adamant you stop looking for your mother?'

That makes me mad. What has Dad been saying to Darcie? If I can't talk about her, he certainly can't, especially not when it's being leaked as pillow talk. Mothers and daughters tell one another everything, surely he remembers that. Mum and I were just the same: for a very long time, I totally believed that.

'You're on your own,' I tell her.

She disagrees entirely. 'Have you seen our new family set-up in there? You might be OK with a new mum, but my new dad comes with some serious skeletons. Then there's you and the muscle Mary. It's a dysfunctional Brady Bunch.'

That does it. I grab her arm. 'We're going inside. You need to share your thoughts with the group.'

'I do not.' She pulls her arm free, plants her feet firmly, becomes as entrenched as a tree stump.

'It'll be fine,' I reassure her. 'Dad becomes entirely ineffectual in heated discussions.'

'Nope,' she says curtly, digging at a pocket in her skirt, pulling free a small envelope. 'And you won't be saying anything either.'

'What's that?'

'George didn't put it in the usual pile. He popped it into the box on the wall. He thought nobody was watching. I rescued it, out of curiosity.'

'Have you opened it?'

'I run your post office. That would be illegal.'

'Quite right.' I attempt to snatch it from her.

'You, however, have a different work ethic.'

My heart races, hungrily. 'I'm discovering that our moral compasses have significant points of crossover.'

She drops the letter on the floor in front of me. Takes a step back as though I'm a rabid fox. Dropping to my knees, I tilt the airmail envelope at the moonlight.

'Thank you, thank you, thank you,' I tell the cosmos, because one glorious word sits in capitals at the end of a foreign address.

ITALY.

'Do you know her?' demands Annie.

Her? I read every line of the address, three times, but neither the name nor the address means anything.

Paola Aggi
Via XXIV Maggio, 31
Casella Postale 5225
89011 Bagnara Calabra, Reggio di Calabria
ITALY

I'm unable to place Bagnara Calabra. 'Calabria's south Italy, right?'

'South-west. On the toe.'

There can be no quibbling over the penmanship. Dad's writing tilts back on itself and his capital letters are full of unnecessary flourish. 'Any other information?'

'Just that.' Again she asks: 'So do you know a Paola?'

Ignoring her to put the letter into the waistband of my jeans, I explain how things are going to be from now on.

'You look at my brother funny and I will sack your sorry arse for gross misconduct. Under the Postal Services Act 2000, you could face up to six months in jail. And should you be contemplating stealing anyone's sperm, it won't be Michael's, do you understand? For that, I will kill you.'

She laughs once, sadly. 'Michael wouldn't make many people's list, Florence. Certainly not mine.'

Enter the Dragon on fast forward. My knife-hand strike to her vagus nerve is a corker. She yelps like a whipped dog, then sinks to her knees, grasping the side of her neck. In her defence, it's a thoroughly unpleasant sensation; acute pain and involuntary spasm. On the upside, the agony is momentary and unlikely to leave bruising. Unless you do it too hard, then it can result in unconsciousness and death.

I rub my little finger and wrist. 'Now play nicely, Bates.'

Leaving Annie on all fours, I hurry back inside.

From then on, Annie behaved consummately. Re-entering the dining room five minutes after me, hair brushed, wearing an untroubled smile, champagne flutes in her hand. Together, we poured bubbly and proposed enthusiastic toasts.

May misfortune follow you the rest of your life, but never catch up was mine.

Annie's was, *Friendship – may differences of opinion cement it.*

Michael's was the most earnest, *Guests make us happy; some by coming, others by going.*

A pleasant enough hour and a half passed. We spoke about a pregnant great white spotted off the Dorset coast. Ebola. The legalities of picking bluebells.

'According to Schedule 8 of the Wildlife and Countryside Act, it is not illegal to pick a bluebell, as long as you do it gently.' Michael had stated the conclusion of his investigations. 'You can't sell them, though. That's corrupt.'

'An excellent spot of googling,' Annie had said encouragingly.

'Now we know.' Dad had elbowed Darcie proudly, oblivious to the fact I'd stashed his stolen letter in the freezer. Two hours is enough to alter the electrostatic bonds between polymer molecules, enabling me to open the letter and reseal it. For more information, see van der Waals' thermodynamic equation – he won a Nobel Prize for his work on 'attractive forces'.

The time passed quickly. Suddenly, there was a flurry of air kisses and promises of future get-togethers. Door shut, peace restored, Dad had given me a huge and clumsy hug.

'Thank you.' He'd breathed a heady cocktail of fermented grapes on me. 'David Attenborough's on catch-up. Fancy it?'

'Give me an hour,' I promised, safe in the knowledge he'd be snoring like Darth Vader in twenty minutes flat.

There's no lock on my bedroom door, but I have a makeshift one. Fashioned from a fork as part of a DT GCSE assignment back in 1995. Over the years, I've found it extremely useful – especially when wrapping presents, abluting and diddling the skittle.

I turn the light off, gently manoeuvre my bed away from the wall and squeeze into the gap. This gap was once my secret hiding place. That is, until Uncle Fergus found me and squeezed in too. The gift he gave me that day was a round pink vanity case, just like Mum's. My gift to him, he whispered, was to be a kiss on the lips.

Fergus's penchant for the under-aged was inexcusable, yet the vanity case was a boon; for the last few years, I've kept PI equipment in it. Tonight, I pull it out from under the bed, use my fingertips to search inside, extract a small metal tube.

'Hello again,' I tell my LED torch, then tug the duvet over my head.

For lone women out and about of a night, this little flashlight is a must. As with much spy gadgetry, it has the secret power of high resolution night-time cinematography – eight hours' worth. It's also heavy enough to use as a blunt instrument, enabling you both to self-defend and collect evidence for the prosecution.

A red light blinks. Just a small amount of charge remains. Hastily, I shine the torch at the front of the cold blue envelope. One line stands out for me –

Casella Postale 5225

A postal box?

I examine the envelope's flap. The process of freezing has reduced the glue's tackiness, but I'm keen not to leave a tear. So, first, I find my jeweller's loupe and dig it at my eye socket. Torch between my teeth, I remove an earring – it has a shepherd's hook wire which I use to tease a breach in the corner of the envelope's flap. Once the opening is big enough, I search my case for a tongue depressor, tongue depressors being the CIA's suggested instrument for illegally opening letters. Easing the cardboard spatula into the gap, I rock it softly, applying only the wispiest of pressure.

The flashlight stutters throughout, though I don't let it rush me. When, finally, the envelope gapes, its booty ready for the taking, I find I'm too scared to look.

I do. In the end.

There's one page only. Cigarette-paper thin, it's been tugged from a Basildon Bond airmail writing pad. In the faintest pencil, Dad has written:

To let you know, after much thought, I've decided to replant the African daisy. The badgers have returned, happy and well. God bless x

I re-read the note. It feels both tender and perfunctory. Slightly distant, yes, but exactly how a couple might communicate forty years into a marriage from which they've both moved on.

On the third reading it comes to me – what if Dad's writing in code and Michael and I are the badgers? That would make this firm evidence that she cares enough to have jeopardised her safety by remaining in touch. But what of replanting his daisy – is he telling Mum he's moved on carnally?

I'm not sure I care. Finally, I have something concrete. A woman lives in Bagnara Calabria to whom my dad sends secret messages. Her name: Paola Aggi.

The tears arrive suddenly, in short, disorganised bursts. They make me reckless.

Critical rule: when returning stolen mail, never leave DNA evidence. Especially don't hold the letter to your chest, kiss it repeatedly and put a single hair in the bottom of the envelope.

But I want Paola to have a bit of me – without her ever

knowing it, because, suddenly, it's ever so important that I keep this woman safe.

Using a dash of spit and my finger, I reseal the envelope and place it under my mattress. The torch performs a beleaguered blink, then dies, leaving me to ask myself a dangerous question:

If this were a paid case, what would I do next?

Easy. Strike while the iron's hot. Re-post the letter tomorrow, giving me four days to travel to Italy's toe to wait outside the post office on Via XXIV Maggio and see who it is that wanders out with this little blue letter in their hand.

Failing that, I could outsource to an Italian investigator, pay them to undertake the due diligence and surveillance. That, of course, is assuming I am swimming in readies.

In the absence of cash, however, I have a friend. One who owes me an explanation. One who had firmly told me to visit if I was passing through. One who has money, influence, friends in high places – a well-connected assassin for a godfather and an aesthetic philanthropist for a dad.

The thought of seeing Tommaso again gives me quite the adrenalin rush. It'll be a fly-by visit, mind you, before I make my way south. Because behind every great PI is an even better contact – I always hold on to them for dear life.

There's a secret knock at my bedroom door. It's the theme music to *Happy Days*. Michael does it quietly but musically, using a mixture of palm, knuckle and finger. It makes my stomach sag, the effort he's putting in to it.

Motionless, I remain on the floor under my duvet.

'Are you asleep?' he shouts.

'Yes!' I shout back.

'David Attenborough's on.'

'I'm too totally asleep.'

His footsteps retreat. And I rub my face, because I can't

leave him this soon. Nonetheless, I pack a suitcase and pen a note.

'I've gone undercover for the Hannigan case,' I tell them all. Five days, tops, then I'll be back. Nobody need know a thing.

Two a.m.

The television blares from the living room downstairs. I imagine Dad, eyes closed, opened-mouthed, looking a few hours' dead, his respiratory structures telling a noisier story.

Yes, I should pop down, jerk him awake and tell him I'm off. But he'll just look all failed. Then say something like: *What about the leftovers? We'll never eat them on our own?* And I'll feel extra bad, even though eating the leftovers is not my responsibility.

As instructed, the taxi driver phones when he's at the bottom of the lane. Opting for the easy way out, I leave via the loft window, shimmying down the stone wall, consoling myself with untruths.

What does Dad care, anyway? He barely noticed I was there this evening. He was doing love-eyes at Darcie – when, technically, I was the guest, and the only one completely out of the loop: I didn't know about Suzy-Ann's death, Bates running *my* post office . . .

Halfway down the wall, I drop my suitcase to the ground. It lands with a blunt thud. I jump the final couple of metres on to the grass.

Yep, if ever there was an excuse to be angry with Dad, that's it. He has appointed his lover's child as acting manager-ess; that's short-sighted, and terrible business sense. Jacket straightened, the case in my arms, I jog towards the taxi's dimmed lights, sticking to the lane's shadowy edge, determined to flounce back to Italy vindicated and devoid of guilt.

With twenty metres to go, however, a hooded figure swings around the side of me and blocks my path.

Instinctively, I chest-pass him the suitcase, dig at a pocket for my torch, hold it with two hands and point it like a pistol.

My attacker drops to his knees and complains, 'You have so winded me.'

I pull his hood off. 'Michael? What are you doing?'

'What are *you* doing?'

'New job,' I tell my brother.

'I knew it. You said you'd have one within a day.' He's pleased with himself; we punch fists. 'So what's the dope?'

'There's a problem, Michael.'

'Go on,' he says maturely.

'The job's a distance away.'

'That's OK, we're partners. I'm the front guy, but in the background.'

'No,' I tell him firmly.

More quietly, he reminds me, 'We're a neat combo.' He shows me his back. 'I've packed a bag.'

'I'll be gone for a week, tops.'

He shakes his head. I'm wrong. 'You're home for quite a bit of a bit. You promised.'

'It's just boring stuff – the due diligence, all that malarkey. It won't take long.'

Relieved, he nods. 'I'm in. Where are we going?'

I take both his hands. 'I can't let you come, sweetheart. Dad will go ape. And what about Sébastien? You need to spend some time together. *Alone*. No me and, especially, no Annie.'

'I don't like her.'

Michael fact: when it comes to expressing physical affection, he is differently abled to most. Specifically, he likes to show me none whatsoever. Unless things are extremely dire, like tonight.

Without warning, Michael grapples me into a body lock. His heart thumps urgently at my cheek. For a while, I cuddle him back. But when I try to pull free he refuses to budge.

The taxi driver has the liver of a chicken. He flashes his full beams to frighten Michael off and/or hurry me along. I wriggle maniacally, slip free of his hold and jog towards the car. But Michael's not done. It's his turn to wring me free of wind. Grabbing me from behind in a waist lock, lifting me off the floor, I fully anticipate a slow-motion body slam. Thankfully, Michael is very ticklish, so I go for his obliques. The tactic is as effective as a water cannon. Michael releases his grip and I bolt for the taxi.

We reverse at speed.

Michael refuses to exit my line of sight. Limp-shouldered, he remains in the moonlight ahead.

Your original training stated that you should choose your professional partner very wisely indeed. Living in the shadows is brutal. The only true witness to your life, your professional partner can become your everything.

I quote: 'It's best all round if you never love them back' (source: *Introduction to Entrapment 101, Tip # 3*)

Now you're retired, you'll agree that was a ridiculous ask. The likelihood is that your partner and you are too mentally meshed. It's the by-product of a career in private investigation; for a long while, you operated on the same quirky plain. But times move on. You cannot be conjoined by the mind for ever.

This is how to say goodbye to your partner:

  • *Close your eyes tightly and play the alphabet game.* In stressful situations, my go-to is Celebrity Children or World Religions.

  • *Remember your motivation.* The past doth love an arse to bite, so never revisit it – certainly never ever without a professional partner.

Part III

Nape

Hotel Ronchi, Ronchi dei Legionari, Italy

Ronchi dei Legionari is a faceless European commuter town a ten-minute walk from Trieste airport and populated by people passing through. I like the anonymity it proffers. Most of all, I like this hotel – a three-star homage to the Italian seventies. It was fully booked, apart from the honeymoon suite, which I had no intention of paying for.

Cosmo, the landlord, is not fond of his job. Sitting at the hotel's front desk, he prefers to ignore the clientele and stick banknotes into a scrapbook. I tried to wangle a look at his collection, but he was unnaturally possessive of it.

He's also dreadful at English. The dominant language of his guests is the dominant language of the modern world, yet when non-nationals attempt to engage in chit-chat, Cosmo shakes his head as though we're the ones in the wrong.

Eventually, I'd sweet-talked the landlady, Rosa. Wangled a discounted room in the staff quarters, underneath reception. You get what you pay for. One small window with PVC shutters and korma-hued nets. No TV. A telephone with rotary dial (dead). Cardboard walls, necessitating that you speak and ablute as quietly as a squatter. I dumped my bag, then made my way back up to the hotel bar.

While Rosa polished the optics, we bonded. Covered a lot of conversational ground, chuckled too often, because the woman secretes pure joy, her pheromones tickling my tummy and sides. Plus, she has the girth of a Swiss ball – I had an inexplicable urge to launch myself at her.

The best bit of all: when my stomach rumbles, she asks, 'Florence, my girl. Can I get you an espresso? Biscotti? Bigoli in salsa?' as if it's a matter of life and death.

I nod. 'I'm not sure the last time I ate.'

It was last night. Dad's shepherd's pie. But Italian women love to feed their daughters. She doesn't have one, I'm famished: everyone's a winner.

Rosa takes a pastry from beneath a glass lid. Puts it in front of me. 'Antipasto. Now, stop worrying about your brother.'

'I can't help it.' I sigh. 'Michael's not ready for children.'

'Nobody is ready,' she points out.

And I wonder if that's why childbirth passed her by. I also think about my own biological clock – which especially gets my goat. Progeny is not an issue I intend on addressing imminently, yet Sébastien sowed that seed, leaving me unnecessarily aware of deadlines.

Ovum fact: they are finite. Fertility's closing date is less movable than death.

'My brother's special,' I explain.

'Boys, they all special.'

'In an educational psychologist's type of way.'

Rosa flaps a hand. 'Just boys.'

'I make you right!' The ed psych was too hung up on ticking overly pedantic boxes.

There follows a very laboured tut.

Rosa and I glance at a booth in the bar's corner. A lanky man, mid-thirties, sits hunched over the melamine table, rustling his *National Geographic*.

Lowering my voice, I say, 'Who's that?'

She rolls her eyes, places a coffee in front of me. 'Lancelot. He study the mountains.'

I smile. 'Lancelot?'

What he'd remind you of: a slightly fluey ultra-marathon runner, one so Caucasian he verges on translucent. Which serves as a valuable lesson: give your child a name you are certain they can live up to. Lancelot's parents' expectations were grossly off course. With the benefit of hindsight, they would have opted for Colin or Dave.

My brother, on the other hand, wears his name like a Savile Row suit . . .

Michael Love.

Look at him now. He enters the bar, showered and coiffed, announcing dramatically, 'I am dying of starvation.' Then he points at a cake stand. 'How do you make that?'

Rosa leans forward, puts a squat finger in the air and tells Michael conspiratorially, 'I use the sugar, the eggs, the butter – the no salty butter – the flour, the liddle bit of lemon and the *lievito chimico*.'

'And what's that one?' he states.

'The Italian chestnut cake.'

'And that one?'

'The panettone.'

I sigh. 'He's never been to Italy before.'

'I haven't been to many places,' Michael tells us both. 'I don't usually fly.'

'You not like the plane?' asks Rosa.

'I do like the plane. I just don't like Flo on a plane. She makes me practise the brace position. And she tests me on escape routes.'

Rosa smacks my hand. 'You make your brother all jumpy.'

'You are allowed to travel alone,' I remind him.

Michael looks at me as though I'm utterly heartless. 'It's my hen weekend. You said you'd show me a better time than Lymington. It was too tame.'

'I bought you a Twix.'

Michael tells Rosa, 'They've got a post-box made of gold.'

'Real gold?' she asks.

Michael nods gravely. 'It's in honour of Sir Chris Hoy.'

'Ben Ainslie, and it's just paint,' I tell her.

Lancelot mutters at his magazine, 'Great, two of you.'

'This is not the library,' Rosa says sharply.

I try to smooth things over, make conversation. 'I hear you're a geologist?'

Without looking up, Lancelot nods once.

'I *love* scientists,' I tell everyone. 'What are you studying, specifically?'

'Fossilised reef mountains.' He looks at me fleetingly. 'I'm actually quite busy. Could you keep it down?'

'No problem.' I put an appeasing hand in the air. 'You're from Reading, right?'

I'd recognise it anywhere, the Reading accent being the default setting for the whole of southern England, the base note to which accentual colours are added. When Lancelot speaks, it's a bit of home from home, but without any linguistic bias whatsoever. It's reassuringly middle England, achingly magnolia.

'No,' he says flatly.

That makes me squint, because he's wrong.

'How you find your room?' Rosa gives Michael a pastry and a coffee.

'It's very romantic,' nods Michael.

When Michael told her we were here on a hen weekend, Rosa insisted he stay in the honeymoon suite, for the same price as mine. The noise that had come from Michael's throat was new to me. It was the gasp an actor might make having landed the James Bond gig. Knocking over the leaflet holder, Michael had leant across reception to give Rosa an extraordinarily tender hug.

I was hugely proud and entirely jealous, because I was the one who had spoken to Rosa first.

Important note: we're not here for a jolly, regardless of the spin I've put on it for Michael.

My plans . . .

To take Michael to Portopiccolo, where we will sit on a king-size canopied beach bed that overlooks the northernmost arm of the Adriatic Sea. While so doing, I will secretly research the Tyrrhenian Sea on my iPhone – situated to the south-west, its waters lick Bagnara Calabra, a seaside town that Paola Aggi calls home. Also while so doing, I will accidentally bump into and update my good friend Tommaso Bellini. Furthermore, while so doing, I will be looking extremely attractive.

That's such a long-lost sensation, being excited to see a man. It makes me jittery, like I'm about to walk on stage. I've been planning my outfit since we checked in at Bournemouth airport.

Though, first, I'd had to return to the cottage to pick Michael up. The taxi driver had been reluctant. I told him straight: leaving my brother had felt as brutal as fly-tipping a baby.

I'd been gone a good twenty minutes, yet I found Michael in the same spot, limp and all out of tears. There was only one way to deal with him. I gave him strict instructions. Told him to creep up the lane and back into the cottage to grab his passport like in *Ace Ventura: Pet Detective*. His enthusiasm in re-creating the scene made even the cab driver giggle.

I watch Michael now, hunched over the bar, like he's been frequenting the joint for ever.

'So how about tonight we check out the nightspots?' I ask Michael.

He first turns to Rosa. 'You hanging here for a bit?'

Doggedly, she points at the floor. 'I stay for twenty-four hours of the day. It's my job.'

'I'll look after her then.' He's blowing me out for the landlady.

'Let's not go too wild, eh?' I frown.

'It has been quite a day.' Pointing at a plate of curabiè, he asks, 'What's that one?'

And even though it's infinitely better this way, I feel aggrieved. Rosa can tell. I ask her, too snippily, to order me a taxi.

'OK, Mariah Carey.' She rests her little hands on her massive hips.

I overstep the mark. 'A working phone in my room would be useful too.'

Rosa points. 'You pay more if you live in a kennel for dogs.'

'I'm joking.' My smile is wide.

Hers is more sincere. 'Me too.'

I return to my digs, a huge plate of bigoli in salsa in one hand, a large glass of Friuli in the other. The next hour is spent getting ready for my reunion with Tommaso.

This evening, I wear less clothing than on our date in Piazza Montevecchio. Black tailored trousers and a plunge V-back jumper, chunky jewellery, heels, a fur-trimmed wrap over my arm. I also wear more make-up; specifically, a big lash of mascara and plum lipstick – the former suggests a highly evolved debris barrier; the latter, fecundity.

While waiting for my taxi in reception, I use the hotel's computer, which Lancelot had been using, until I started hovering. I didn't over-invade his space, just mooched around enough to hurry him along.

Out of professional habit, I check out the PC's history. That's always enlightening, especially in this case. The geologist has something to hide – he's cleared the computer's history. Not all of it. Just the last hour's worth.

So I gather a potted history of north-east Italy. Am halfway through a Wikipedia extract on Friuli-Venezia Giulia, the region in which we're staying, when Cosmo shouts, 'Taxi!' at his scrapbook.

In the back seat of the cab, I get into character. Project

from the diaphragm, which slows speech, lowers the pitch of your voice and makes you instantly sultry.

'Portopiccolo, *per favor.*' I'm good at voices. Then again, I practise like an opera singer.

It's wasted on the taxi driver. Impatiently, he heads for Route SS14, quickly putting distance between me and the Ronchi Hotel, driving through the Friuli countryside.

According to Wikipedia, this region is within the northern temperate geographical zone and a bit confused – ancient spruce, vineyards, out-of-town supermarkets, a community melded by ship building, Serie A WAGs, furniture factories, Italians, Slovenians, Pakistanis, Croatians and Brits. All barricaded in by the Alps and a fat finger of sea.

Interesting fact: they make 40 million chairs a year here – that's one in every three made in the entire world.

A more conscientious taxi driver might proffer such facts. My one even fails to point at the gigantic dining chair to the left of us; he's busy jumping a red.

Another interesting fact: the gigantic dining chair to our left is made of red oak, weighs twenty-three tonnes and is the height of a seven-storey building.

If I was a taxi driver, I'd be much keener to please. One of the things I would say is: *The big seat to your left is completely impractical, other than to serve as one-upmanship between global chair manufacturing communities. Metaphorically speaking, it's a giant penis extension.* That's a conversation starter.

But my driver's not a tour guide, and I can guess his problem. He works in and around Ronchi. Travelling past the big chair is very inconvenient. He'll have to come all the way back again.

At the coastal road, I open the taxi's window. My chin totters uncomfortably on the window's edge while I inhale the Adriatic. It twinkles a cold ink-blue. The cliffs that stave it off look beaten and anaemic in the moonlight; a billion tonnes of water collide with its shins, drumming at its Achilles, day in, day out. There's no respite.

I count shadowy mussel farms. And cruise ships – that reminds me of Jesus and his boat, *Santa Maria*, and suicide at sea. Trouble is, self-murder was never her destiny. I'm almost sure of it. Rubbing my face angrily, I examine the back of my eyelids, summoning thoughts of Tommaso – each recollection serves as a delicious slap.

Then the taxi driver forgets to slow down at a speed bump.

'Portopiccolo?' I demand.

'Portopiccolo,' he confirms.

The cliff face to our left becomes increasingly manicured, its limestone more up-lit. Eventually, bare rock is replaced by wire netting and pebble walls enclosing streets that become too narrow for cars.

I don't tip the driver. I smooth out the creases in my trousers, then use the ten-minute walk to the infinity pool to practise my slink.

I stop at a few eateries on the way. Just to read their menus and peek inside at the staff, but Tommaso's not there. Eventually, the walkway steers me to its premier bar and restaurant. I lean over a barrier made of glass and chrome to stare down at it.

It's a buoyant auditorium on a cliff's edge, and tonight a private party is in full swing. It's attended by footballer types and colt-like girls in colourful bandage dresses and designer shoes. They pose by the infinity pool, taking selfies. An enormous badge on one girl's breast confirms she has reached the ripe old age of eighteen.

Individually, Italian women are not the most beautiful in the world; as a collective, however, they sparkle like a bevy of Benetton models. It is utterly demoralising when you're the wrong side of twenty-nine.

Instinctively, I retaliate. Exude an ingredient they cannot – self-mastery. I'm helped, admittedly, by the fact that there's a lot of them and just one of me. Solitude provides a pedestal. Take advantage of it – study how I descend the staircase to the pool area as though arriving for my own wedding. People stare – of course they do: self-mastery is compulsive viewing when done well.

Reality check: I have *never* met a person who has achieved mastery of the self. I have, however, watched a few women who can style it out. How do they do it? They use their necks.

My backless jumper helps. Hair loosely up, exposing my nape. The neck's nape forms a perfect V of naked skin that alludes to the form of a female's genitalia. The Japanese called this tantalising triangle of hairline *komata no kereagatta hito*. Once upon a time, that was an astonishingly romantic phrase. These days, it means a geisha with a lovely fu-fu.

I also pretend to drag an exquisite wedding train behind me, because – orthopaedic fact – everybody with self-mastery has a long neck. Apart from the Dalai Lama, who slouches. As do the young women below. Hunching over desks, laptops and iPhones all day, they have lost their natural vertical position. Growing your neck returns the body tonus to a healthier state, unlocking a poise at which men can't help but stare.

Look at them ogling. Then again, the Italians refuse to watch people slyly. I'm half tempted to stop on the fourth step up and use it as a platform from which to give them a lesson in evolutionary biology . . .

The neck contains vital connections between mouth and stomach, nose and lungs, brain and spine, heart and brain. By exposing it, we flaunt a potently attractive asset – the ability to produce healthy children with strong-looking vital connections between mouth and stomach, nose and lungs, brain and spine, heart and brain.

That promise is as potent as China white.

Entering the spacious poolside bar, I leave a small wake. I also wind my neck in a bit. In crowds, avoid leaking too much self-mastery: it's intimidating close up. While maintaining my neck's length, I lower my chin, become the doyen of coyness, allowing those around to admire my *komata no kereagatta hito*.

I recognise the bar from the website photographs, though it's beyond stunning in 4D. Walls of sliding glass – to the south, sea; the west, yachts; north, residences – a view for every mood. The sofas are cowhide, the glass tables are bevelled, tea-lights float in tiny crystal baths. The Gypsy Kings play on the sound system, which I decide is fate: '*Djobi Djoba*', a total favourite of mine. Were Michael here, we'd have spontaneously started clapping at supersonic speed, refusing to stop until forearm burn kicked in. My brother is faster by miles – he does plyometrics, so his twitch muscles are explosive. He could palm-clap to the whole of *!Volaré! The Very Best of the Gipsy Kings*, which is two hours thirty-one long.

A tip for the gatecrasher: make a friend, quickly. In an ideal world, go for the hard-to-please. Everybody avoids them, when, in reality, more than anyone, they long for a wingman. There are two candidates at the bar. A morose teenage girl, sipping cola from a straw and texting; and a middle-aged guy, sixty, tops, scruffy, pigeon-grey hair and moustache, dressed, against his will, in somebody else's best tucker.

'*Buonasera*.' I smile and sit beside him.

The man is bored rigid. Until I arrive.

'*Buonasera*, signora.' He looks at me straight on.

The side of his face I'd seen when approaching is taut, with an upbeat eye and pert nostril. The right side of his face, however, is lax enough to sway in a breeze. 'Are you here for the party?' He summons the bartender, then points at me.

'Vodka martini, thank you. I am.'

When the door to the kitchen swings open, I power-pry inside.

The man makes conversation. 'You're staying in Sistiana?'

'With a cousin in Udine.' The chef isn't Tommaso. Neither is the sous chef, nor any line cook I'm able to clock.

'Where in Udine?'

'Via Duino 8.'

'I know it,' he declares.

When I turn to look at the man, I see he mimics me, looks into the kitchen, intrigued. While so doing, he leans conspiratorially in my direction. 'My mistress lives in Via Duino.'

That makes me grin. And him. Lifting a chin at the barman, he says, '*Per favore?*'

First, the waiter checks the coast is clear. Taking a cigarette from his own packet, he places it between his lips. The man can't do it himself – his right hand is weak from embolisms; his left, I now see, is low on middle fingers. When he itches his nose, it looks like he's doing the sign of the horns.

I give the waiter a look: *he's prone to inter-cranial bleeds, they could use him as a warning on the packets: a before-and-after shot; you shouldn't be encouraging him.*

I'm a hypocrite. I insist on lighting the cigarette for him. 'Do you know the birthday girl?' I ask nonchalantly.

'She's my goddaughter.' He exhales smoke.

'Really?' I ask.

His nod is exhausted. 'The rituals we go through in the optimism of a moment.'

That is deep. And true. My godfather, Bernie, was my dad's pal from primary school. Having denounced the devil and promised to bring me up a textbook Catholic, should my parents simultaneously die, he'd fucked right off. I have never seen him since. Not once.

'How did you lose your fingers?' I ask.

His face drops. Both sides. 'I was too nosy.'

Proudly, I show him my middle finger. The left one. 'See there?' We squint at the top couple of millimetres of the digit. 'Chopped it off when I was nine. Caught it in a door hinge. They sewed it back on.'

'They couldn't sew mine back on. When the dog shat them out, there were only the bones left.'

I giggle. 'A dog bit them off?'

'Giving them to the dog was the grand finale.'

Here's a truth – everybody in Italy has a mafiosi story. Of course, I humour him; sip my martini and say, 'A finger snack.'

My new friend guffaws. While my immediate perimeter becomes infused with Tom Ford Neroli Portofino; instinct swings my head to the left.

But the man who stares down at me isn't Tommaso, though he has an unnervingly familiar face. The strawberry-blond curls, meat on his muscles, minimal melanin count.

It comes back to me far too slowly . . .

I trailed him from the tabaccaio to the Hotel La Barcaccia. He'd given me evils on the roof terrace. I'd nicknamed him the Polar Bear.

I've not seen him smile before. But today his grin exposes oversized canines. I don't like it one bit.

'Hey, man.' The Polar Bear stretches across me to shake my friend's hand, all the while his eyes planted steadfastly on mine.

Adrenalin makes my bile spume, yet I style it out. 'Don't mind me.' I do big eyes at my wingman.

My wingman gives me a secret wink back, before declaring, 'Jason, you look – how do the Essex girls say? – hot to trot?'

Jason and I laugh, competitively; until Jason stops and says, 'Who are you?'

That throws me. More so when my wingman jumps to my defence, presents me too loudly and protectively.

'Apologies, signora. Let me introduce you to Jason Marl. And this, Jason, is . . .'

Fleetingly, the whole place quietens. The smile Jason gives me is expectant and awash with king-size cuspids.

'Marissa.' I finish my wingman's sentence and look for an exit.

Thoughts sprint through my head . . .

Is that why Tommaso did a runner? The phone call during dessert. Was the Polar Bear giving him the heads-up? Calling to tell Tommaso that, finally, it had dawned on him – he knew who I was.

The woman who entrapped Scott Delaney, then sold her story to the paper. Which I didn't, but that's the universal consensus.

The Polar Bear would then have come to a fair assumption: the son of a moneyed aesthetic philanthropist is good for a bribe.

An even worse case scenario: Tommaso has a girlfriend, and the Polar Bear had put two and two together and assumed I'd been hired by her. Entrapment fact: a target on a stag-do is a textbook set-up.

Whatever, Jason seems to be having a complete mental block now. He squints and grins. 'How *do* I know you?'

I long for a joint, quite badly. In the absence of class Bs, I order another vodka martini, three olives.

'What's your name, again?' I ask.

'Jason Marl. Jay.'

'That doesn't narrow it down.' I fan myself with the wine list. 'Are you a footballer?'

He laughs like I'm deluded or stupid. 'No, I play the guitar.'

I have no idea if he's being sarcastic, but the atmosphere is suffering and gatecrashing is most successful when you're not getting interrogated.

I play dumb. 'That's cool. Are you in a band?'

'No.' He laughs, folds his arms, scrutinises my face like he's the King of Siam.

Then it gets worse. The small, bald one turns up, although he doesn't know me from Adam. 'I'm Freddie.' He shakes my hand like I'm his bank manager.

'Are you in the band too?' I ask him.

'I'm not in a band,' interrupts Jay.

'Football coaching.' Freddie's smile is apologetic. 'Just kids.'

The noise I make is completely overexcited. 'Your accent? Bristol, right?'

Freddie laughs. 'Off the Gloucester Road.'

'I *love* Bristol,' I tell him. 'A uni friend of mine used to live there.'

Bristolian-people fact: they're too friendly and probably the easiest to entrap. It rarely enters their psyche that someone could be that calculating. See how generous Freddie is with his personal data . . .

'I'm near the Bristol Flyer.' He even gives me directions to his house. 'Come out of the pub, do a left, past Atomic Burger, first left into Berkeley Road, then a right into Arundel.'

'That's near Bishopston Books. I picked up a first edition of *The Soccer Tribe* there.'

Freddie looks genuinely fascinated by me.

I show off. 'Football is a modern counterpart of the primeval hunting pattern. A match is a historical re-enactment.'

Jay interrupts. 'I do know you.'

My wingman reminds him: 'Marissa.'

'What's the name of the book again?' says Freddie.

Jay says, '*The Soccer Tribe*.' Because he's not going to leave me alone.

A fact about vulnerability: it's only ever a matter of perception.

So what if Jay recognises me? That's not the end of the

world. I've not done anything wrong. I simply need to stick to my guns. I'm here visiting a cousin who lives at Via Duino 8, Udine. I can't help it if my reputation precedes me. PIs go on holiday too. It doesn't mean I stitch up every man I meet. Very often, I don't.

What am I saying?

If Jay has recognised me, I'm in trouble. Because the Polar Bear's a Leo (I'd bet Michael on it), and Leos suffer from competing personality disorders: Alpha Male Syndrome versus an acute inferiority complex. Particularly, they are prone to vindictiveness. And tonight Jay's need to belittle is further spiked by some industrial-grade marching powder – there's a coke-bat in the cave; his little finger is having a party of its own.

'No point arguing with him,' Freddie mouths at me.

'Have you been in the paper?' says Jay.

The concentration required to keep my eyebrows gently raised, the corners of my mouth facing cheek-ward, is immense. But I can't do a thing about my neck – the blood pumps furiously, threatening to break free of my jugular. My earlobes and eyelashes dance to its rabid beat.

'Probably,' I say. 'I'm big in manga circles.'

This makes Jay roar.

'Manga are Japanese comic books and graphic novels.' I turn to my wingman, who looks quizzically into my eyes.

'I know what manga is,' says Jay.

'I don't.' My wingman shuts him up.

'It translates as "whimsical drawings". My eyes plead a little.

His good eye twinkles. 'Where did you train?'

'Kyoto Seika University. The faculty of manga.'

Freddie is a fucking sweetheart. 'They do degrees in everything these days.'

'They do,' agrees my wingman.

'You're in films!' shouts Jay.

It's the final straw. 'Mate, that's enough,' says Freddie.

My wingman tells the waiter: 'His tone is grating at my bloody balls.'

Jay puts his hands up. 'Rocco, mate, I'm sorry. No offence.' Then he points at me as if I'm a blow-up doll. 'It's just she's got a memorable face.'

I look around. *Rocco?*

My wingman puts a placatory hand in the air. 'Rest assured, offence has been taken. Enjoy your fucking evening.'

This I know for a fact: if Rocco Bellini were pre-stroke and twenty years younger, we'd have been soulmates and lovers.

United, we watch Jay do a mission-march to the infinity pool. Freddie follows him, though turns to look at me, his smile thin and disappointed. Mine too: we've so much more to talk about. Bristol's Art Trail, for example – you follow a map and visit artists at home, which is unworldly yet indicative of Bristolian naivety. If I was a robber or a sociopath, I'd get my arse on that tour.

For a few moments more, Freddie and I maintain a cheerless eye contact. It's accompanied by '*Un Amor*', a devastatingly sad Gipsy Kings' classic. The poignancy is palpable.

OK, it's not. But I'm a single woman abroad; I get my kicks where I can.

'Now, *Marissa*.' Rocco Bellini makes me jump. He juts his chin at the waiter, who inserts a fresh cigarette into the operational side of his mouth. 'Tell me again, where do you stay in Italy?'

When giving fabricated information to strangers, make sure it is watertight.

'I told you, signor. I'm staying at my cousin's place.'

Rocco dabs the left corner of his mouth with a napkin. 'You told me the address of a guesthouse.'

He's not wrong. I'd looked at the little boutique hotel on the internet at Bournemouth Airport. At 300 euros a night, it had gone straight on to my bucket list.

'Well, that's where she lives,' I state defensively.

'You're very trusting,' he says. 'A woman alone, giving out her address.'

'I'm not alone,' I remind him. Point at the hinterland. 'My friend is running late.'

For a lot of reasons, I can't now tell him that his son is the friend. Particularly, I must honour the promise I made to Massimo.

'Marissa is a pretty name,' Rocco says. 'Do you have any others?'

I'll give Rocco this: insinuating that I'm using a false name is a good punt from a seasoned professional. My head-bob is extremely apologetic, because I've dug myself too big a hole; the only way out is to carry on lying.

'My name, signor, is Marissa Carvel.'

'And you draw mangoes?'

'Hentai manga. I'm giving it up.'

Rocco makes a suggestion. 'Maybe it's sensible you give up chasing footballers as well.'

'I am not.'

'Freddie is engaged to be married.'

I say this, very earnestly, 'Freddie has good foot–eye coordination, end of. There are a lot of other things to life, especially when it comes to choosing a partner.'

He smiles, intrigued. 'Like what?'

The answer presents itself as a vision. Through the bobbing heads, I spot him outside. Just his profile – one ear, a beauty spot, pink gum and a refulgent molar. It makes my insides do an *entrechat*.

Tommaso Bellini is even prettier than I remember.

The warm and whippy wind tosses his hair about his crown. His shirt, a brilliant white, billows against a black sky. A post-makeover Heathcliff, currently Tommaso is enchanting a terraceful of people.

For a while, I can't stop staring.

Then I examine Rocco's good eye. Its twinkle isn't as energetic as his son's, but I spot the vestiges of it. 'Signor, could you excuse me for a moment?' I ask him quietly. 'I do believe my friend has arrived.'

I make my way out on to decking that hovers supernaturally above the choppy sea below. Circumnavigating the guests, I attempt to catch Tommaso's attention, but each time a new person arrives in his face. The Shakira-lookalike, especially. Long, blond, shaggy hair, breasts that are small and humble, hips that don't lie; she refuses to fuck off. And how I wish she would because, physically, there's no denying that she and Tommaso make the perfect match. In an unimaginative way.

I study their body language.

He touches the side of her head. She snuggles her ear into his palm. And when he laughs, she does too. As do I. His is a contagious type of happy – that's the upshot of genuine self-mastery.

Florence Love Commandment No. 1: Thou shalt not be a relationship wrecker. (Not unless it's in a professional capacity and there are very good reasons.)

That doesn't mean I can't look my best, though. Scratching volume into my hair, straightening my breasts discreetly, I weave a route to a table close to him. The biggest aphrodisiac in the world is unattainability; Tommaso is becoming perilously attractive.

I take a note out of his book; I'm laughing with a stranger when Tommaso finally clocks me. His reaction is one of confusion, followed by unabridged pleasure. I forget to be coy. Grin back, too freely. Despite being mid-sentence, Tommaso leaves Shakira to come and inspect me close up.

'It is you,' he says.

For the first five seconds, we look at one another in the firm knowledge that, were it not for the girlfriend, we would be kissing with tongues.

'What are you doing here?' Tommaso's voice is a little high-pitched. He pecks my cheeks quickly, holds my wrists in case I escape.

'I have more information about my mum.'

He looks around, shakes his head. 'Not here.'

Feeling foolish, I backtrack. 'That's not the reason I've come. You said if I was passing . . . I thought I'd say hi, you know, look at the view.'

He nods, looks around. 'I know a better one. It's the best around here. You can see the whole of Italy.'

His eyes make me shy. 'All of it?'

'Only if there are two of you.'

'Where is it?' I squeak.

'Castello di Friuli.' He points somewhere inland. 'A short ride into the foothills of the Southern Limestone Alps. Meet me there in an hour.'

'Tonight?'

'I need to talk to you. To explain. Have you seen my father?'

'I do not know your father,' I lie.

'Good.' He flicks a look back at Shakira. 'Don't let anyone see you.'

'Tom! *Vuoi una birra?*' a friend shouts over to him.

'Take a taxi.' Tommaso whispers strictly, then shakes my hand. When he lets go, I discover a folded fifty-euro note in my palm.

I have no idea why I mustn't see Rocco. In truth, I feel

like a dirty secret. Paranoid and edgy, I assume an unattractive posture, leave the resort swiftly, decide that it's best all round if I return to Ronchi Hotel, collect my brother and head south in search of Paola Aggi first thing in the morning. I am nobody's bit on the side – not even when acting in a professional capacity.

The trouble is, Cancerians are dangerously curious. It's often the death of us.

Acrophobia

Castello di Friuli.

It's a thirty-minute taxi ride away, and twenty-five of them are spent on precipitous roads in second gear. When, finally, we stop in a layby, the cabbie gesticulates that I must do the last five minutes on foot.

Utterly alone, I look up at a huge stone house. Situated on the apex of a steep hill path, candles flicker at its windows; now and then, the wind wafts clinking glasses and laughter my way, but I can't see a soul. It's like an old, haunted film set.

Before my ascent, I read a tourist information board at the bottom of the steps. In six different languages, it tells me that Castello di Friuli is within the National Park of the Dolomites of Friulia, an area of huge significance, if you're into limestone, sinkholes and junipers. The villa's converted barns serve as a small museum and study centre specialising in the region's unique geology.

I climb the rubble steps without looking backwards once, and remind myself of basic limestone geology: you get a lot of caves. I like a cave – they're much closer to mean sea level.

To clarify: I don't have vertigo. I suffer from acrophobia, which is similar, but not the same at all.

Vertigo is an inner-ear issue triggered by height as well as almost any other type of movement. Acrophobia is psychological – you arrive in a high place and become too agitated to get yourself down. It's a by-product of our mammalian preference for not falling from trees. I don't feel too ashamed – a state of high alert is a useful defence strategy.

Lakes are even closer to mean sea level.

Athabasca, Baikal, Crummock Water, the Dead Sea . . . I play the Alphabet Game until I reach the house on the hill, which, far from a folly, is an early-seventeenth-century Venetian-style villa that now operates as a guesthouse and restaurant. At reception, I'm welcomed warmly and sent further skyward, up a central staircase the colour of oak barrels, to be, finally, awarded a table on the large stone balcony.

I order a carafe of Merlot and fan my face with a paper napkin before glancing, sheepishly, at the panorama. It's cloaked in darkness. A skinny moon too busily admires itself in the sea. Leaving the land in the shadows, the towns shine feeble as sparklers. I'm relieved. Tommaso had promised me the whole of Italy, which is an awful lot of view.

It also reminds me how irrelevant I am. Michael. I should call him. Tell him where I am. Ask that he track my phone. Just in case.

But, as Noah instructed, I left Darcie's on the hall table in Laurelbridge.

I'll phone Dad when I return to the hotel. Explain that Michael totally hijacked my work trip yet is having the time of his life; he'll be marginally soothed by that. *I don't care what you do, as long as you're happy*; he's told us that enough times. And the last time I saw Michael he was extremely happy, having usurped Rosa, who should have been my friend, mostly.

Tommaso's arrival gives me an ectopic beat.

I watch him pause at the top of the oak stairs to talk with a member of the bar staff, who subsequently relocates me to a better table – one at the balcony's edge – then provides me with a bowl of triple-fried veg. Leaving Tommaso to make his entrance.

He sits opposite me and immediately rests his ankles against mine. It's as though no time has passed. He may well have just walked back around the corner of Piazza Montevecchio, phone call over, returning to his seat for the rest of our date.

I pull my feet free. Hold up a bit of cauliflower. 'These are nice.'

'It's a speciality of the place.'

'It's also one of your five a day.'

'A win–win situation.' He tries to tangle ankles again.

'I love vegetables.' I kick him off.

'And food in general, I seem to remember.'

'Not everybody like vegetables, though. It depends on genetics.'

Tommaso gives up on the foot tussle. Sits back, points triumphantly at the view. 'Beautiful, huh?'

'Aren't you going to ask me how come?'

'How come, what?'

'How come not everybody likes vegetables?'

'I wasn't,' he admits. 'But I will now.'

'Phenylthiourea. You find them in cauliflower, broccoli, cabbage – anything that's a member of the cruciferous family. It tastes of nothing at all *or* is unbearably bitter, depending on the person's genes. Phenylthio*urea*. The emphasis being on *urea*.' I put a hand in the air. 'You asked.'

'I did.' He nods seriously.

'Now. Are you and Shakira an item?'

He squints. 'The pop artist?'

'The blonde girl who was all over you when I arrived.'

Tommaso looks slightly appalled. 'She's my half-sister.'

That takes a while to compute. He pushes deep-fried broccoli at my lips. 'Only she's not called Shakira, and she has a huge problem with you.'

'Since when?'

'Since Jay told her you were chatting up our father.'

'Ah.'

'Sophia is protective of her mother.' He frowns at me, amused. 'That's Italian women for you – you're all crazy loyal.'

And although I should chastise him for being both sexist and racist, I feel an utter sense of completion. Tommaso spoke as if I were Italian. As Italian as Paola Aggi. As Italian as him. As Italian as Shakira, who is called Sophia. And the stepmother, too. Lucia, that's what Massimo had called wife number five.

I am an intrinsic part of the Latino theatre. I'm also a modern woman, now Shakira's not a threat; 'Your sister's very pretty.'

'If you like that sort of thing. Personally, I prefer my women worldly. And not so skinny.'

I laugh. Rest a breast on the table. 'How old are you?'

'Twenty-seven.' Our glasses are refilled. 'You?' he wonders.

'Twenty-nine.' I pat the table indignantly. 'You just fucked off.'

'I did.'

'With no explanation or apology.'

He places a palm on his heart. 'It was an unprecedented emergency.'

'I left my telephone number with reception. A text would have been polite.'

Tommaso ignores this to squint and say, 'Freddie asked about you after you left tonight. My father said you were chatting him up too.'

I laugh defensively. 'The Bristolian?'

'I told him you were out of his league.'

'You sound jealous.'

'Nope,' he says. 'But Jay is.'

I frown. 'Of who? Of Freddie? Is he gay?'

'No,' he states impatiently. 'Jay's just possessive of his friends. He said your name was Marissa?'

I squint at Tommaso, as though he hasn't got a clue. 'Jay bamboozled me. No sane woman would give him their real name. Tommaso, his behaviour's not normal.'

'No, it's not,' he agrees quietly. 'Then again, he came off a motorcycle at 140 kph. That's not normal either. Never ride a superbike.'

I place a palm on each breast. Because that is terrible. And fascinating. And an excellent example of why it's prudent not to forejudge. Connections between the cerebral cortex and the limbic system have to be in tip-top fettle; the smallest amount of damage can make for unstable behaviour. I was premature, took Jay for a drug-addled Leo, when the truth is a brain injury had turned him into one. I wonder what star sign he was prior to the accident.

'Is he medicated?' I ask Tom.

His nod is unequivocal. 'That night in Rome, he was drunk and disorderly. I was advised to remove him from the city.'

I laugh. 'Are you serious? By who?'

He takes my hand – his palm is heavy and persuasive. 'I am serious enough to want to help you. Before we were inter-rupted, we spoke about your mother. Bambi of the Bluebells.'

'Don't make fun of me.'

His expression becomes funeral-director serious. 'Prior to my being disturbed by Rome's Commissioner of Police, I was telling you about my godfather – Massimo Satori.'

Tom shuffles his chair closer. Our foreheads almost touch; I wish they wouldn't. I feel uncontrollably disloyal to Massimo.

'My godfather worked closely with the police,' he tells me. 'He helped take some nasty people off the streets.'

This admission makes me absolutely livid. Massimo attempts to live out his days in anonymity, the only thing keeping him from death, a murderous sidekick and intense secrecy, yet Tommaso's loose lips endanger him. I could be anyone.

'If your mother left Italy via official channels, changed her name, went to England, then he will know the procedure. Specifically, he'll have contacts and access to information.'

Predicament fact: I have a massive one.

'First, however, I *must* speak with my father.'

'No.'

'Rocco liked you. He won't let you go unless it's safe. It has to be safe for all of us.'

Massimo had been unequivocal: 'For many people's safety, most especially your own, today never happened.'

I had sworn on my mother's life: nobody would ever know we'd met. That was the agreement. He had then told me to get the fuck out of Italy.

I frown. 'Why are you so keen to help me?'

Tommaso gives this some thought, before saying slowly, 'Three reasons. The first –' He takes my hand, traces my forefinger along his goosebumps. 'The second, I have a mother too. The third, because I can.'

He points beyond the balcony, past the moon; it's backlit by a gazillion galaxies. 'Now, have you caught a glimpse of Bambi yet?' he asks.

'I think so.' I too admire the universe. 'She's in Bagnara Calabra.'

He squints. 'That's very far south. How do you know?'

'I don't. I have a lead.' I dig a hand at my handbag, pull free my spy torch and USB lead. 'It's out of battery,' I explain. 'You'll have to watch the footage on a laptop.'

Tommaso looks at the flashlight in his palm and laughs. 'This is a video camera?'

'Audio Video Interleave. Thirty frames per second. Seventy-two-degree angle of view. Though it's just a recording of me opening a letter. My dad sends one to a Paola Aggi every month. Maybe. He did this month.' I nod at the torch. 'I reposted it afterwards. It'll reach Heathrow Worldwide Distribution Centre tonight. British Airways will fly it on to Italy most likely tomorrow.'

'You've been back to England?'

'Briefly, then I found the letter.' I lower my voice. Give him insider information: 'When posting a letter to the continent, add one day for it to arrive if your letter's destination is a city with an airport, two days for a major city, three days for an average-sized town, and four for a settlement in the countryside. If my calculations are correct, the letter will arrive at PO Box 5225 in the postal region of Calabria at some point on Tuesday.'

I don't know if he's overtaken by lust and/or delicious confusion, but he holds my cheeks in his palms, kisses me firmly on the lips, and says, 'You are extremely weird.'

And although his mouth is closed, saliva molecules sneak in through my lips. I know this because the testosterone in his spit is chemically compatible with my own signalling molecules. I have to stop myself from groaning.

Quickly, I continue. 'My plan is to go to the post office in Balgara Calabria and see who picks it up.'

He nods, says nothing, just strokes his arm.

'Don't you have any suggestions?' I ask.

'"Kisses are a better fate than wisdom."'

I palm-clap. 'E. E. Cummings said that.'

'Yes.' He leans forward, pecks my nose. 'A very wise guy.'

His spit smells divine, as though he's gargled with a Peroni-and-Listerine infusion. That's the cortisol and oxytocin – it can shape-shift an aroma, because other people's spit only ever smells nice if your chemical systems are in courtship.

'You are definitely on the run,' he tells me.

'I'm the littlest hobo, remember.'

'Who has missed an important point.'

'About what?'

'The postal system in Italy – it's very shit. You and Paola Aggi could be waiting for your letter for weeks.'

I shrug. 'Then Paola and I will be waiting for weeks together.'

'Your plans until then?' he asks.

'To show my brother a good time – he's about to become a runaway bride.'

He ignores this to peck my mouth gently once more. Before he pulls away, I accidentally run a tongue around his lips.

Tongue fact: where the lips are labial, the tongue is entirely phallic. A moist, open mouth, a penetrating tongue and the simulation of intercourse is patent, which is why you shouldn't French kiss in public. You are also agreeing to the risk of infection and disease; that is intimate viewing for a diner, unless you're from the continent, where food, sex and voyeurism are happy enough bedfellows.

He neatens my hair, traces the muscles of my neck, talks to my lips. 'Now you must do something for me.'

'How did I get indebted to you?' I laugh.

He examines my clavicle. 'You will be, after Massimo.'

I wish he'd stop mentioning Massimo. I fold my arms. 'Shoot.'

'It's my mother,' he states. 'She's embarrassed I'll turn up alone.'

'To what?'

'Lunch tomorrow.'

I smile. 'I'm looking after my brother, remember, but thank you for the invitation.'

'It's not an invitation. I'll pick you both up at midday precisely. I will need your take on things.'

'On what things?'

'He's after her for her money.' His eyes twinkle deliciously, like we're six and playing make-believe.

'Your mother's boyfriend?'

'Look at the place.' He points around us.

'This belongs to your mum?' I whisper-roar. 'Do you live here too?'

'Wouldn't you?'

'Good god, no. But if you've a head for heights, you'd sacrifice family members for a pad like this.' I look at it properly: the ceilings, the huge oak beams, the balcony and its Renaissance stone work. Particularly, I squint at a customer I've spotted at a table inside. Hidden in a corner, he and a woman talk over beers. 'Will there be food?' I ask Tommaso.

'It's lunch. You're in Italy.'

I take another deep-fried vegetable. A carrot. Look again at the geeky couple, because that is Lancelot, on a date, definitely, with a young, speccie, serial-killer type.

'Go on, then. But my brother and I will be attending for purely culinary reasons.'

'Good. Now drink up. I need to get back to the party before Papa goes home. I'll talk to him about Massimo.'

'No,' I snap, then touch the beauty spot beneath his eye. It's risen surface is smooth and velvet-soft. 'I'd rather we did this my way. I have other leads to follow first.'

He nods respectfully.

'And don't forget to watch the footage of my letter.'

'It's at the top of my things-to-do list.'

When I catch Lancelot and the bespectacled serial killer frowning at me, I pull the fur wrap around my shoulders. 'And I'll be needing a car home.'

'I can do better than that.'

My legs wrapped tightly around Tommaso's hips, we zip along mountain roads lit dimly by his Vespa's headlight. Tonight, my acrophobia fails me. After a while I hold on to his waist less tightly, lean back a little, ignore the sheer drops and let the wind work my hair into a tangle. On a hairpin bend, I whoop, delighted, because, momentarily, I'm entirely free of existential angst.

At Hotel Ronchi, we don't kiss immediately.

First, I touch one of his eyebrows, trace the curve of his nose to its tip with a nail. Intently, he watches me. When, finally, we touch tongues, I forget where I am. It's a kiss we may have well been jointly choreographing since childhood. So in synch, it's like I'm kissing myself.

I have no plans to stop. Ever.

Then Rosa comes out and tells me off like a mum. Because we are leaning against a brightly lit tree in front of reception and there are children around.

'You're very accomplished,' I tell Tommaso as he hops back on his scooter.

He agrees. 'I have awards.'

'A little less velocity next time, though.'

'I'll bear it in mind.'

Without looking back, he waves and disappears around the corner that takes him back to Portopiccolo.

Face-plant

Michael pats his knees. Pristinely turned out in cotton trousers and a short-sleeved shirt, he's seated in reception, excited. Tommaso won't be here for half an hour at least – so, for a bit, I spy on my brother from an armchair in the wi-fi corner.

When Michael's phone beeps, he checks to see who it is, then becomes instantly irritated. Placing the handset face down on a side table, he refuses to watch it fit and spasm its way towards the edge.

When I returned last night, Michael told me he'd heard from Sébastien and Dad. 'I'm having some me time,' he'd explained. Annie has been trying to call too, but he's ignoring her, just as we'd agreed.

I watch Michael stand up and I focus on his face. He is deciding to micromanage the reception desk, to reposition its leaflets, phone and pen so they're equidistant.

Cosmo sits behind it, watching him over the top of his glasses.

When he's finished, Michael points at Cosmo's banknote collection and enunciates, as though Rosa's husband has mental challenges, '*Buongiorno*, signor. I used to collect rubbers when I was little. The ones that smell of fruits.'

My brother's such a jammy bugger – Rosa's husband nods, then turns the scrapbook around to show him. Michael is all about the moment; I'm able to walk past him and swipe his phone from the side table.

Today alone, he's had six missed calls from Annie.

Hiding behind a wall, I use the opportunity to read every

text she's ever sent him. Fifty-three in all, which verges on persecution. They've known one another for less than a month, yet the messages are relentlessly shouty. And unnecessary, given that she, Sébastien and Michael have formed a WhatsApp group. The Three Musketeers, they call themselves. The messages here exhibit an altogether warmer tone. They make me feel both excluded and murderous.

A selection of icy texts meant for Michael's eyes only:

Don't be late.

You were very selfish today.

Need a lift to work tomorrow. Be here for 8.

Please note you've upset Seb AGAIN.

For a while, I plot her assassination, then remember to call Noah.

'It's Florence,' I tell him quietly. 'Give me an update.'

His ego is fragile as a soap-bubble. 'I'm well, thanks for asking. Whose phone are you using?'

'Michael's. We're on a case.'

'Where?'

'Abroad,' I whisper abruptly. 'What's going on at your end?'

'Are you back in Italy?'

'I can't talk. Can you just update me?'

Noah nails a voice that infers imminent and grave danger. 'I have just spent the last thirty-eight hours watching the Weymouth office.'

'Really?' My first love is turning out to be worth his weight in gold. 'What are your findings?'

'There are no customers. Just three employees – two men and a woman. They appeared to be on staggered twenty-four-hour shifts. The impression I get is that the office is a hub, for clocking in and out, maybe. I don't know. What I do know is, it doesn't sell wind technology. That doesn't involve around-the-clock staffing. Or a video entry system. Or a complete lack of advertising, signage and clients.'

'So we're clear the business is a ruse.'

'Affirmative. Then there are the briefcases.'

'What briefcases?'

'Most people wouldn't notice the difference, not at a quick glance. All three employees had the same one. It's standard issue. A brand called Camelot.'

'Is it a good make?' I'm a little confused as to the relevance of this.

'They're made of steel, have a metal tether and barrel locks. We're talking high-level security. And expensive – a grand a piece. Without a key, you'd need a bomb to open it.'

'How do you know all this?'

'I am a courier,' he says with dignity. 'I know my document holders.'

I *love* that level of professionalism.

'It doesn't end there,' he continues. 'I followed one of the guys home.'

'Go on,' I say, quickly.

'A male worker – middle-aged, nondescript.'

Nobody is nondescript, not ever. 'Give me a proper description.'

'It was dark.'

That is irrelevant. Michael always provides full and florid rundowns; so full and florid, I'd recognise the target in a football stadium from behind. Admittedly, my brother's helped by the fact he has OCD – that gives you an eye for the little things. There's also the fact that I made him commit the CIA Identikit process to memory.

'Private investigation is always about the small print,' I tell Noah. 'Now, what about his car?'

'A Ford Mondeo. The 2004 model.'

'No full registration? Colour, bumper stickers, paintwork damage, cushions on the back ledge . . .?'

'His wife was putting the bins out' is his best offer. 'Kids' bikes in the porch. I'd say he's a normal family man. Who's also very attached to his briefcase. He locked the thing to his arm to walk twenty steps inside.'

'Where does he live?'

'New Milton. Twelve kilometres from Laurelbridge.' Noah's eager to please. 'The house is a bungalow.'

'Email me the address. I'll do some checks – title deeds, electoral roll – I need to get the nondescript guy's name.'

'Roger,' he tells me.

'How do you know?'

'No.' He coughs. 'I meant, understood.'

'Over and out. But next time, think *details*.'

I go back to the wi-fi corner, wave at Michael as if I've just arrived and indicate that I'll be ten minutes.

His finger-wave back is perfunctory. He's now sitting next to Cosmo behind the reception desk and they are communicating silently via an ad hoc sign language.

Firing up the PC, I consider the evidence so far.

Employee No. 1 drives an old, nondescript car, is himself nondescript-looking, lives in a nondescript bungalow, yet totes around an extortionately priced briefcase day and night.

I type 'Camelot briefcase' into the search bar. Noah was right about the price – this piece of luggage is top-drawer. Developed specifically for the secure storage and transportation of sensitive documents, cash, passports, paperwork and/or firearms, its construction is twelve-gauge cold-roll plate steel and the test tether cable can withstand 9,000 kilos of force. The website states: 'We supply the public and private sector clients, including police forces throughout the UK, government bodies and security services.'

If Eric Steensen was in the force while working for ACME, he was not undercover. Not *completely*. Undercover agents don't carry bomb-resistant briefcases – it gives the game away.

Noah's email is already in my inbox. Employee No. 1 lives at: 24 Cull Lane, New Milton, Hampshire.

Immediately, I carry out an online Land Registry check.

Employee No. 1 is called Gary Rose. He owns the property with his wife, Dawn, and has done for eight years. An ancestry check shows that the couple are married with two boys, aged four and six. It also allows me to establish the rest of Gary's family tree – parents, brother, sisters, in-laws. Using the electoral roll, I trace his past addresses back to his childhood home, along with the addresses of his nearest and dearest.

A firm conclusion: Gary and his family's details are too freely available for undercover work. I even chance upon a photo of him batting for the New Milton cricket team.

Michael's phone makes me jump. It's a message from Sébastien.

Big bust-up with Annie. U were right. She's evil. Am going to block her. U have to promise u will too??

I'm frowning at the phone when I feel a nose in my neck, then lips. I giggle. Tommaso looks over my shoulder at the PC screen, nods at Gary Rose in his cricket whites.

'Should I be jealous?'

Michael arrives beside us at supersonic speed. 'No, you should be ashamed of yourself. Get out of my sister's neck.'

'It's OK, sweetheart.' I clear the PC's history and present Tommaso. 'Michael, this is a friend of mine.'

'Michael! It's very cool to meet you.' Tommaso clicks his feet together and bows like a nice Nazi. 'My name is Tom, and your sister and I are much more than friends. We are lovers.'

That makes me snort, loudly.

Michael pats his shoulder. 'Good. I thought I was going to have to fight you.'

'Do strangers kiss your sister's neck a lot?'

My brother points at me, like I'm so beautiful it's tragic. 'Look at her, Tom.'

I stand up, give his arm a hug and tell him, 'I hope you've packed your crampons. We are about to have an authentic Italian lunch with a view.'

Michael is consumed with disappointment. 'You didn't tell me to bring crampons.'

Tommaso waves a dismissive hand. 'If she wants to do the scenic route, let her. We'll just use the steps.'

On our way to the car, I send a quick text to Noah.

Whatever they're doing, they're doing in plain sight. Watch ACME like a hawk.

An unnoticed office space above a community hub. A company with no marketing team and a penchant for bullet-proof suitcases – of course this is the key to our parents' story. In my absence, I instruct Noah Steensen to proceed in haste.

Michael sits in the front of Tommaso's convertible Mercedes. Whenever we get over 30 kph, my brother puts his hands in the air, like he's on a rollercoaster.

'We have let him out of the attic before,' I tell Tommaso in the rear-view mirror.

'It's Flo who lives in the attic,' Michael states. 'She's very messy.'

'Untidiness is my slant on aversion therapy,' I explain. 'I come from a long line of neat freaks.'

Michael ignores me. 'Do you know, Flo has told me nothing about you?'

'Good,' Tommaso replies. 'You'll hear it from the horse's mouth and make up your own mind.'

Michael nods like our dad. 'So what do you do for a living, son?'

'I wait tables.'

My brother becomes immediately limp. 'I'm an actor, I know all about waiting tables.'

That makes me laugh. He's not waited a table in his life. But I bite my lip because Tommaso looks so impressed with Michael it makes my heart do a loop-the-loop.

'You're an actor? Wow, man. Are you famous?'

Michael nods. 'I was in *Coronation Street*.'

And he was. As an extra in the Christmas special. To his credit, he did a marvellous impression of a stranger having a drink in the Rovers.

Michael pats Tommaso's leg; apparently, he has passed a lacklustre grilling with flying colours and is deemed boyfriend material. 'If you like my sister, it's best you play hard to get.'

Whereas I do a high-pitched laugh, Tommaso takes it much more seriously. 'I can't, Michael, it's against my culture.'

'Be it on your head,' says Michael.

'I am here!' I remind them.

'Just know this: my sister is difficult.'

Defensiveness is not an attractive trait. I am, however, notoriously self-justifying. 'Since when have I been difficult?'

It's a dangerous question – I certainly don't want him to qualify his statement out loud. *Since Dad called you it every day of your life growing up.*

'See what I mean?' Michael is telling Tommaso through the side of his mouth. That fucks me off more than him saying, *Since Dad called you it every day of your life growing up.* I could burst into tears.

'It's her Latin temperament.' Tommaso Bellini makes excuses for me.

'Latin temperament' is the exact phrase Dad used to explain away my mother's foibles – her periods of deep thought, her need for domestic order, the tears and her discomfiture around strangers. In fact, Tommaso makes me feel so vindicated, I hide out of view of the rear-view mirror for a moment and have a power cry; a short and weighty weep to restore mental stability and alertness.

Today, we approach Castillo di Friuli via a different route; one where we're able to drive further up the incline, although the view's full impact is veiled by the imposing stone villa.

'It was built during the Renaissance,' Tommaso tells us as we walk towards his home. 'It was first a country home for a countess. Then it was a monastery. Now it's a centre of geological and culinary excellence.' Fifty metres from the villa's walls, we can certainly smell the evidence.

'I work here sometimes when Mum needs me,' Tommaso tells my brother.

Michael looks ever so sad. 'Your mum works here?'

'She does, my friend, very hard. Once she was an environmental studies lecturer at the University of Bologna. This is her life now.'

'How the mighty have fallen.' Michael scrunches his nose at the magnificent mansion.

'How did she afford it?' I ask.

'A divorce present from my father,' he confides. 'He's very generous with his ex-wives.'

Today, we enter via the back door, straight into an open-plan living space the size of a barn. Stone walls, marble floor tiles, walnut furniture, shutters and ceiling fans. A large, rustic kitchen with its own courtyard and view. Staircases everywhere alluding to the private quarters above.

'This is incredible,' I mutter.

'Howard calls it the granny annexe.'

'Howard the boyfriend?'

'Technically, fiancé,' he admits. 'This is their engagement party.'

'You said it was lunch!'

He shrugs, chivvies us up a staircase. 'Now, Howard is quite the charmer. Don't be fooled.'

This time, we enter the restaurant via a private door.

The guests have congregated on the balcony. Loudly, they talk over one another: arguing, jubilant, having an academic debate – it's impossible to tell. Neither does it matter a jot. The balcony heaves with a very Latin disposition, and it feels liberating.

I don't know Tommaso's mother, but I spot her immediately.

Oblivious to the garrulousness, she watches me intently, like a mycologist studies a mushroom. On the occasions I allow our gazes to meet, she doesn't look away, or smile, or frown. That level of dispassionate scientific attention from another woman is entirely unnerving. Especially one whose prevalent thought is: *you are fucking my son*.

I want to tell her the truth: *I'm not. Not yet*. Because she's more than I expected. Extremely graceful, high cheekbones, a ballerina's neck and short pudding-bowl hair – she's in her late fifties, yet her willowy presence usurps everybody else's. Mine especially.

Always become obsequious in such situations. Because, as Sun Tzu famously said back in 5000 BC, know your enemy. And here stands a woman who could take me down in a second with a withering look. Ignoring etiquette, I don't wait for Tommaso to introduce us.

'*Scusi, scusi . . .*' I make my way through the people.

Eye contact now locked, I decide she reminds me of Ingrid Bergman in *Joan of Arc*.

'*Buongiorno*, signora.' I realise I don't know her name – not her first name or her last. She was a Bellini once, but she looks the enlightened type, quick to bin a redundant epithet. I do my best imitation of an Italian. '*Mi chiamo* Florence. *Come ti chiami?*'

'Jolana.' She touches her chest. 'Or Jo-Jo, depending on your mood.'

Jo-Jo of Arc, I don't say out loud, even though she's totally nailed the voice. Not the martyr's, the Ingrid Bergman version.

I smile. 'I like your accent.'

She nods her thanks. 'And you are from London?'

It's not her fault. I've worked diligently to disguise my roots. 'Not far,' I say.

She extends both hands, shaking my right one so warmly I feel grateful.

I also quite fancy her, in a totally platonic way, which is an interesting sign. Family members share pheromones. Attraction to potential in-laws confirms it's the real thing and that mating with one of them is a foregone conclusion.

'Jolana, I'm embarrassed,' I tell her, because I genuinely am. 'I should have brought a gift. Tommaso invited me late last night. I arrived in Italy unexpectedly.' I show her all the people who have turned up too. 'It turned out to be perfect timing.'

'Tommaso and his friends being here is gift enough.' Jolana makes me feel a billion korunas. 'One moment, darling,' she says, waving behind me. 'Howard, come and meet Florence. Howard is British too,' she tells me, as if it's a delicious secret.

Howard is quite the surprise.

Sixty, medium height, salt-and-pepper hair and beard, cords, short-sleeved shirt and tie, two pairs of glasses on his head, he looks like a lovely geography teacher, one who works at a failing school in the inner city. Because when Howard speaks, his accent evokes the sound of Bow bells.

'Good to meet you,' he tells me confidently.

'And you.' I point a thumb behind me at the view. 'Wow.'

'Beats Bermondsey.' He winks. 'Where do you hail from?'

'South coast,' I nod.

'And who, Florence, is this?' Jolana interrupts us, delighted.

I look to my left. Michael stands beside me, arms flaccid, a dispassionate stare.

'My brother, Michael,' I explain.

'Tom really wanted me to come, didn't he, Flo?' he tells them defensively. 'I'm an actor on the telly.'

Jolana is a wonderful judge of character. Her eyes are entirely relaxed, her chin gently tilted to the left. 'I think I recognise you.'

'I'm moderately famous.' Michael nods.

With polish, she kisses both his cheeks. 'Then you are especially welcome.'

Howard is a bit of a hippy. He kisses Michael's cheeks too. Holds his shoulders like a stage hypnotist. 'What you been on, brother?'

Tommaso approaches Howard from behind, gets him in a gentle throat lock. 'He was on *Coronation Street*.'

'That'll explain it,' says Howard, hugging Tommaso amiably. 'I'm more into the big screen.'

Michael counters Howard with comfortable aplomb. 'Then if I were you, signor, I'd watch this space.'

I have *never* been more proud.

Tommaso, Jolana and Howard laugh in unconscious harmony. How I'd love to elbow my way into their circle and do some accidental synchronised laughing too. So much so, I realise I've forgotten about Mum, that I've had my back to Bagnara Calabra the whole time I've been here.

Lunch is a raucous, delicious affair – plate after plate of Italian and Slovenian delicacies. If there's any order to the courses, I don't notice or care; their arrival is as relentless as the chatter.

The party is made up of Jolana's extended family, work colleagues, mutual friends and a member of the Department of Agriculture. Thirty-five of us sit at a table ten metres long and fight for airspace, because if you don't talk fast, you don't talk at all.

By dessert, I am clear on the following three observa-
tions . . .

Tommaso's life in 4D is endlessly surprising.

When he speaks colloquial Italian, for example, I see new
gestures and facial expressions that display an emotional
intelligence I'd not expected. It's libidinous. By the time I
catch him having a conversation in Slovenian, I am hook,
line and sinker in lust.

Jo-Jo and Howard are absolutely delightful.

Their subliminal connection is patent to anybody with a
background in kinesics. They eat at the same pace; have
acquired each other's most nuanced facial expressions; their
knees and shoulders are always aligned, even when they
occupy different rooms. And when they talk between themselves, you can't help but ogle like a voyeur, theirs being that
rare frisson that has been honed during previous incarnations.

*Howard could not exude more humility and fondness towards his
stepson-to-be if he tried.*

It's a far cry from the set-up back at home with Darcie
and Annie.

'I wish my own boy was more like Tom,' I hear him tell
guests. 'He's got a good work ethic, that one. And he loves
his mum. I'm proud to be a cog in their little unit.'

Me, too, I think. Even though I'm not.

Not yet.

It's extremely confusing, therefore, when Tommaso kisses
the inside of my wrist and whispers, 'Do you see what I mean?'

'About what?'

'The fiancé.'

'Howard?'

'He's an arsehole.' His headshake is apologetic. 'I don't
trust him one bit.'

I frown. '*Really?* What's he done to piss you off?'

'Nothing.'

'Not ever?'

Tommaso's look suggests I should know better. 'The Bellinis are very intuitive. If we feel something is wrong, there's usually something wrong.'

I laugh. 'Are you jealous?'

'I'm Italian.' He shrugs.

'You're also an Aries.'

'Scorpio.'

I bloody knew it. I kiss his lips. 'In your defence, Scorpions are an excellent judge of character.'

Point cemented, he stabs his fork at the torta.

'Have you managed to watch the letter footage?' I change the subject.

'Yes,' he says. 'I think I can help.'

'Not Massimo, though,' I state.

'Yes, Massimo.' He makes his eyes big. 'Because what I can't get you is *any* information whatsoever myself. Papa will get wind of it – my sources are his sources. Rocco must not know you're here.'

'Because of *Sophia*?' I let go of his hand. 'Christ, Tommaso, I have not got designs on your father. Or Freddie. Or anyone else. There must be someone you can call on. You know people. Rome's bloody police commissioner . . .'

Tom becomes impatient. 'These *people* are friends of my father's.'

I reassure him. 'I would never tell a soul.'

He doesn't answer, gives me no other option. That leaves me deflated. We're mute for thirty seconds. It's the longest silence we've had. And I hate it. Am extremely relieved to discover that Tommaso's ego is more evolved than mine.

'Are we having a domestic?'

To which Michael pops his head between ours. 'Par for the course. Told you she was difficult.'

For what happens next, I intend to pray, a lot. Because

there was Michael having a wonderful time. Effortlessly, he'd butted in and then butted out of our conversation; something I've not seen him do successfully before. He was just a microsecond from leaving us be, while exhibiting a confidence, maturity and level of assimilation that would make my father weep with joy.

Then I go and stick a leg out. Like I'm six again.

God punishes me. Slows the world right down. Enabling me to watch my little brother launch forward, chest proud, as though he were about to commence an acrobatic sequence. I watch his eyes grow from tapered to dangerously bulbous. His feet hang in the air. The face-plant feels like it lasts for a good twelve minutes.

Whitey

Jolana patches my brother up efficiently and reassuringly. She reminds me of Ingrid Bergman in *The Inn of the Sixth Happiness*.

His injuries are alarming yet conducive with falling arse over tit, she explains: a split lip and broken tooth, ruptured nasal capillaries, widespread grazing and internal bruising.

I'm not sure how she's come to such a firm diagnosis, but I accept it completely, because possible alternatives are: he's decimated his spleen, or suffered a blood clot which will strike him dead during the car ride home.

God gives me a chance to redeem myself. Wipes Michael's memory, leaving him convinced he'd got his feet tangled in a chair.

If you were an honourable woman, you'd put them right. Our Lord suggests methods of atonement. Forgets that I have to consider the occasion. My hosts will prefer it if I don't turn their engagement into *The Jeremy Kyle Show*. Neither does Michael need to know the truth, ever – he'll use it as ammunition for the rest of my existence. Worst of all, he'll tell Dad.

Damned if I do and damned if I don't, I excuse myself. Go downstairs to sit outside on the villa's steps and have a tête-à-tête with Heaven. Hands clasped, I start with a Hail Mary to show I come in peace. In return, Our Lady sends an attaché.

A pair of brown loafers arrive in my eye-line.

I look up. Howard tips a cigarette packet at my face. 'Are you praying?' he asks.

'A bit.' I sigh.

'To who?'

'Thor, fairies, leprechauns, the Flying Spaghetti Monster . . .'

'Where have I heard that before?'

'Richard Dawkins.' I nod. 'I'm useless with blood.' Taking a cigarette, I remember the state of Michael's face. 'It's his hen weekend. My dad is going to kill me.'

Howard sits beside me on the step. 'Look at it as fodder for the best man's speech.'

I half smile. 'As it turns out, I am the best man.'

'There you go. It was meant to be. Give yourself a break. You're a good girl.'

I am not.

I suck hard on the cigarette, but it's a dud; the nicotine rush doesn't come up to scratch. 'What are these?' I complain.

'Some rubbish out of a machine. I don't normally smoke.'

Things not to say to a potential stepfather-in-law to be: 'Neither do I – not cigarettes, anyway.'

Luckily, Howard's on the same page. 'I've been banned from all that,' he confides. 'Jolana says I've got to look after my heart.'

'Do you have cardiovascular issues?' I ask gravely.

'None whatsoever.'

Instinctively, we look at one another with exhausted eyes. Dope-smoking fact: a couple of puffs never killed anybody.

'Some people are such killjoys.' I shouldn't be encouraging him.

No matter. Howard is having a conversation with himself. 'Plus, I'm very much supposed to be celebrating.'

I squint at him. 'Have you actually got some?'

'Just the one. An emergency supply.'

'Like an EpiPen?' I squeak.

'Exactly.'

'And this *is* an emergency.'

'Our secret, though,' he double-checks. 'She'll have my guts for garters.'

'Us Brits have to stick together.' See how quickly I discard my Italian roots, because it's been months since I last toked on a joint, and it could certainly put things into perspective. Plus, I'm in a lot of shock. On medical grounds, I'm totally due a break.

Parental warning – smoking dope is illegal and definitely doesn't suit those with innate mental issues. If, however, you are sane and enjoy a healthy and balanced lifestyle, its consumption is much like drinking a fine wine and can be appreciated thus.

A rough guide to cannabis:

1. 'Solid' is strong and mellow, like a large glass of red, and looks like an Oxo cube.

2. 'Grass' is giggly and as banjaxing as a bottle of Prosecco, and can be mistaken for putrefied broccoli.

Parental word of assurance – either variety is safer than taking an aspirin. The National Institute on Drug Abuse is unequivocal. To the possibility of overdosing and dying, their response was (and I quote): 'No, it's not very likely.'

The worst that can happen? You chuck a whitey. This is best described as having a very unexpected nervous break-down, followed by vomiting, incontinence and a strong desire to die.

I am not an advocate of drugs. I am, however, a pragma-tist. If you're inexperienced, stick with the Nepalese brown, like Howard, who's at a family party and cannot risk red-eye.

Currently, we're sitting behind a car-sized outcrop. It hides us from the house while providing a three-sided panorama. The effects of Nepalese black can be compared to a light pre-med. This, thankfully, makes the view ahead very palatable. I'm able to lean against a boulder and experience philosophical serenity.

Three tokes in, and Howard becomes very beatnik too.

'This strain is from Manali in the Himalayas. The closer to the sun you are, the more resin you get.'

'Are you a potographer?' I ask.

This makes him giggle. 'Just your common-or-garden anorak.' He passes me the joint. 'What do you do, Florence?'

'I used to work in a post office.' I'm not sure Howard believes that; his eyes watch me too wisely. 'I was very high up,' I reassure him. 'What about you?'

'Garden centres.' He sighs. 'Not very rock and roll, but it pays the bills.'

I remember what my dad wrote about replanting flowers in his letter. 'Tell me about African daisies,' I ask.

'OK.' He smiles. '*Osteospermum*. Part of the *Asteraceae* family. Big flowers, can be over a metre tall. An annual – in UK climes. A tender perennial in Italy.'

'It's definitely an annual in the UK?'

'If you're lucky, you'll get a couple of years out of it.'

'You don't replant an annual?'

'Not unless the conditions aren't right in the first place . . .'

I stop listening, because my conclusions are this: if Paola and Dad are not speaking in code, they've had contact before; within the last year or two. It is top of my list on my return – to scour the grounds of Cowslip Cottage for *Osteospermum*.

'Gardening's very calming,' Howard is telling me. 'Therapeutic.'

Just six tokes in, I become loose-lipped. 'Calm is a pipe dream, Howard. Especially in a job like mine – you need to be on your toes, or it's game over.'

'I'd no clue the British postal system was so cut throat.' He pokes an indiscreet tongue at his cheek. That makes us both laugh out loud for a good four minutes, until Howard hears voices in the distance.

'I'd better get back.' He looks at me with guilty eyes.

'Yellow-belly,' I tease him.

'Guts for garters,' he reminds me. 'Now, hide that roach.'

I swear on my life and shoo him away. Old hippies can be complete fusspots.

A whitey fact: I have not pulled one since the year 2000. It was New Year's Eve, and I presented myself at A&E with a self-diagnosed heart attack and stroke. When discharged, it was with a complete flea in my ear.

Parental warning: Nepalese brown is stronger than I remember.

My spatial awareness is shot. Having hidden the joint's butt, I found myself on a different side of the villa – the side over which the house might as well hang.

I see a vast, red sun slipping down the back of the world. The Karst plateau ahead has a Martian hue. Apart from the river – this high up, the Isonzo appears as emerald puddles that sit idle and luminous in the bottom of an alpine valley. And in the far distance the sea is as murky as a plunge pool. A plunge pool into which valleys, rivers, Trieste and the whole Adriatic tectonic plate appear to collapse.

It's a lot of view. Far too much. Which is the crux of my problem with altitude. Along with acrophobia, I suffer from a philosophical condition called barophobia – a mental reaction to very heavy shit, like existence. Dad used to tell me it's the variety of vertigo that clever people get.

I've been here for thirty minutes – face down, spread-eagled, distributing my weight evenly and remembering survival techniques.

No. 1 basic field-survival technique: breathe. Even though your whitey is telling you that your brain, heart and central nervous system have ceased to communicate. That it's a matter of moments before your fingers loosen and you slither into a thousand-metre freefall.

Face to face with an ant, I tell it the God's honest truth.

'I didn't mean to trip him over. It was like a Tourette's moment. I don't even have Tourette's. It was like when I shouted, "Fuck!" on a bus. I told myself not to, but impetuousness got the better of me.'

Ants are dreadful at listening. This one notices neither the view nor me, and it certainly has no concept of its own mortality, which leaves one of us at a distinct evolutionary advantage. I stab it with my nose, then make a disturbed screech like a mating fox, because I just killed.

For the second time today, I pray and receive word via a harbinger.

'Are you stalking me or something?' says a pair of feet. Different feet to Howard's, they are donned in black vinyl shoes with Velcro straps; the type you get in the back-to-school section of supermarkets. I recognise his middle-Englishness. Do a victorious sob when I gather the courage to lift my chin and confirm the identity of my rescuer.

Lancelot stands above me. An Adam Ant strip of sunblock streaks his nose.

'Hello, again,' I say.

He asks, confused, 'What are you doing?'

'I'm being a guest at Jo-Jo's engagement party.'

He looks up towards the villa and frowns. 'How do you know them?'

I'm snappy, because this isn't the time. 'I'm enjoying a dalliance with her son, but it's early days. Lancelot, I am not a stalker. I'm just properly stuck.'

'On what?'

'A cliff. I haven't much strength left.'

Lancelot sits beside me. Pulls an apple from his rucksack.

Takes a bite. Pushes it at me. 'A cliff is a near-vertical exposed rock. Gradient-wise, this isn't even a mountain.'

How I want to suck it dry of moisture.

Cannabis side-effect: the parasympathetic nervous system can't be arsed to tell the submandibular glands to produce saliva. Add abject fear to that, and you're likely to experience a horrendous case of cotton mouth.

Sharing apples, however, is as intimate as French kissing.

I have no choice but to shake my head at it. 'Whatever we're on, I can't stand up on it.'

'It's a hill.'

I push myself on to my elbows so he can see my eyes. They relay exactly how vulnerable I am. But Lancelot doesn't give a shit. He stares me out for a bit. Finally, he puts his apple beside my face and stands up.

'You are putting me in a very awkward situation,' he mutters.

'How exactly?'

'Let's get you up.'

'I need a helicopter.'

'You don't.'

'I *really, really* do,' I tell the ant's surviving family and friends. But they are hell bent on scurrying towards a skyscraper of fruit. *There is a God: St Adam of the Ants*, they cry with gay abandon and not a whiff of barophobia, climbing to the apple's apex, diving headfirst into its sap.

Dehydrated spit collects in the commissure of my lips.

Lancelot sighs reluctantly. 'OK, watch closely.'

He stands a few metres away, chin aloft, a gymnast about to mount some apparatus, hands in the air. There follows an enthusiastic forward roll down the cliff.

I scream. Point-blank, at rock, apple and ant. Then Lancelot is back beside me, knuckles on hips, the white strip of suncream smudged and dotted with lichen and pebble.

'So, you see,' he says, 'it's virtually impossible to die here.'

'Why would you do that?' I whimper.

'To prove a point. It's not that steep.' He offers me an impatient hand. 'Now get up.'

'I'm too paralysed.'

Lance turns his back on me and walks upslope.

'Don't leave me!'

Abandoning me, however, is not his intention. Lance lunges backwards to perform three balletic back flips. I've barely the time to start shrieking again before he's beside me once more, ready for his next routine. The one that involves him running full pelt up a mountain for a good fifty metres.

'Watching?' he shouts down at me.

'No!'

Expertly, he falls like a stunt man, smiling as he tumbles past me. Then he's back at my side, catching his breath. 'I won't let you fall. Now give me your hand.'

Furious, I sit up. 'Who the hell are you?'

'A geologist,' he states, grabbing my wrist.

As focused as a bear dragging a petulant lover, he tells me to concentrate on the ground beneath my feet. I am not allowed to complain, simply to listen, which I do diligently, because Lancelot issues me a lot of instructions on how to live my life.

'You did *not* see me today. I'll get you back to the main house, then you make your excuses and go home. Immediately, do you understand? Most importantly, you did *not* smoke weed on a hilltop.'

He called *me* a stalker, when he'd been eavesdropping on Howard and me all along. 'It was resin, and it was just the once.'

'I don't suppose you inhaled either? Why are you spying on me?'

I squint. 'Are you in a circus?'

'Go home. Unless you want Michael to sue you for attempted murder.'

'You are an actual bastard.'

'An actual bastard would go on to tell Tommaso about your day job. I read the papers. Scat Delaney, eh?'

'Scat De-what?' I ask impatiently.

That makes him snort. Pointing at the house, he tells me what to do next. 'Make your excuses, take Michael with you and go back to the hotel. Then think about moving to another one.'

Finally, he deposits me on a path. I am full of questions, but Lancelot's having none of it.

'This is the path normal people use to stroll up and down the hill,' he says, then brushes his face like a mime actor, and changes expression. 'Oh, hi there. We're staying at the same hotel, right? What brings you here?'

I totally frown. 'I'm here for my friend's mother's engagement party.'

'Well, have a lovely time. I'm a geologist, who's off to a study shed to work on my PhD in peace. Good day.'

Baffled, I stare at Lance. His glutes, especially: tight melons of muscle. Nimble as a mountain goat, he trots up and away.

Michael doesn't say much during the car ride home; most of it is spent looking in the wing mirror, mourning the loss of his upper lateral incisor.

'I liked that tooth' is as much as he can mouth.

'I'll get you a new one, I swear.' From now on, he will see the embodiment of textbook siblingship. The upside of a whitey: it results in a lot of firm promises to yourself.

I even phone Hotel Ronchi, speak to Rosa and explain that Michael's had a fall. When we arrive, she and Cosmo stand on high alert outside reception, like an emergency care team, brandishing a pre-Cold War wheelchair.

'His injuries aren't physical,' I reassure them. 'It's the aesthetic and psychological shock of tooth loss he's struggling with.'

Rosa translates for her husband, who immediately shows Michael all the gaps in his gums.

'But I liked that tooth,' he tells Cosmo.

Rosa nods at us all. 'It like losing your womb.'

Feeling responsible for her childlessness too, I insist on pushing the wheelchair. It's not a smooth journey. The contraption has a tricky bias to the left; Rosa scurries ahead of us, moving the chairs and tables into which I keep ramming Michael.

The elevator is too small for us all. So I take the stairs two at a time, wait for the doors to open. But Rosa has the wheelchair now, and she refuses to relinquish control. Pushing past me, she treats Michael like he's three and biologically hers.

This is the problem with Michael.

Left to his own devices for one evening, and he bags himself a surrogate mother. The same thing happened in London. He started going out alone and now is engaged to be married. When it comes to emotions, my brother cannot be trusted.

And this disproportionate pandering feels especially disloyal to my mother – a mother who would never favour Michael, not like everybody else. She would love us precisely the same, but for different reasons – a noble instinct that Rosa could do with honing.

I'm a hypocrite.

Bambi and I well know a secret truth – that firstborns are a little bit extra-special.

It's not yet seven o'clock, nonetheless, I watch Rosa tuck Michael into bed with promises of subtitled movies, cold compresses and food.

By the time I walk Tommaso to his car, I feel very unchristian indeed.

'Is anyone at home?' Tommaso knocks on my temple.

'I'm sorry. I'm a nuisance.'

'Yes,' he states, leaning against the door of his car. 'Now, give me your full deductions concerning Howard?'

I'm too tired, so put a solemn hand on my heart. 'Tommaso, in my humble opinion, Howard from Bermondsey is as sound as a pound.'

You, however? I don't say out loud . . .

Because Lancelot has muddied the waters there, what with his being so acrobatic and bossy with regards to my welfare. One thing is irrefutable . . .

Tommaso's father, Rocco Bellini, is a big-arse don.

There will be a lot of people interested in the goings on in the Bellini family. Whether Lancelot is a crackpot with a personal vendetta, a terrorist or in the Secret Service, social-ising with a crime family is not the cleverest publicity for a girl like me.

'Listen, Tommaso, I'm going to get some sleep then travel to Calabra tomorrow morning.'

'No,' he complains, pulling my hips towards his groin. 'I miss you already.'

I wriggle free. 'You said you'd help me out.' He nods. 'Then look after Michael while I'm gone. Make sure he's happy, occupied, but mostly happy. Whatever it takes. Three days, tops, and I'll be back.'

No nonsense this time, he grabs my waist. 'He will have around-the-clock care and entertainment – between me and those two in there.'

'Swear on the Bible.'

'I'll do better than that,' he says earnestly. 'I'll give you my word, Tommaso Bellini's word.'

I want to kiss his neck, because I believe him. Instead, we

shake hands, so as not to upset Cosmo, who is loitering in reception.

Tommaso is about to drive away when I shout that he stop.

'You said you'd help me out, right?'

'We just had that conversation.'

'I need transport.'

He shakes his head, once and firmly. There is not a millimetre of wiggle room in his response: 'Not my car.'

And I agree entirely. I'm a terrible driver. I do, however, have a Staged Access A2 licence, which permits me to operate any motorbike (with a pillion) up to 47 bhp anywhere in Europe.

Saddle Sore

From Ronchi Hotel to the southern town of Bagnara Calabra, it is 801.9 miles. That is 198.1 miles off me winning membership of the Iron Butt Association, an organisation which admits motorcyclists only if they complete 1609 km in less than twenty-four hours.

Tommaso's Vespa, however, has a top whack of 50 kph. I have to stop too often, mostly to recalibrate my courage – scooters are overtaken a lot, often by professional road cyclists. I manage 160 kilometres on the E70 before I stop at a service station on the outskirts of Venice. Relinquishing speed for comfort, I buy a cycle helmet and a wooden-beaded seat cushion.

Ahead of me looms the Autostrada, also known as the Motorway of the Sun (and, most commonly, as the A1). The spinal cord of Italy's road network promises horizontal plains, rolling hills, rivers, poplars and vineyards. My other purchase, a guidebook, tells me I'll be on that road for 650 kilometres.

In actuality, it feels twice the distance; which it is, given my top speed . . .

I watch the fat swathes of cork oak, cypress and cherry laurel peter out, in *Six Million Dollar Man* slow motion. Deposed by agriculture and industry, the once forested floodplain has been remodelled. To be fair, the latest landscape is a triumph – verdant and regimented as topiary, the fields are living billboards for the region's cuisine. Its beauty is relentless, especially when you're on a scooter that loves to dawdle.

I take a comfort break at Occhiobella. Observe the River

Po – a panorama that's been immortalised by painters and lauded by naturalists. Sadly, the guidebook warns against skinny dipping. The olive-green water is a lava flow of human effluent and chemical fertilisers. Its current anthropic use: irrigation, HEP, industrial transport and the illegal mining of construction materials.

That takes the shine off.

Far too early in my journey – at Bologna – I hit 'the wall'. My coccyx is in trouble. My face is as dehydrated as a sheet of seaweed. The journey ahead feels unachievable. I consider ditching the bike to jump on a train. Scooters, however, are terrific for surveillance. In Italy, especially. Plus, it's not my bike to dump.

I'll treat it like my own child, I'd promised Tommaso, with very sincere eyes.

Bologna, it turns out, is my saviour. It encourages me onwards. The St George's Cross is its city's flag too. The red roofs may herald from the Renaissance; they're also the exact same colour as English construction brick. I even spot a pub called the Empire English.

Survival technique: always look for tenuous alliances when you've hit a psychological block. You might, for example, turn to the crowd for support. Interact with those on the sidelines – a sports psychology fact: that releases endorphins. Some runners blow kisses as they run past spectators. Currently, I am proffering thumbs-up at people I pretend are out to support me. It causes smiles and confusion in equal measure, which I decide is hysterical and would make an excellent scene in a film.

Then I head south-west.

This is mostly what I now see on the Motorway of the Sun – tail lights and motorway signs. Lorries overtake me incessantly. Windy and cold, there's a spiteful spit in the night air.

The blue boards keep me focused: Firenze, Arezzo, Monte San Savino, Roma, Napoli . . .

Bit by bit, I become aware of changes in the landscape. The horizon no longer undulates as gently. New landforms appear in the shadows – angular, lofty and bald.

When a signpost signals that I'm passing Praia a Mare, I allow myself an air-punch, because this is the home stretch – 230 kilometres of coastal road that takes me straight to Bagnara Calabria.

The air tastes new here. Salty and fresh, it cleanses my respiratory system of diesel fumes. Yet it's not until the sun rises, pulling away the blanket of night, that the landscape is revealed to me.

To my right, the Tyrrhenian Sea, infinite and vivid, the same dazzling colour as the oceans in old pirate films. *Sinbad and the Eye of the Tiger, Jason and the Argonauts, The Golden Voyage of Sinbad.*

To my left, parched mountains which forget to peter out at the coast, instead preferring to stop dead just at the water's edge.

Mezzogiorno fact: it is entirely alien.

That fills me with hope.

6.37 a.m. I arrive much later than hoped in Bagnara, exhausted, windburnt and in receipt of an angry perineum. I've no time for a sleep, so get straight on with a whistle-stop recce of the neighbourhood.

First impressions.

Bagnara is small, cliquey and basic, with a tradition of terrace farming, fishing, earthquakes, swordfish and subsidence. In the main, it's tourist free. I also get the feeling the locals intend to keep it that way, fulfilling their wish to slip down the hillside and into the sea privately and at their own pace.

With regards to communications, I'm left wondering how

they receive any letters at all. The Poste Italiane on Via XXIV Maggio is a travesty – a tiny concrete box of an establishment that nestles in a silent and steep backstreet. It has one counter, a bell and a front wall of glass that would contravene a whole host of UK Data Protection Regulations.

I ended my recce at a seafront guesthouse, where I noted boarded-up houses, unimaginative graffiti and empty car parks. People may wander up and down the esplanade happily enough, but it's clear that Bagnara's soul defected many years ago.

My guidebook fills me in. Neither nature nor history has worked in the region's favour. Contending empires and dynasties considered southern Italy their theatre of war. Invasions were annual, genocide, enslavement and rape commonplace.

Ordering an espresso, I smile sadly at the waiter. His ancestors endured a lot of shit. For what? I watch the comings and goings of the harbour ahead. Low-key boats, middle-aged and utilitarian, the Mezzogiorno's staple diet being seafood; it's a world away from Lymington Yacht Haven. Some vessels float north towards the Tyrrhenian Sea, some in the direction of Sicily. Entry and escape from Bagnara is as regulated as a fart.

Sicily.

This is my first time seeing her in the flesh. So close, a sea swimmer could make it. The island looks as isolated as a snow globe, a gunmetal mushroom cloud above her head like a bad-arsed mood. The sea around her is ruffled too; waves swirl and break without method and with a lot of madness.

I pull my jacket around my shoulders, do up its zip and ask the waiter if there's a room to rent. There is. A single with internet connection, a seaview and communal bathroom.

I take a quick shower, ice my groin and then pack a surveillance rucksack, including Michael's phone, which I've retained on health-and-safety grounds. Then I reopen my longest and most important case to date.

Case No. 0001/Operation Bambi Love.

8.17 a.m.

During all cases of surveillance, the aim is to remain as invisible as a radio wave. Immediately, I have a problem. There's no bench on which to read; no bus stop, shops or tourists to blend in with. Plus, it's starting to spit and I don't have an umbrella.

Stand out and it's case closed.

In an ideal world, a PI has their own car – one with pinhole cameras drilled into the bodywork – allowing them to park up in prime positions and hide in the back. Very often, however, PIs don't work in an ideal world.

In the absence of my own car, I borrow someone else's.

A legal truth: when breaking into a car, never drive it away. That's stealing. What you can do is sit in the passenger seat and stay out of the rain. Assuming the owner has left their vehicle open, that is.

Today, my method of breaking and entering is the Tennis Ball Technique. Be warned: it works exclusively on old cars – the very type that southern Italy is awash with. I take a ball from my bag. Like my fork-lock, this was part of a GCSE assignment too. It's a common-or-garden Wilson Championship, and I drilled a hole into its side using a 6mm bit. Placing the hole over the car's keyhole, I punch it flat.

The pressure forces the door lock up.

Once inside the Fiat, I hunch in the back seat, my mini spy scope snuggled invisibly into a palm, and watch the post-office counter directly.

Just eight people visit today. Three pick up a letter. One woman leaves with nothing at all, but she's forty, with a lot of rug rats, so is definitely not my mum.

Then at one o'clock, the single employee – a bored barrel of a teenage girl – pulls the shutters down and goes home. If it weren't for the dirty red box on the wall, you wouldn't know there was a post office there at all.

Nobody has collected Dad's little blue airmail envelope.

Disappointed, I return to the guesthouse and, for the first time in months, allow myself an indulgence. I remember my training and try to evoke my mother's face.

Sex: female.

Race/complexion: Italian/an iron-deficient beige.

Height: one metre seventy to one metre seventy-five.

Weight: a hundred and thirty pounds or thereabouts.

Build: Charlie's Angel.

Hair colour: Jaclyn Smith out of *Charlie's Angels*.

Hair length and style: Jaclyn Smith out of *Charlie's Angels*.

Fashion sense: Jaclyn Smith out of *Charlie's Angels*.

This is the very reason I banned myself from remembering her. I was eight when she disappeared, so I didn't know how to retain and document a mental picture of a target back then. I didn't mean to turn my mother into a caricature.

Will I even recognise her?

This is a dangerous track. As is asking myself, *How much of her actual personality was a façade?*

Bambi said she loved detective shows and, as a direct consequence, I loved them too. There was her own fantasy to be a PI – wouldn't that be an irony, me living a dream that was never really hers?

I pull the sheets up and over my head, squeeze my eyes shut, recall only *very* tangible data:

Fingernails: Bambi's were lovely – they were as long and tickly as almonds.

Teeth: she had the gentlest buck – that's orthodontic proof that she was benevolent through and through.

Jewellery: a golden cornicello worn around her neck, day and night.

She forgot to leave that necklace to me. Her little lucky horn. I imagine she regrets that now. Fingering my Adam's apple, I make excuses for her. Because she did disappear in a bit of a rush.

Michael's phone tinkles. The message tone is 'Sci-fi', which is twilight-zone sinister, and very funny, because I see it's Annie. Of course, I indulge in some therapeutic snooping.

As is traditional, her text is succinct.

https://twitter.com/camille tremblay/status/840222764511902736

Untraditionally, it's just a Twitter link. It should take me to a post belonging to Camille Tremblay. But Twitter refuses to play ball. I refresh a lot of times, while racking my brains as to whether Sébastien's ever mentioned a female relative. Then I give up, because Sébastien says a lot, and the journey here has knocked me for six . . .

For a moment, I'm unnervingly dislocated. Have no idea where I am. Consciousness arrives too slowly. My knee-jerk reaction – I am Guy Pearce in *Memento*.

I collect facts fast:

1. It's a different day to the one I went to sleep in.

2. 'Night Owl' warbles on someone's phone.

3. It's been warbling that tune, on and off, for quite a while.

4. Sicily is still outside my window.

I sit bolt upright. Shake my head free of a dogged sleep. Focus on Michael's phone – it's slipped off the bed, is currently fitting on the floor. Rescuing it, I press Accept and shout, to appear alert, 'What's happening?'

'I can't see you,' whispers Noah.

I squint at the mobile. 'Are you FaceTiming me?'

'I thought it was better this way.'

I rub my eyes. 'It's five a.m.'

'In the UK it's four. Put the light on, hen.'

'No.' I'll be looking like shit. Plus, I'm frowning at Noah's nasopharynx – it's glittery with snot. 'You're very *Blair Witch*. Are you shining a torch up your nose?'

'It's dark. Now, if you don't mind, I haven't got all day. Assuming you're not too busy, of course.' This conversation is a potential recipe for disaster. Virgos have great difficulty being the bigger person. Cancerians are very cranky in the mornings.

'Just fucking shoot.' I get him focused.

He jumps straight in. 'The employee with the Mondeo is called Gary Rose.'

'I know,' I sigh.

'Unfortunately, I won't be watching him any more. We made eye contact. He called me a few choice words, then deleted the photos from my camera.'

'You what?' I try to turn the bedside lamp on; knock it off the table instead. 'I need details and some semblance of chronology, Noah.'

Oh, the melancholy with which he speaks – he could be delivering a eulogy: 'Sunday afternoon. Gary Rose took his wife and children to Poole Park. An hour in, he received a phone call, kissed his wife goodbye and left. He stopped at Lidl's, did a shop – milk, teabags, that sort of thing – then drove to Shorefield Leisure Park.'

'Where's that?'

'Milford-on-Sea. Caravans, log cabins. Huge place.'

'That's near Lymington.'

Noah wipes his nose on his sleeve, looks either side of him and continues. 'He was in there for half an hour and left without the shopping, going back to Poole Park to meet his family.'

'You didn't follow him on to the site?'

'Err, security cameras everywhere,' he scoffs, like I'm the Sunday-afternoon PI. 'Monday, Gary arrives at the office at seven a.m. He had the briefcase back on. He left the office almost immediately, with a second employee.'

'Did he have a briefcase?'

'Will you stop interrupting me?'

'I'm very excited.'

His eyes are unforgiving. 'The second employee had a briefcase too. Together, they drove to Shorefield Leisure Park again. Ten minutes later, Gary and his colleague exited the site with a third person lying in the back footwell, under a blanket.'

'Who was it?' I interrupt, then suck in my lips.

'Naturally, I didn't get a good look. Not until they arrived at Newport County Court.'

That's in Wales? I might not be allowed to speak out loud, but he cannot control my mind.

'Gary and Employee No. 2 bundled a woman into the court building – while being attentive to what was going on around them. It was almost military.'

Gary Rose is a witness-protection officer! I want to shriek.

'My conclusion?' He pauses for dramatic effect. 'Gary Rose is a witness-protection officer.'

ACME Technical Services is a witness-protection office.

'ACME is a hub for undercover police officers.'

Your dad was looking after my mum. Like Kevin Costner out of The Bodyguard. *Only without the love affair (regardless of what the local papers said at the time; and regardless of how much Dad failed to obliterate that particular rumour).*

'It seems obvious now,' Noah is telling me.

Don't you dare say it, my eyes warn him. *That your dad was like Kevin Costner out of* The Bodyguard, *and he was having an affair with my mum.*

'Bambi Love was a very dangerous woman indeed.'

I might not have seen her in twenty-five years, but my instinct is to slit his throat. 'What are you insinuating?' I ask his nostrils.

'Dangerous to someone *big* – in Italy, I mean. Enough for the British authorities to agree to protect her.'

I look at Sicily – an ominous shadow against an inky sky, a law unto herself. Homeland of the Cosa Nostra, the original and baddest mafiosi. I won't argue with Noah – normal witnesses aren't relocated abroad. Not unless it's extremely heavy shit.

'We're talking intergovernmental cooperation, Florence,' he says, milking his point.

I argue, weakly, 'Why the hell would you take a photo of a witness-protection officer?'

'I wasn't. I was trying to get a shot of the three of them together. The woman was white, overweight, in her thirties. You said you wanted *details*.'

I did. But now I know the important job they did for Mum, I feel ashamed and disloyal. 'So they caught you and deleted the photo – that's it?'

'I told them I was a freelance journalist. There were a few of us.'

'Find out the reference number of the case. It'll be on a board in the courthouse reception. I'll do some research. See who the witness was.'

'No need. It's all over the local papers.' He provides the following information even more solemnly than before: 'The woman they were protecting, Florence, is Nina Darvil, the girlfriend of Oliver Crane.'

'He killed kids.'

'She aided and abetted. Was released from prison last year. Is back in on a parole violation.'

My mother may have come to England as a protected witness, but she fled it a vigilante. Because our parents – Noah's mum and dad, and my mum and dad – avenged their children. Plotted the perfect murder and took out a kiddy-fiddler.

'What was your mum's name again?' I ask Noah.

Entirely offended, he snaps, 'Elaine.'

I look out of the window, watch the bobbing lights of a fishing trawler on its way home from the Messina Strait.

'Did your dad sail?' I suddenly frown.

He shakes his head.

'But Eric knew people with boats, right?'

Noah's face is buffering, but he's still shaking his head. 'He hated the sea. Dad wasn't a fan of sharks or rip-currents.'

'But you lived in Sandbanks?'

'He wasn't allergic to looking at it.'

'What about Lymington?' I ask.

'No, Dad didn't go in the sea there either.'

'How do you know?'

'I don't. We never went. My mother was born there, but I don't remember visiting.'

Elaine Steensen was born in Lymington? I slap my thigh and ask, 'Does the name Bob Hannigan ring any bells?'

'Bobby.' He nods. 'He went to school with mum. That's a lot of years ago. He died a long time back.'

And I smile, very widely indeed.

The reason I love this job: you collect snippets of driftwood here and there and, before you know it, the stern of something tangible presents itself.

'Noah,' I ask ever so apologetically, because I genuinely can't remember. 'What was your mother's maiden name again?'

*

Assiduously, I look at the photos I took on Michael's phone – the ones from Lymington Lawn Tennis Club. There are a lot of names on the Championship Boards. I don't rush. Deep down, I know the answer already.

Bob Hannigan and Elaine Benn won the mixed-doubles championship in 1977.

Victorious, I punch a pillow. And although I don't see an Eric or a Bambi among the many names on those boards, I know for certain this is how our parents met.

My dad knew Elaine from the tennis club. Elaine was engaged to Eric, a witness-protection officer – one of his wards was Bambi. Too busily I romanticise their friendship in my head, wonder if they double-dated. Until other scenarios present themselves. Maybe my parents were in a marriage of convenience, George simply a patsy enlisted to validate her new name, identity and fake history. That makes me feel terrible for Dad. And for Michael. But mostly for me, because I don't want to know that I was part of a game plan; a convenience-baby, discarded the minute my status changed to 'baggage'.

An abrupt fear arrives. It sends crude twangs to my stomach. *What the hell did my mother actually do to end up in Dorset?*

Very important PI rule: do not become emotionally embroiled in the case.

I refocus.

One thing is for sure: they should not have remained such firm pals, the four of them – it could have compromised everybody.

Maybe, in the end, it did.

The bare bones. Theirs was a special friendship. So special that, when someone in their circle abused their children, they murdered him as a clan.

I use my smartphone to investigate Eric Steensen's job. According to the National Crime Agency, he will have provided those under his protection with a 24/7 personal package including:

- The eradication of the protected person's old identity

- The creation of a new one

- Late-night phone calls when they feel unable to cope with their new life

- Keeping them alive in the face of death threats

- Arranging their funeral, should the situation arise

- Keeping their loved ones safe.

As a consequence, the witness-protection officer must also live a mystery-shrouded life – they're key to finding people with vengeful bounties on their heads.

Here's a quote I struggle to wrap my head around: 'Without prejudice, they become a guardian angel to some of the most despicable elements of society.'

For a long time, I lie on the bed looking out at Sicily, and contemplate which side of the fence my mother sat.

Rug Rat

I plan not to spend another day car-jacking. Luckily, the morning sun is fierce. It burns off lacklustre clouds.

So I blow-dry my hair and plait it loosely, the aim: radiant locks that appear full of androstenedione. I wear no make-up other than my plum lipstick, to simulate lip engorgement. Then I find my motorbike helmet.

Tucking its straps inside the dome, I wrap it in a lot of masking tape, because every ridge must be concealed. Thoroughly taping the helmet to my stomach, I squeeze a strapless bandeau bra over my bump to keep it firmly in place. To finish off the look, I wear a bohemian sunhat, a once loose-fitting shirt-dress, black leggings and white pumps.

Having discreetly exited the guesthouse, I return to test my disguise. Ask the waiter for directions – the same waiter who served me coffee at breakfast and rented me a room.

He speaks differently now I'm someone else and do not have a sexual bone in my body. But that's not a bad thing at all; he's so magnanimous I might as well be expecting his child.

That's an extremely nice feeling: being revered, biologically.

And even though I'm not a huge fan of newborns, I quickly grow to love my bump. Ovoid and ergonomic, I can't help but use it as a resting place for my wrists.

A downside of pregnancy: personal space goes out of the window. Even the most parochial Italians pet a swollen uterus – which is why, in cases of subterfuge, you should attach your bump very fastidiously indeed.

But what if it's a serial killer? I want to ask them, with big eyes. Baby-scan fact: they don't test for psychopathy.

But I don't speak Italian, so can't play devil's advocate:

People cooed over Frau Hitler's bump. And Mrs Hindley Senior's bump. And Cneajna of Moldavia's bump – a bump so cruel, he became known as an impaler and, latterly, Dracula.

Another question the midriff-molesters like to ask: *bambino o bambina?*

Bambino, I can't help but frown, because growing a boy-foetus is tough to get your head around. They have doll-sized genitals that are actually inside you. You're a biological squat for a creature slightly limited by neural wiring.

This is not sexist. It's science.

Women have four times the number of neurons connecting the right and left side of their brains. As a result, we can multitask while enlisting logic and intuition. In their favour, boys have impressive connectivity between the front and back portions of the brain. This means they excel at drawing triangles and parallel parking; just not both together.

I'm not sure I'm doing the world any favours, I'd joke, if I were bilingual.

Even the bored barrel of a teenager becomes heart-wrenchingly maternal when I enter the post office.

'Do you speak English?' I ask her.

'Yes. Liddle,' she tells my belly, dropping her head to the side, utterly in love with a bicycle helmet. '*Bambino o bambina?*'

I stop her there. 'Boy or girl?'

'Boy or girl?' she repeats.

'A little boy. Your accent is excellent.' She's delighted that I humour her in her attempt at English.

She giggles. 'I help?'

I lean on the counter. 'May I just sit down?' I nod at two wooden chairs in the corner and dig my helmet with the heel of my hand. 'The *bambino* is doing zumba.'

'Yes.' She's half imploring, and I feel instinctively protective towards her. Hidden beneath the cheeks and jowls is a very pretty face indeed. I was never a midnight-grazer like her, but I was plain compared to the other girls – which is why, by her age, I was married and grateful that someone had asked.

I sit as if balancing on a fitness ball – back arched, nipples proud, legs akimbo – and do a power-audit . . .

A wall of notices – some handwritten, some official Poste Italiane posters. Offical leaflets in a wall-mount. A shelf selling post-related stationery. I stand up, pace a little, take a pamphlet and fan myself with it.

'Do you have any water?' I ask. 'I've gone all wobbly.'

Unreservedly, she nods. Then disappears into a back room, apparently to divine it herself, because she doesn't return for ten minutes, by which time there's a rush on.

Four of us now, and the space feels tight. Especially as customers nos. 1, 2 and 3 unnerve me.

Hubble, bubble, toil and trouble . . .

Their cataracts glow like milky pinhole X-ray machines; the women stare at my abdomen of polycarbonate and polystyrene. Luckily, when Counter Girl returns, they forget me instantly to barge simultaneously to the front, because Italians don't queue. Which I like. A thicker skin allows the circumnavigation of bullshit. They all want serving – so what?

None of the X-ray-eyed women collects a blue envelope.

'I've phoned my husband,' I tell Counter Girl, once they've gone. 'He'll be here to pick me up in an hour.' I show her my watch and mobile phone. 'He's in Sicily,' I elucidate.

She doesn't ask any questions. Her English is actually piss-poor. I'm not sure how much she grasps of what I say. But she seems to enjoy my company. The attention, maybe; I get it, I've been there. So I tell her my backstory. Why not? I've been devising it since sunrise.

'We're travelling the Mezzogiorno in a Winnebago,' I explain. 'After thirty-six weeks, it's not advisable to fly, so we've opted for a road trip. The Garden of Ninfa, Pompeii, the Amalfi coast – we've seen them all. It's a dream come true. I've always wanted to tour southern Italy.'

I brush an imaginary stain from my shirt-dress; that wasn't true until I just said it out loud.

Absence makes the heart fond and philosophical. I remember how I felt about Tommaso, before Lancelot had sown any seeds of concern. I pretend it's a Bellini boy I'm carrying.

'My husband has caught a boat to Sicily for the day. I was feeling lazy, so decided to stay and have a wander around Bagnara. We're very independent that way. Just let each other *be*, you know?' I tell her my most special hope: 'There's a slim chance we're soulmates.'

She looks at me as though I am mesmerising.

I put a precautionary finger in the air. 'I know I should have stayed closer to the van, but I'm having the type of energy burst that's common in the third trimester.'

I don't know why I make her giggle, but it's nice when someone shows an interest. Sometimes, I guess, you just click. The next hour is spent chuckling at one another's linguistic heritage. I teach her Old Dorset words:

Joppety-joppety: jangling with nerves.

Dunch: a bit deaf.

Slommock: a slatternly female.

She teaches me southern Italian profanities:

MEEN|kee|ah (penis-related).

MEET|tsee|kah (penis-related).

TES|tah dee KAHTZ|soh (penis-related).

FEHS|sah (front-bottom-related).

11.03 p.m. – Customer No. 4 arrives.

It's the forty-year-old woman with rug rats. Only today,

she has just one in tow – a swarthy four year old who immediately sits beside me and swings her legs impatiently, allowing her mother to launch into a heated debate with Counter Girl.

The adults talk too fast and in a vernacular that's confusing. I can't decipher the issue between them. Suffice to say, the little girl's mother is a feisty piece of work and I'm pleased that Counter Girl remains so stoically proud-chested. Were I not pregnant and on a case, I'd have totally bowled in.

A detailed description of Customer No. 4 from the back: her hair is a coccyx-skimming explosion of black curls, matchstick tight. If you pulled it out straight, it'd skim her calves, the walls and the ceiling. Underneath it all is a slim and sinewy woman, like a vegan yoga instructor who's been clean from crisps for a decade at least. Though yoga's not her job. Career-wise, I'd say she was a professional of some sort, who certainly doesn't have time for this; impassioned, she points at the back wall, in the direction of the sea and up at a picture of the Madonna herself. I'm sure I catch a penis-related word or two.

Throughout, the small girl gawps too – not at them, at me.

In the end, I have to frown down at the infant. Her curly hair is a mini-version of her mum's, only shoulder length and more of a soft Afro. The infant is plucky, refusing to dodge my gaze. Instead, she shakes her head slowly, like she's a thousand years old. Covertly, I roll my eyes at her, to show her that grown-ups are an enigma to me too. She mimics the gesture; rolls her eyes back.

I want to smile, but don't; we live in cynical times. Plus, her mother doesn't look the sociable type. Having said her piece, she faces me, without seeing me, and summons her daughter.

When she's face on to me, I decide she would be exponentially more attractive were it not for the bitterness residing in her forehead. She would also look her true age – today, I'd put her at thirty-seven.

Her daughter sighs, gets up and trudges slowly out after Customer No. 4.

The bicycle helmet's giving me sympathy hormones. I like the kid, so call out after her, '*Ciao*, Piccolina.'

Counter Girl follows suit, bids the child a fond farewell too: 'Ciao, Paola,' she shouts.

Without looking back, little Paola does a finger wave.

And I sit motionless for a good ten seconds.

The private investigator must never show a flicker of excitement, interest or surprise. Train your micro-expressions so that when a revelation occurs, you acquire a meditative state: a face that says nothing.

'What was her problem?' I ask, too quickly.

Counter Girl flaps a hand dismissively. 'No letter.' Then digs a hard finger at her temple – the universal signal for 'bat-shit crazy'.

For a little while longer, I point, noiselessly. Then I leave the post office, fast.

I follow Customer No. 4 into a narrow street that winds downhill, back towards the seafront.

Paola is a little way behind her mother, and stops briefly to steal herself a flower from a windowbox. It resembles a small sunflower – the exact type a four year old draws. I watch how mindfully she pinches the bottom of the stalk, as though she's been taught how to harvest a bloom humanely.

Burglary successfully executed, she spins into a sort-of Michael Jackson moonwalk, before her mother calls back to her. Paola's shoulders slump, exhausted; obediently, she jogs to catch her mother up.

Why is my father sending coded letters to a little girl?

Logic tells me: he's not. That I'm jumping the gun and

should return, pronto, to the Poste Italiane and continue my case. The one where I locate the correct, grown-up Paola.

Trouble is:

1. This girl has got my attention.

2. I have spritely occipital lobes (that's as close to psychic as you can get).

3. I'm a private investigator, so am obliged, ethically, to follow my gut.

The seafront.

Mother and daughter sit on the steps of a pizzeria. I use an alley between two houses to change, swiftly removing my shirt-dress. The helmet too. It comes away easily, the masking tape slippery with sweat. Burying my makeshift bump in shrubbery, I scrape my hair into a severe bun and change my clothes.

The smallest physical alteration knocks a person's recall facility. My advice: go lightweight; the best disguises are those kept in a jacket pocket. In mine I have a vest-top and wrap-around sunglasses.

Back on the street, I limber up out of view, do some hamstring stretches on a railing, while watching the girl. Under the deep Mediterranean tan and flare of curly hair, her features are small, like a Victorian doll's.

I keep a firm core and do not exceed 9 kph. Padding along the promenade, I rest after fifty metres, stretch and run back. I'm repeating this process along the pebbled beach when a bus pulls up beside Paola and her mum. Resisting the temptation to watch them, I wait until I hear the bus crunch into second gear.

Then I turn on my heels and run after it.

Paola skips to its back seat, her harried mother following.

For a lot of reasons, I cannot get on that bus. Yet I follow it for quite a while, coming to a breathless halt as its exhaust disappears around the corner, its direction south, towards Reggio di Calabria, the main port serving Sicily.

A few deep breaths, and I continue a beleaguered dash along the seafront. Just before the guesthouse, I take a sharp left. Tommaso's Vespa is parked up in a side road.

I spark it so its engine roars furiously and get back on to the coastal road.

Sicily spits a brackish wind at my cheeks, but she doesn't frighten me. When I turn a bend and spot the bus's tail lights in the distance, I yelp. And more so when I'm close enough to confirm that two curly heads – one little, one large – still inhabit the back seat.

I hang back, ensure there are cars between us.

Logic reminds me that I'm supposed to be following the owner of a postal box. Four year olds don't have postal boxes. It's illegal.

Her name was at the top of a letter, I argue with myself. *That doesn't mean she owns the fucking thing.*

I make myself very angry sometimes.

The bus surprises me when it takes a left at the town of Villa San Giovanni, bypassing Reggio di Calabria entirely, heading inland instead. Sicily is replaced by a girthy river, its job to top up the Messina Strait. And I like this new bit of Italy a lot: the valley bottom is forested, there are fields and a sky that feels ever so slightly like England. The land ripples gently.

I don't know the name of the village at which Paola and her mother alight. But it's forty-five minutes from Bagnara. A hell of a journey, and the second day they've done it. No wonder the mother's pissed off. Especially as we've passed other post offices en route – ones that look perfectly legitimate and professionally run and have postal boxes of their own.

Keeping my distance, I watch mother and daughter wait at the side of the road. I also undertake a quick empirical study of the place.

Square concrete houses with tiny square windows painted peach or pink, dotted along a wide main street. Dirt tracks between them, leading to other houses, also small-windowed and painted peach or pink. The middle distance is higgledy-piggledy fields; a patchwork of olive groves and citrus trees. Fields growing Mediterranean rocket, escarole and cos lettuce in strict stripes.

Sign of life: none.

The sun is at its high point. Italy's shutters are down.

My heart pauses when a Fiat Punto honks loudly, then comes to an abrupt stop beside Paola. The man who gets out is extremely tall and, from the side, shaped like a 'C'.

Paola shouts, '*Nonno!*'

Throwing her arms around her grandfather's thighs, she presses an impassioned cheek at his groin, then marches directly to the front passenger seat, leaving her mother to get into the back and harangue her dad from there. Father and daughter are identical: willowy with curly hair – though his is short and a pannacotta white.

Logic reminds me of the basics.

It's a professional no-no to follow people into areas you know nothing about, especially when your vehicle is as noisy as a hand-dryer and you have no helmet, leaving your face completely on show. And when you're so dehydrated you consider boiling your own urine – which is an excellent example of histrionics *and* why surveillance is inadvisable without prior reconnaissance and a full contingency plan.

I throw logic to the wind. For this reason, do not copy what I do next. Put your notepads down and turn a blind eye. In my defence, I've come too far.

*

The Fiat takes a zigzag of lanes, and comes to a halt in a hamlet.

Ten small villas. All detached. All painted terracotta.

The house in which the Fiat parks is set back from the road. Reminiscent of the colourful pads I saw in Monte San Savino, it snuggles in a private oasis of dazzling fauna and blossom.

That feels a lifetime away, the day I trekked to a lonely church on a hill in Ciggiana, to the safe-house of Massimo 'The Eradicator' Satori.

Your mother is not in Italy. I would know.

A realisation stabs me in the stomach: was he trying to tell me she's dead? Then a second stab: how had he been so sure about anything, given we didn't even discover her real name? A third and final stab: maybe Massimo *did* discover her real name.

I park the scooter out of sight and walk, weakly, among the villas. Should anybody ask, I'll pretend I'm lost; a silly strategy given that eye contact equals case closed. But I'm in trouble – so parched, I struggle to swallow. My oesopha-geal lining has reconstituted itself into cellophane. The sun shoots solar flares at my cranium; it makes my head pound. I haven't the wherewithal to bolt between trees and bushes.

And all the while my heart hammers ruthlessly at my neck.

Because, finally, I have an address. Maybe not the right address, or a remotely relevant one, but an actual address. The implications alone are enough to make an abandoned daughter keel over.

By the time I approach the house's front wall, I am light-headed and nauseous. I lean against the cold brick. Push my face, forearms and shins against it too. Then, dragging a shoulder along its surface, I follow its cool angles around to the house's side. Broad, shallow steps wind down into a flower-filled terrace below. There are people down there, I can hear them: they're around a corner and out of view.

I also hear chickens.

Bambi never let us have chickens, I remember, then smile. I've been sent on a wild-chicken chase.

I allow my back to slide down the wall and my glutes arrive heavily on the stone floor. My chin drops into my neck. It's imperative that I stay alert. Try to listen to their voices. But the curly-haired woman steals the show.

She says, '*Bla bla bla bla bla bla . . .*'

I make myself promises – to become fluent in Italian by the end of the month. But unconsciousness creeps across my vision, like blinkers. Panic burns the back of my throat. I tense and squeeze my large muscle groups to get the blood pumping back to my head.

The little Paola girl. I definitely hear her. She's being very demanding.

'*Che fai? Che fai?*'

I decide she's well looked after, despite her mother's bad mood. There's no fear in her voice; it's full of unbridled resolve.

'*Che fai?!*'

My chin shoots up.

Paola stands above me. One hand is on her hip; in the other she holds a blue plastic cup.

I fling a hand out to the liquid. 'Water, please?'

She pulls the cup defensively to her chest. '*Dove è il tuo bambino?*'

'I hate backwash too.' I try to make friends. 'But this is quite an emergency.' I do an impression of someone in an emergency – fan my face then pretend to vomit.

'*Bambino?*' she demands.

I look at my stomach. Then at her, wordless.

Alarmed, she runs down the steps. '*Mama!*'

That gives me an energy shot. I get up. Back on the road, the heat hits me like a cartoon shovel. But I'm strict with myself. I stumble single-mindedly back towards the trees and Tommaso's bike.

Logic is a fickle bastard: suddenly, I'm one of the best private investigators it knows. If anyone can concoct a story and claw a route out of this vat of shit, it's Florence Love . . .

You're lost, remember? Turn around, go back to the house and ask for water. Tell them Paola is mistaken – you weren't pregnant less than an hour before, nor do you have a clue where Bagnara is.

There's no need. Paola's mother is intent on finding out for herself. The footsteps behind me are furious.

I increase my pace, but she catches up with me easily. I look to my left, then down, to see Paola padding beside me, comfortably matching my speed.

I tell her solemnly, 'I normally run much faster than this.' Then stop dead.

Because Paola looks *nothing* like me: apart from the eyes.

And I should know, I've studied mine a million times in the mirror.

'Sweet fuck,' I tell her face.

She nods, like Yoda, and hands me a bottle of water. I drink it in one, eyeballs rooted on her. The liquid, her familiarity – they're as energising as cocaine.

She's persistent on the baby issue. '*Dove è il tuo bambino?*'

Her facial-recognition skills are off the scale, like mine were at her age. I want to ask what gave me away. How could I improve my performance next time? On a scale of one to five, where would you rate my ability to fool the general public?

'That wasn't me,' I mumble, and wipe my mouth, glancing back at the villa. '*Grazie*, Piccolina. *Grazie* for the *acqua*.'

It would seem my Italian is funny. She now uses those

eyes to communicate in a way I recognise inherently – like she's the tiny protagonist in the story of every other fucker's life. Apparently, I'm to watch her, which is fine. I'm already transfixed.

Paola has the worst voice. I've no clue what she's singing, but she's doing 'yogurt', which is when you try to sing in a foreign tongue, using nonsense sounds to fill in the words. By the end, I'd take a punt that she's singing, 'Do You Want to Build a Snowman?' And I clap, like she's a new breed of simian. She's not; she's the only other one of me.

Succinctly, she indicates that I'm to give her the empty bottle back. Then says curtly, '*Arrivederci*, signora.'

I wipe my spit from the bottle's neck. Pass it back. Nod. '*Arrivederci*, Paola Aggi.'

She doesn't argue. I inhale, because there's the proof. Then I accidentally pat her head, ever so gently.

I don't see the mother, but she totally overacts. Screams as though her child is being mauled by a boar. I don't know what to do other than run. Yes, I do: don't run – because that makes it look worse.

Yet these are *not* the circumstances under which I want to learn why Dad has an underage pen-pal in Calabria with my exact eyes, singing voice and attitude to life. And if there's no sensible reason, I'll be arrested and extradited, because, I admit, it looks like I'm abducting her. But I don't even like children and I was, honestly, just feeling her hair.

'*Vieni qui, Paola!*' the mother wails, with the most disturbing passion. '*Subito! Sbrigati!*'

When the child is back in her mother's arms, I turn quickly to check that she's OK. This serves to stoke the mother's fury. Brushing Paola inside, she decides to pursue me. Angry as a heron, her approach builds momentum.

For a split second, I consider my escape. Turn my back on her. But I have bugger all left in the tank.

And so I, Florence Love, stand stock-still. Assume a lack-lustre defensive position and close my eyes. Await an almighty shove, or a punch to the kidneys, or a frying pan to the head. Whatever my fate, a part of me welcomes it; I need an excuse to lie down.

Instead of physical pain, however, I am delivered a word. A killer word. Not from Paola's mother's mouth but from a second, older woman.

She is some distance behind us both. And the word she squeals is aimed squarely to my assailant:

'Maria!' she shouts.

'*Mamma!*' Maria calls back, urgently. '*Mamma! Entra dentro!*'

Her mother is uncompromising. '*Torna subito!*'

Logic is back again. Do *not* hyperventilate, it tells me. Voices are a weak cue to identity; not unless you add other variables, like a face and a name.

Yet I cannot turn around. Not when I know there are exceptions. Newborns, for example – they're wired to recognise and imitate their mother's voice. Of course, I'm hamstrung – I was a newborn once, and the older woman's voice is as familiar as my own.

For more than twenty years, I've been trying to remember that pitch, rhythm and timbre. I mourned its loss as though I'd mislaid the only photo of my mother left in the world. When all the time, her voice was mine.

Rigidly, I stare ahead in the direction of my scooter.

As long as I don't actually see her face, I will not be able to confirm or deny that Paola is my niece. Neither can I conclude with any degree of reliability that my mother is married to the pannacotta-haired man. Certainly, I'll remain none the wiser as to whether I have a sister, who is older than me, but not by much. Most importantly, I'll be unable to entertain the possibility that, for her entire adult life, my mother has been a bigamist.

I don't look back. Neither do I hear them utter another word. Nobody comes after me. Not Paola, not Maria, not the mother formerly known as Bambi.

Yoko Ono

A day and a half on the open road. That's a lot of thinking time.

At the beginning, my thoughts tumbled among themselves destructively. By Venice, I had no choice but to start filing facts into boxes . . .

Maria.

Bambi's firstborn. She would have been a toddler when our mother left for England. I don't know the reasons for her particular abandonment, and don't give a fuck. Because that's a monster of a sting: *firstborn.*

For thirty-three years, that was me. I had other roles too. Like, *only* daughter. Like, favourite female relative in the whole world. Like, the one whose job it was to eventually deliver her a little Paola. That makes my loins feel cruelly redundant.

Bambi (current name unknown).

An unchristian truth – I'd hoped she'd be a fraction of the woman she once was. Certainly, I hadn't wanted her to be happy, married, with grandchildren. It's beyond my comprehension that she managed to achieve any mental serenity whatsoever.

I can't cut a lawn without thinking about her. Which is exactly what I had to do from the age of six. Olden-days Bambi didn't like going outside that much. Not even into the garden. Dad said it was her Latin temperament.

Dad.

Categorically, he is a perjurer. The letter to Paola is proof. My guess is, when they married, he was aware of the family she'd left behind. In retrospect, he pussyfooted a lot around her. I thought it was his job to keep her the right side of sane. Perhaps he was trying to deter her from running home, back to her first love.

Latin temperament, my arse. I don't remember her ever being irrational or volatile; her true condition involved a beautiful imagination, tearful introspection and a soupçon of agoraphobia. And when it was just me and her, she was properly happy, which leaves a daughter convinced she's not just enough but indispensable.

Many hours of my drive back to Ronchi were spent wondering how Dad gets up in the morning. The heart-break. Knowing the body in Mum's car belonged to his brother.

Now I understand, of course – I understand why he failed to scream obscenities at the journalists who hinted at his wife's infidelity, why he let the village gossips whisper en route to his post-office counter. My father's reticence was contrived. The general public jumped at an unimaginative MO: that the dead lovers killed themselves out of over-whelming guilt. What other option could there be?

That's ironic, what with the truth being far worse. I bypass the fact that they gassed a child-abuser. I refer to how will-ingly my mother took a bullet. Uncle Fergus's murder was Bambi's ticket home.

For sanity's sake, I close Case 0001.

It's early evening when I arrive back at Ronchi Hotel.

Emotionally deplete, I don't care about blistered loins or spasming lumbar regions, or the fact that my internal organs are vibrating fiercely, despite me having dismounted ten minutes ago.

In reception, I bob respectfully at Cosmo and say, 'Michael?' very clearly.

Cosmo refuses to look at me. Just points upstairs. About

to see my brother, I feel a weak injection of relief. Michael is everybody I need now. And this is the plan.

To make him lie on the bed, his back to me, remaining absolutely still – no talking, snoring, throat clicking or (discernible) breathing. This enabling me to assume the foetal position, snuggling my knees and shins into the long crook of his spinal column.

That's where I feel safest, in the cradle of his back.

And that is where I will sleep until dawn. Just as soon as I've used the hotel's computer.

http://twitter.com/camille tremblay/status/840222764511902736

I frown at the post Annie has forwarded to my brother. It is a photograph of Camille Tremblay and her son. Taken at a Canadian Football League game, the accompanying message confirms their relationship to Sébastien.

Look what we're up to, @seb.tremblay89. Can't wait to see you. Little Louis's stoked ur back again so soon!!

Tremblay fact: they all look the same.

Though Sébastien's sister pulls off the onyx hair and ashen pallor best. Small and trendy, with an elfin haircut, boho summer dress and sandals, she looks fun and proactive. Her son, Louis, is an eight-year-old version of his uncle – only he wears a Montreal Alouettes hoodie and grins as maniacally as Camille, arms outstretched, two thumbs up.

It's a happy pic. It's also an old one, posted the summer before last. I'm confused as to why Annie has forwarded it to Michael.

I browse Camille's other Twitter feeds . . .

Louis at the dentist. Louis doing tae kwon do. Louis on a Space Hopper.

Just one of Camille and Sébastien, taken six years previously: they're blowing out the candles on a twenty-first birthday cake. My conclusion: their parents are exceedingly tight or the siblings are precisely the same age.

I rack my brain, but can't remember Sébastien ever mentioning a twin sister. In my defence, his voice has a sinisterly soporific quality. I often zone out when he's talking.

Though one thing remains certain – if Annie sent this post to Michael with the same contempt as her previous texts, she is being an unmitigated bitch.

Both sides of Michael's bed are occupied.

Michael wears pyjamas (white), Rosa, a pinafore dress (white). They sit beside one another under the eiderdown (white), arms folded, watching TV, with a selection of cheeses.

For the first time in forty-eight hours, I smile. 'It's John Lennon and Yoko Ono.'

Michael is too angry to make eye contact. 'I think you'll find John Lennon was hetero.'

'That makes sense, Yoko Ono being his wife. Hello, Rosa. Room for another?'

'No,' says Michael. 'You can sit on the floor.'

I frown. 'Not much of a welcome.'

'He not happy,' mouths Rosa.

My immediate thought: Lancelot has blabbed. Michael looks choleric enough, turning his head towards me, one agonising inch at a time; squinting at the naked skin between my eyebrows – which is exactly how I taught him to deliver genuine emotion without making eye contact: you glare at the glabella.

'You want answers?' he asks.

'Yes.'

'You want answers?' He says it again, because I'm not playing along with him.

'I think I'm entitled to them.' I sigh, because *A Few Good Men* is in Michael's top 500 films.

'You want answers?' he triple-checks.

For fuck's sake. 'I want the truth.'

'You can't handle the truth!'

Rosa reassures Michael. 'She a big girl.'

I put a hand on Rosa's shoulder. Take a moment to compose myself and build a defence.

There's no need. 'Flo. You took my fucking phone.'

My smile is unconstrained, as is my sigh. 'Yes, Michael, I did.'

'My phone,' he reiterates.

'I needed to stay in touch with you.'

Rosa squints, because I haven't called once. I ignore her to pull a chair up to his side of the bed, take his chin in my hand and examine his face.

One side is tinted blue and haematoma-yellow.

'You look like shit.'

'*Mamma mia*,' Rosa complains.

I will not lie: I'm not good with wounds or general suffering. That and borderline blood-injury/needle phobia are the reasons I never considered medicine. Or heroin addiction.

'It not that bad,' Rosa reassures him.

'It is,' I tell her flatly. 'My father is going to kill me.'

'I liked that tooth,' adds Michael.

Rosa shows me her little brown ones. 'If I can, I give him mine.'

'I almost died,' Michael reminds us.

And I grab his shoulders to make him stop making me feel guilty. 'You did not almost die, do you hear me? And you cannot be telling Dad that either. He'll never let you out again.'

'Ignore your father. When people get disappointed with their own hearts, they blame the duck, the chicken, the cat.'

I can undermine my dad, but she can't. 'Rosa, why are you in bed with my brother?'

She flattens the bedspread over her legs and scores a line down the middle to demonstrate that no impropriety has occurred or will ever occur.

'Michael give me lesson in being an actor. He very good teacher.'

I demand evidence. 'Show me now.'

His headshake is frank. 'She's not ready.'

'Don't be embarrassed,' I reassure Rosa. 'It's just me.'

And she confides, without a sip of complaint, 'We not got to the acting bit yet. I just watch.' It makes me want to spoon my heart out and show her how engorged it is with gratitude.

So I stand up. Put my money where my mouth is. Messing up my hair and waving an imaginary samurai sword, I deliver my next line with unblinking fervour . . .

'"I am gonna ask you questions. And every time you don't give me answers, I'm gonna cut something off. And I promise you, they will be things you will miss."'

Rosa looks concerned, while Michael applauds and explains, 'That's The Bride out of *Kill Bill*.'

'*Volume 1*,' I clarify. Then it goes quiet because, unexpectedly, I suck in sobs that have come from nowhere.

'And this, Rosa, is why acting mustn't be rushed.' My brother presents me as a case in point. 'The Method is very depleting.'

'You need food, Florence.' Rosa gets up, neatens the bedclothes around Michael. 'I got the mushroom risotto; the jota; the costolette alla Valdostana.'

'Yes, please,' I sniff, taking her side of the bed, ushering Michael on to his side and burrowing my knees into his lumber region.

'Why are you upset?' I hear Michael mumble into his pillow. 'Did the case go badly?'

'You could say that.'

'Don't worry, you'll get us a job soon.'

And that's that. The conversation is done and dusted, with

a line underneath it. I wait pointlessly for questions that will never come. Try to think of a time I've felt lonelier. How I wish we could swap places. His faith in me is too exhausting.

'Tell me about Sébastien?' I ask his shoulder blades.

'Five-three, black hair, fair complexion.'

'Things I don't know.'

'Strawberry birthmark on his lower back.'

'His family back in Canada?'

'One mum, one dad and one twin sister.'

'Nieces and nephews?'

'A boy, Louis.'

Christ, I did zone out. 'I bet that's hard – the distance between them all.'

He shakes his head. 'They don't talk. Sébastien was a challenging child.'

'Why? What was his problem?'

The following information is apparently a huge secret: 'His sexuality.'

'No way,' I state, because Camille looked hip and open-minded and seemed genuinely keyed up at the prospect of seeing her brother. 'Even his twin?'

He sighs, turns around so we face one another. 'His sister was the worst. Sébastien's never even met his nephew – she's frightened it'll rub off.'

I squint. 'That what will rub off?'

He whispers again: 'His sexuality.'

'He's not seen the boy *ever*?'

'*Never.*' He stares at me, unblinking. 'He has no one, Flo. Which is why I feel extra bad about calling it off.'

I nod slowly. 'It sounds like Sébastien's had a rough deal.' What was it Camille had said?

'Can't wait to see you. Little Louis's stoked ur back again so soon . . .'

I loathe Annie with a passion, but her craftiness is undeniably impressive. The stolen airmail letter to little Paola. Holding Sébastien ransom over a Twitter post that could liberate a worm farm.

Michael says guiltily, 'I have had the best hen ever, though.'

'And that's the main thing.' I chivvy him along. 'Now it's time to nip this in the bud. You won't be as strong as me at surviving divorce. And that's where you're headed, because when you love someone, it's quite a *definite* thing – even when they're as unattractive as Sébastien. Rule No. 1: you don't just go off them. You have to genuinely believe they're as perfect a life partner as you can get.'

'Annie says marriage is not all coffee beans and rainbows.'

'How would she know?'

Michael shrugs.

'Exactly. The attraction thing in any relationship is extremely key. Love can't be that flighty. It's anthropological law. Look at swans.'

'Sometimes it's flighty.'

'And when it is that flighty, you're allowed to have a wonderful but doomed fling. It's knowing the difference.' I speculate as to whether that's how Bambi felt about Dad, then stop myself right there to talk like a Sergeant Major. 'Sit up, Michael, and look at me.'

We face one another, cross-legged, knees touching. I get straight to the point. 'Did you know Sébastien wants children?'

'Yes.' He nods. 'And he can't have any.'

'Is it something you could ever contemplate?'

The hand to his throat suggests he's already entering anaphylactic shock. 'Like, *never*. I've told him. Children make me discombobulate.'

I pat his knee. 'That's the best word you've ever used.'

'I know.'

'Do you also know it's a deal breaker? One of you wanting

a child and the other not? It's an insurmountable barrier to fulfilling one another's potential.'

'I don't care,' he says. 'I don't want one.'

'Excellent.' I rub my face, relieved. 'I'll sort *everything*. Phone the registry office. Speak to Dad. I'll even explain why it's off to Sébastien – I'll put it nicely.'

'Can we just stop talking about this now?'

A hand to my sternum, I give him my oath. 'Not another word about Sébastien until we're back home.'

When Rosa returns with food, Michael and I show her some more acting. Re-enact scenes from *Thelma and Louise*, then, our *pièce de résistance*, *Butch Cassidy and the Sundance Kid*, the final scene.

Eventually, I decide to take the leftovers to my room and pack. Though first I ask, 'Where's Lancelot?' Because there's a very important conversation to be had with St Adam of the Ants.

Rosa shakes her head. 'He's gone home.'

'When's he back?'

'A week or a month.' She shrugs her shoulders.

The PI in me wants to ask a shedload of questions, but I've decided to bail out on that bit of digging. Lancelot, the geologist, has mud on me. I don't intend to make an enemy of him. He also has a neat repertoire of acrobatic moves – that's the hallmark of a potential nemesis.

What am I saying? I'm on it like a car bonnet. I need to return Tommaso's Vespa before I go, anyway. I leave Michael and Rosa, but not before issuing my brother with instructions.

'I'll see you at breakfast. Oh seven hundred hours. Be packed and ready to leave – it's time we put a stop to your marriage.'

Somebody has been in my room.

I know it instantly. The handset cord is resting on the

wrong side of the phone; it's coiled in a tight tangle, as opposed to a loose figure of eight. The pop sock I left draped on the window ledge has fluttered to the floor. But the biggest give-away: an envelope with my name on it is propped against the pillow.

First I check the bathroom, then under the bed, in the wardrobe, then I sit on the mattress's edge to open the envelope. Inside is a folded sheet of Hotel Ronchi notepaper. Its handwritten message is pithy.

Florence,
*   Your choice of boyfriend is inadvisable. For your family's safety, I beg you return to England and stay away from everybody Bellini-related.*
*   You will not see me again. Please destroy this letter.*
Lancelot

I do no such thing. I read it over and over, then put it in a pocket to show Tommaso. Because Tommaso told my brother we were lovers. And being someone's lover has its responsibilities. Always erring toward candidness, for example.

There hasn't been enough of that on my part.

And Tommaso makes me feel safe. Maybe safe enough to come clean about everything. About smoking a joint with Howard. About half killing my brother. About being rescued from a cliff's edge by a man who's reconnoitring his family. About my PI past.

On second thoughts, I decide to tell Tommaso nothing. I wouldn't come out of it well.

Though I will show him Lance's note – it's only right, what with the geologist having a beef with his nearest and dearest, who I happen to like.

The landline does a brief and unexpected *ding*.

I squint at the hotel phone hard. Take the handset. Bang

it on the side table and put it to my ear. It's dead, so I return it to its cradle. Thirty seconds pass. I hear it again, a faint tinkle.

Personal experience has put me here before – a private investigator's phone promises to be compulsive listening. In the absence of counter-surveillance equipment, I use a one-cent coin and brute force.

Things you should not find inside your handset: a UF capacitor, alligator clips and hearing-aid batteries. It transforms the receiver into an eavesdropping device – which is illegal, unless a high court has evidence you're involved in subversive activities.

This particular wire tap, however, is non-agency. Antiquated and amateurish, it's the type a middle-aged nerd might cook up after watching a YouTube tutorial. Its major upside – it transforms the handset into a microphone; my every sniff, snore and sigh will be monitored, whether I'm using the handset or not. Major downside – the receiving equipment has to be within ten metres of the tap.

Quickly, I put the shower on full whack, aiming the spray so it beats rowdily at the PVC curtain. Selecting 'Happy' by Pharrell Williams, I place the iPhone next to the landline, its volume on max. Silently, I sweep the room for a transmitter.

Unable to find one, I squash my belongings into my wheelie suitcase. At reception, I show Cosmo my baggage and indicate that I'd like to leave it at reception.

'Saves me hoicking it down in the morning,' I tell him.

Cosmo points a jowl in the direction of the back office.

Once inside, I head straight for the key cupboard. Take the key for the room next to mine.

It's identical to mine in layout and size, and I know immediately the transmitter is in here. Towers of bedlinen and towels, bottles of bleach, a thousand toilet rolls – it's current use is as a storeroom, and it's the perfect place to hide a receiver. I haven't the time to pull the place apart and put it back together again.

Suspect fact: Lancelot is not the culprit. My phone was tapped after I'd left for Bagnara; he's gone so can't physically listen in, making the equipment useless to him.

Plus, genuine prowlers never leave a note.

Nepotism

Like many single women, I've imagined having a stalker, one who's mesmerising. Tommaso, for example. I'd encourage him to audition for the role in a heartbeat, were he in a much better mood.

Disappointingly, Tommaso tonight impersonates someone who works for an insurance company. He's walking around his scooter, inspecting the chrome, polishing its mirrors with his sleeve.

'I haven't had time to clean it,' I explain.

He squints at the odometer. 'Or fiddle with the mileage.'

'It's not like you didn't know where I was going.'

'You didn't give me time to think it over.'

'I can't help your sluggish processing skills. I'd only mentioned Bagnara four hundred times that day.'

Honestly. I am gutted.

We'd parted on a biochemical high note. I'd expected a heroine's welcome: being swung by the arms, a firm hug. The accidental brushing of groins. Though no kiss, not immediately. Rudies would be off the menu until he'd ignored his scooter to demand every last detail about my trip.

Which he hasn't. That's confusing.

Because I thought it was romantic that he'd suggested we meet on the coastal esplanade – a walkway leading into Portopiccolo. Maybe we'd watch the sunset from a bench and promise one another things. Like, wherever we are in the world, and whoever we end up loving, the moonrise will remain ours. A secret wink to the other.

Yes, I know that we're here to say goodbye until next time.

No, I had not realised that the farewell would be terminal. Or quite so swift. And lacking in drama and narrative.

My back to the sea, I perch on the railings, swinging my feet in a feeble attempt at nonchalance. It's wasted on Tommaso. He won't even look at me.

'So, am I still not allowed in then?' I ask childishly.

'To where?'

'Portopiccolo.' I point ten minutes to our left. 'It's definitely not shut. People are strolling past all the time. Look, there's one.'

He mumbles, 'I'm not in the mood.'

'For what?' I ask quietly.

At last, he looks at me directly. His eyes are so humourless I barely recognise him. 'You went to see Massimo.'

'Ah.' I hop free of the railings and put a palm on Tommaso's face. 'It was a massive set of coincidences.'

'Meeting Massimo is never the result of coincidences.'

'I bumped into a friend of his. Sister Bernadette.'

'Father Benedict's mother?' he gasps.

'He's her son?' I start to cry for a lot of reasons, but mostly from delayed shock. 'He put a gun in my mouth.'

'You told Massimo I'd given you permission and directions. You mentioned my father.'

'*He* mentioned Rocco.'

'He told you to leave Italy.'

'That is true.' I brush away a tear.

'You're still here. Do you know who he is?'

'We got on well,' I reassure him.

'Massimo gave you a break. Trusted you to disappear. Are you completely stupid?'

That's rude. I punch him on the bicep.

Outraged, he rubs his arm, then points at the Vespa. 'And you put three thousand kilometres on my bike.'

'Which is exactly what happens when you drive to Bagnara and back. Can I be honest, Tommaso?'

'Have I a choice?'

'Massimo was wrong about Mum. He told me she didn't exist.'

'For a reason,' he states through gritted teeth.

'I knew it,' I say triumphantly. Nonetheless my shoulders dip. I'd wanted Massimo to be more honourable than that.

I don't know why Tommaso's shoulders dip too. But suddenly he's pulling me into his chest, kissing my forehead hard. 'It's only because I have a mother too, that you are still alive,' he concedes.

'You *what*?' I wriggle free. 'Tommaso, what the fuck are you saying?'

Reluctantly he nods. 'It's Rocco. My father.'

My whimper is involuntary, because I knew my wingman would die. People you meet and like – for no reason tangible enough, you just do – always go and croak. It makes you feel robbed. You end up mourning a death you've no business to.

'I'm sorry for your loss,' I say.

Tommaso shakes his head, holds my shoulders, suddenly keen to keep me upright, or at a distance.

'He just needs to step down.'

'Meaning?'

'I get a promotion.'

I try to take a step towards him, but his elbow joints are locked. So I make him feel better. Tell him private things about me . . .

'My dad's laid that one on me too. That the post office needs a change of leadership, a more youthful perspective – but it wasn't my dream . . .'

'Yes, I know all that,' he snaps.

I examine Tommaso's feet. He's sporting tan wingtip dress

shoes; Fratelli Borgioli, handmade, 700 euros a pair. The exact type an aspiring mob boss might wear.

'So what's your new job? Head waiter, right?'

Agitatedly, he taps a Blakey. 'Something like that.'

For a farfetched moment, I pretend it could work. Even the most ruthless mobster is allowed love in their lives. A woman who knows them like no other and loves them accordingly. Yes, such women lack scruples. They also exhibit first-rate survival mechanisms – blind purpose, creativity, a touch of psychopathy, the wherewithal to perpetuate their own myth, the intelligence to break convention's bonds, an innate dynamism that imperils the status quo.

On paper, that's a kick-arse legacy.

I commemorate evil women . . .

Bonnie Parker. She wrote poetry and murdered while wearing high-end fashion. Ma Parker's brand of evil became iconic in twentieth-century films, literature and music. The Pretty Pants Bandit made her hostages strip to their Y-fronts, which is funny in retrospect. But not at the time.

There's the crux. Violent crime is never funny at the time.

'You've got the right name for the job,' I say. 'Tommaso Carlo Massimo Bellini.'

'Shut up,' he says.

That makes me mad. 'Listen to you. The new Capo Famiglia. That's quite a promotion.' I point. 'Tommy "The Ice Pick" Bellini. You can have that one.'

He looks around. 'I said, shut up.'

I will not. I will very much point at his footwear and ask ridiculous questions. 'How much do non-Capo Famiglia people spend on shoes? Because these are obscenely expensive, when all you're doing is walking around a scooter and telling me off.'

I don't know what I'm saying. Yes, I do. I'm reacting to being unceremoniously dumped, because he and I know the truth – I could never be a gangster's moll; I don't have the personality disorder for it.

Suddenly, I need confirmation that Tommaso's not got one either. 'Have you ever popped anyone off?' I point two fingers at my temple. 'I mean, properly?'

Roughly, Tommaso grabs my arm and pulls me in the direction of the beach. We stumble over pebbles the size of cars, down towards the water, coming to a stop in a damp nook between rocks, where Tom pushes me into a sitting position.

'It's my inheritance,' he states. 'I have no choice.'

My bow is very sarcastic. 'Your subjects can only hope you use your power for good.'

Tommaso loses his fight. Becomes as reluctant as a suicide bomber. 'I can't be him. My father – that whole generation – they're different from me.'

I try to touch his hand, but Tommaso brushes me off. That makes me feel stupid. I flick my legs free of sand. 'Well, this is all very out of the blue. I pop off for a couple of days and, bam, you're a crime lord.'

'It's not like that.'

'Then tell me, what is it like?'

'I take over the business concerns, that's all.'

'Which are?'

'Private. I didn't ask to see your father's CV.'

'Men like you don't have to ask for permission.'

I'm being facetious, yet Tommaso doesn't argue the point. 'I have too much time on my hands. You turned up, prickled my interest. For a day or two, you were a distraction. Then Massimo threw up dirt on your mother. That has been a surprise to us all. It's the type of dirt that cannot be ignored.'

'Who can't ignore it?' I demand.

'Italy.'

For a minute or an hour, I cup my cheeks and stare at

Tommaso. Because that's a lot of people. And even though I've no clue what my mother did to infuriate them, I become as incensed as her homeland.

These would be pertinent questions: *How? When? What did she do?* Because finally someone has Bambi's backstory, and that someone is sitting right in front of me. Yet I am only conscious of the rawest self-pity . . .

Why the hell does a mother return to a country that wants her dead? What sane woman jeopardises her perfect family unit and their middle-class cottage in Dorset. A nostalgic woman? One with an incorrigible hunk of arrogance? One that remained too hung up on her first and only legal husband?

I know the answer.

Firstborn children are full of grace, God grants to them a special place.

That sentence was printed in my ninth-birthday card from Dad – it was the first birthday I didn't receive a card with her name in it. I thought the words were perfect, though. Told myself she'd magicked the card on to that shop shelf, then sent Dad subliminal messages to buy it.

'I was a distraction?' I mutter words at Tommaso.

He squeezes my wrist. 'Stop it. You're making this worse.'

'What? How?'

'I'm trying very hard to be philanthropic.'

My eyes become wide. 'Did you bug my room, Tommaso?'

'No,' he tells his knees. 'Cosmo did.'

'Cosmo?' A longsword might have been thrust at my back. 'Why?'

'It was Rocco's wish.'

'Well, don't use Cosmo again. He's useless.'

'You have to go home to England.'

'Once I was a distraction, now I'm an inconvenience – you're just shooing me away, like Massimo did.'

'Massimo liked you very much. He gave you a break and a head start.'

'Rocco liked me.'

I'm wrong. 'You were top-trumped by your mother's story.'

Tell me her story! I should shout.

'*You* liked me,' I say.

Tommaso's headshake insinuates I'm again mistaken. But I'm not. He licks his lips. That's the animal side of him showing irrepressible emotion. The gesture is swiftly followed by the pursing of his labia oris, which is indicative of the choking back of passion.

To cement my case, he lays it too bare not to care: 'I knew something was destined to happen between us when I first saw you. You were in the Colosseum. Do you remember that?'

I lie. Shake my head.

'Then seeing you on the Spanish Steps. And in the Barruchia's roof bar. It felt like destiny.' He shrugs. 'I shouldn't have told you about Massimo. And then you came to Portopiccolo.'

'We were friends. I was passing through . . .'

'No.' He places a finger on my lips. 'We're both more intelligent than that. You turned up for selfish reasons. I'm glad. It proved I was right.'

'About what?'

'You. I am hooked. Dangerously.'

Never, ever say: *I'm hooked too. Dangerously.* Even when your love interest is devastatingly Italian and you're feeling the sentiment more intently than they are. I muster every scrap of dignity and look at him with unbridled hatred, because there comes a but . . .

'But, Florence, I'm being the best friend you ever had.'

It surprises me how brazenly I just say it. 'Go on, then. What did she do?'

His eyes say: *Don't.*

I tell him my motivation. 'My aim is onefold. To discover the truth, however uncomfortable that truth may be.'

His eyes say: *It's a truth you never need to know.*

My eyes say: *I have all day.*

His eyes change tack – they dim, like he's turned the fairy lights off. There's no longer an invigorating maelstrom of greens – no twinkling olives, mints or pistachios. Just a mercenary disc of khaki, his pupils are as black as infinity.

I shiver. Even his molars hide behind furious lips. 'Did you find her, Florence?'

When you are lovers, candidness is the law. 'No, Tommaso. I did not find her.'

His new eyes say: *You need to do better than that.*

I tell my feet. 'In my opinion, she killed herself back on 13 February 1988. It was the day the sun-dust stopped dancing. The day she stopped tickling my ears, the actual insides. That's love. And that's when it died for her, way back then . . .'

When I look up, Tommaso's eyes twinkle weakly. *That was the right answer*, they say. Standing up officiously, he now swipes imaginary creases from his trousers and puts an end to the matter. 'Good. We'll leave it there.'

'No,' I say. 'What did my mother do?'

But Tommaso has turned his back. Walks away. 'Get your brother out of this mess. Take him home to Dorset.'

'Stop being philanthropic,' I shout at his shoulder blades. 'Tommaso, stop. Please. I don't get it.'

Ignoring me, he marches back up the beach towards the esplanade and his scooter. And although I'm unable to see his face, I hear his voice. His instructions are delivered with unnerving assurance.

'You have twelve hours to leave Italy, give or take. We're on opposite sides now, Florence.'

266

Getaway

By the time I'm back on the esplanade, Tommaso and his Vespa are nowhere to be seen. So I walk in the opposite direction, to Portopiccolo, for quite a way, wondering what unforgivable thing my mother has done to her people. Realising I can never come back.

A taxi passes me. Stops. Reverses.

'Ronchi dei Legionari,' I tell the driver, an overexcited Bangladeshi called Jiro. Forty-five, married, father of three. A ship's engineer by day, a local studies know-it-all of an evening, he jabbers on – tells me about cliff-reclamation strategies; the Obelisco tram; a signposted stroll to Prosecco . . .

I should be straight up:

I don't give a fig. Now, please shut up, because the tiny amount I thought I knew about my mother has been decimated. She is hated by one and all.

But I'm not straight up. I make mildly interested noises.

When we approach a huge war memorial on our left, I tell him abruptly, 'This is me.'

'*Mi scusi?*' Jiro frowns, because this is clearly not me. It's a monument the size of a pyramid on a dual carriageway with little around it apart from a service station and 500 acres of spruce.

I need to think about my mum. 'Please, just stop,' I tell him firmly.

Reluctantly, he pulls over. When I offer him a twenty, he refuses to take it. 'Tommaso said I get you home safe,' he says.

That makes me frown. 'Job done,' I reassure him.

The car pulls away half-heartedly. No doubt Jiro watches me in his mirror, nosy about where I'm heading. But I give him nothing. Only once the car's headlights disappear around the bend do I turn towards the memorial.

Sacrario Militare di Redipuglia.

It's colossal. Comprising of thirty-two tiers, each tier nearly three metres tall, this place is home to 110,000 cadavers. Forty thousand in alphabetical order. Seventy thousand in no order at all, because the tumble of their bones lack rhyme, reason and a barcode – that fact kills me.

A plaque at the entrance reads: *Im Leben und im Tode vereint.*

United in Life and Death.

It's 8.30 p.m. The tomb is in darkness. I head towards it, begin to climb the Brobdingnagian steps.

The C-section is five tiers up. I'm breathless by the time I find the Campanellas. I stand flush with the inscriptions, as far away from the edge as possible. With clumsy fingers, I dig in my bag, locate my keys and their flashlight fob.

Soldato Campanella Attilio 3 AET. FORT.
Soldato Campanella Cesare 22 FANTERIA
Soldato Campanella Dominico 14 FANTERIA
Soldato Campanella Eugenio 113 FANTERIA
Soldato Guillermo Lorenzo 138 COMP. MITR.

I study each inscription with pained pride. Genealogical fact: all these men are interconnected via love or deoxyribonucleic acid. You just have to go back far enough and, eventually, you'll find the common denominator – the original Campanella from which all others sprang.

I was half-Campanella back in the day.

'Who am I now?' I ask the inscriptions, softly.

I wish I hadn't. A breeze arrives to gee up the spruce,

which promptly chatter among themselves. Like Chinese whispers, their hushed prattle rushes towards me and passes me, disappearing into the mountains beyond. It gets me thinking too much about films – *The Hills Have Eyes*, especially, the 1977 version about an incestuous clan of savages who lived in the Nevada mountains. That makes me uneasy. Nonetheless, I sit on the stone ledge, which is as cold as a mortuary slab, pull my jacket tightly around my shoulders and stay camped among the Campanellas for a while longer.

Below, cars slice through the silent air, refusing to dawdle in this bit of countryside. I'm grateful for the service station ahead; it blares a rude yellow, as reassuring as an accident-and-emergency department. Its forecourt is empty, apart from a blue Fiat 500 – that little bubble of a car makes a dead weight of my heart.

Because Mum had one too – not a Fiat 500, but an Austin Martin 330 which, from this far up, looks very similar indeed. Mum later swapped it for Sunny – a yellow Datsun that had invisibility powers. That's what she told me, and I believed her completely. The irony makes me smile thinly – that little car went on to help her disappear from the face of the planet.

And now, magically, she's back.

Florence, listen to me very carefully indeed. You're dabbling in events that are extremely dangerous. You must not get involved. Do not look for your mum. I cannot help you or talk to you about this again.

Is she even my mother? I ask the Campanellas telepathically.

Michael's phone beeps. It's as deafening as a rape alarm. I yank it from my bag in case it wakes the mountain people. There are three text messages and five missed calls – all from Sébastien.

Text no. 1: *Please pick up. I've had a massive row with Annie. Ignore her if u hear from her. She's evil and a total liar. Call me xx*

Text no. 2: *Did you get my last text?*

Text no. 3: *OMG, I am so sorry. I didn't mean for you to find out this way. Please pick up, I need to know what she's told you?? Xxx*

Annie's cunning knows no bounds. Without saying a word to either man, she provided the kindling and match that would destroy their union. If she were sitting beside me now I'd shake her hand, then push her over the monument's edge, because respect where respect is due.

Annie told me everything, I text back.

Within twenty seconds the phone is ringing. I don't pick it up, just sit on the thing until it shuts up, then put it on mute.

Please pick up, is Sébastien's next text.

Seb. I need to hear it from you.

Not by text, my love x

Yes, by text. I am too distressed to talk out loud.

The response takes a few minutes to come through. I stare at the screen in anticipation of explanation and excuses; reams of them. Instead, just one sentence arrives.

The only reason I didn't tell you is because Louis doesn't know I'm his dad.

What. The. Fuck.

I rewrite my next text a number of times. Because about 400 questions spring to mind. Plus, I chastise myself – I should have seen it before. Sébastien is a bloody twin. And twins are, biologically speaking, a fluke of nature; a lovely one, usually, because from the nanosecond of conception they become each other's primary carer. Yet for some personality types, that skews their value system and has long-term mental repercussions.

I decide to come straight out with it:

Did you have sex with your twin?

Sébastien is unequivocal. *That is disgusting!!! My family found him again. Camille adopted him. Louis was a mistake – a one-night stand.*

We're gay? I remind him.

I was barely sixteen. Experimenting. It was horrible.

So horrible he managed to shoot his load enthusiastically enough for instantaneous procreation.

Why haven't you seen Louis for ages? I demand.

It is the next text that seals Sébastien Tremblay's fate.

That's exactly it, Michael! I met you and realised that if I have kids I want them with someone I love.

My nostrils are flared as a donkey's, but I made Michael a promise – I will put it nicely . . .

Dear Sébastien. As previously stated, I don't want children. Not yours or anyone's. They discombobulate me. I will not deprive you of your opportunity to fulfil your potential. So, I wish you happiness – just with someone else. Preferably, your current son. The one who's been deprived of your attention, love and unmitigated pride in him his entire life. You selfish twat. Michael.

Then I switch the phone off, because there is *no way* my mum would have felt that way about her children.

Bidding the Campanellas a curt goodbye, I make my way down the tomb's steps, head for the petrol station's synthetic light, then swing a left. It's a two-kilometre walk back to Hotel Ronchi, my final pit stop in Italy.

I speak loudly and sarcastically: 'Any phone calls tonight for me, Judas?'

Cosmo's sharp nod tells me: *I am busy.*

Ignoring him, I lean over the reception desk and look at his banknote scrapbook. Cosmo defends his collection with a plump forearm.

Existential fact: numismatics is philosophy in motion. While neatly sticking a rectangle of paper on another, larger rectangle of paper, Cosmo is engaged in *nothingness*; Sartre would say he 'lies coiled in the heart of being – like a worm'. There is no truer state. Which is handy when you don't want to feel guilty about stuff.

Stuff like rooming a single woman in the basement below your desk, then bugging her room. A woman for whom you've developed a nugget of fondness, exhibited by the fact you and your wife nursed her brother for days.

Cosmo frowns, '*Si?*'

The truth, however, is that Cosmo doesn't give a shit about me. He likes Michael. I'm not saying he despises me; there's just nothing he finds particularly endearing. His is the personality type that baffles me the most – the type who can take you or leave you.

'*Buona notte.*' I bid him a curt goodnight, then march in the direction of my room, because it doesn't work like that: Michael and I come as a package. Once around a corner and out of sight, I wait a minute, then glance back at the reception desk.

Cosmo has closed his scrapbook. Already he is wearing a telephonic headset. His pen is expectantly poised above a notepad.

Bugging fact: two metres above my head is an even more excellent place for a receiver than the storeroom.

I don't return to my room. I go upstairs to Michael, who is already asleep. I don't have the energy to check for intruders or bugs here. Or to undress. Or to wash. Only to flop onto my side of the bed and pull the quilted bedspread over my legs.

Within seconds, the baby-kisses of sleep make my body slink away from the tangible. My thoughts become disordered. Too willingly, I plummet, the survival jerks arriving to recalibrate me, to ensure I resume a feather-like descent from stage one to stage two of non-REM sleep.

Then there is zilch.

I'd like to say that stage three, chronobiologically speaking, is as black as death. But death doesn't have a colour. Once you're there, it doesn't even have a name. In fact, the only reason I know stage three has happened to me is that stage four always follows it – which is where I am now. Crash-landed in a place of vivid emotion and contextual hullabaloo.

REM sleep.

I'm six years old. My mother and I watch *The Hills Have Eyes* in the lounge. I'm scared – the film is wrong, as is the light in the room. It's supposed to be afternoon, yet the sun is shining through the patio doors.

A fact from childhood: the sun-dust only ever danced at breakfast time. But I watch it now. And try to ask Mum a hundred questions, the most pressing one, *What is your real name?* But my vocal cords are broken. I sound like I've had a tracheotomy.

Mum fails to take me seriously, just keeps doing childish poses – down on one knee, straight-armed, she points an Afro comb at me, no-nonsense, like Kate Jackson from *Charlie's Angels*.

So I grab the comb, mouth words in her face. *Just tell me your name.* Examine the flap of extra skin she has hanging around her neck – it runs the length of her sternocleido-mastoid muscle. But before I can touch it, she grabs the extra skin herself, pulls it up and away. With it come her neck, chin and face. In utter silence, I squeal. The prosthetic mask she rips from her face is as thick as a pig's hypodermis; how did I never notice it before?

I stare at Bambi's real face.

It's exactly the same one as before – thirty-something, beautiful, ditsy, resolute. I don't understand why she's so shy when the doorbell rings. But she demands I deal with it.

I'm only six. I mime rules at her: *I'm not allowed to answer the door. Not ever.*

It turns ugly. She raises a hand to me. With a jolt, I open my eyes. Stare at a penumbra of orange light around the doorframe. It helps me position myself. Michael's room. Ronchi Hotel. But why the doorbell?

It is, in fact, the telephone, which is *brumm*ing next to Michael, and it's not remotely doorbell-ish at all. I elbow my brother awake.

Irritated, he picks it up, says nothing, then hangs up. Head back on the pillow, he mutters, 'Argh. Six a.m. wake-up call.'

While Michael takes a shower, I pack his bag and order a taxi ride to the airport. The plan, to skip breakfast. I want to get out.

It's Rosa who mans the front desk. I peruse the counter – Cosmo, his scrapbook, the earphones are nowhere to be seen.

'Where's your husband?' I ask.

'He sleep.' She points at the suitcase I've parked in the back room, disappointed. 'You leaving?'

'I'm sorry.' I nod, a little bereft, because we will *never* meet again.

But Rosa ignores me – Michael has limped free of the lift, so she instinctively shuffles to his aid. Taking his bag, she helps him walk, lest he fall and lose another incisor. She even lowers him into a comfy chair in the wi-fi corner.

'He is perfectly OK,' I mumble.

But their moment is exclusive of me. 'You do not move,' she states.

'I won't,' my brother replies solemnly.

Then Rosa ushers me out of earshot. 'Florence, we need to talk.'

I couldn't agree more. If she doesn't know about Cosmo tapping my phone on the Bellinis' behest, she very much needs to.

'We settle your bill.' She winks, then frogmarches me to the reception desk. There, she prints up an invoice and speaks like a ventriloquist. 'There been a man outside all night. He ask to see you.'

I am not oblivious to the enemies I've made, yet my PI

training goes out of the window. Swinging my head this way and that, I search out my assailant.

There are a few candidates I have in mind. Massimo – the Eradicator – I disrespected him badly. Rocco has an especial grievance with my mother, as does the entire land. Then there's Lancelot – he's enough of an enigma to be a genuine serial killer.

'The man speak with Cosmo last night,' Rosa tells me. 'Just after you arrive back at the hotel. But Cosmo not find you. Then, twenty minutes ago, the man come again.' Rosa takes something out of her pinafore pocket. Slides it across the counter furtively. 'He leave this.'

The envelope is an odd size. A small square. My name has been scribbled on its front, but I don't recognise the hand-writing. Using my finger and thumb, I trace the contents – a thin, rectangle of cardboard, like a business card; or the message that accompanies a bouquet of flowers – or a funeral wreath.

Tearing open the envelope, I slip free the card. My knees become immediately colt-like. I take a step forwards, steady myself against the reception desk.

It's the Queen of Hearts. *My* Queen of Hearts.

There's no doubt the playing card has been in the wars. She still bears Father Benedict's footprint. Her conjoined sister's neck has suffered a terminal fold. Yet my queen somehow recovered to make an epic journey – to be reunited with me, and able to proffer information . . .

Because there are a lot of little words written on her back – in fine red ballpoint and hidden among the red swirls of the playing card's reverse. At first glance, you'd miss the secret writing altogether.

I strain to decipher it. Leaning over the reception desk, I pull free Cosmo's hobby eye-glass. Then accidentally sob – the writing is familiar to me.

My mother's 'G's look like '8's.

Paola A88i
Via XXIV Ma88io, 31
Casella Postale 5225
Ba8nara Calabra

My second sob is a result of the pointlessness of it all. She risked her family's safety – old and new – to give me a contact address I already have and one she can never, ever use again.

The upside: there's an outside chance my mother acquired her kooky graphological habit deliberately. Just for me. She knew I'd grasp its significance, just as soon as the time was right. Last birthday she sent me an anonymous birthday card. Only it wasn't anonymous, it was signed 'Con8ratulations'. The time before, it was the posters she'd stuck on to the windows of her magic Datsun Sunny.

Dan8er – Toxic 8as

Suddenly, I want to tell Noah . . .

My mother and I are two peas in a pod. You were right when you said I was probably the only one who really knew her. Maria was ahead of me, chronologically. But it's me my mother has an intimate connection with.

Where is Bambi? I ask the Queen of Hearts telepathically. *You're the pea in her pod*, she ribs me. *Where would* you *be?*

Robotically, I walk on to the street, light a cigarette and lean against the tree under which I'd kissed Tommaso – godfather of a crime syndicate that is plotting my mother's execution.

Surveying the street either side of me, I see only parked cars. No people. Or so I think until, quite unexpectedly, I spot Bambi's messenger. He leans in plain view against the wall of an apartment block opposite. Tall, shaped like a 'C', his hair a rich pannacotta white, he blends in with the hoary stone, motionless as a lizard.

I don't breathe for a long while.

Neither do I hear Michael approach. Nonetheless, my brother is beside me, glowering at his mother's husband. 'Who's that?'

I slap away his hand. 'You swore solemnly you wouldn't move.'

'I did.' He nods.

'Then go.' I tell him off. 'I'm waiting for the taxi.'

He tuts and returns inside.

My mother's messenger has not moved a muscle so, casually, I walk across the road towards him. Given my mother's circumstances, I assume he's used to living in the shadows, will certainly have done this sort of thing before.

I'm mistaken. Rather than staying put, he follows my lead. Walks towards me, emotionally, as though gearing up to a hug, like it's *Surprise Surprise* – but people may be watching, Cosmo, especially. Plus, there's CCTV. What is my mother thinking?

I shoo him away. Whisper urgently, 'They know who she is. Michael and I have been told to leave Italy. You're in terrible danger.'

'Michael?' Flabbergasted, he looks past me, at the Hotel Ronchi, as though ready to bowl inside. In response, I prepare to rugby-tackle him, because Michael will not be able to cope with any of this. Not when I made him a lot of solemn promises and this scenario is unconducive to every one of them.

Mum's husband now looks behind him, searching for back-up.

'You have to stop acting suspiciously,' I beg. 'The Bellinis are on our case. They're looking for your wife.'

He doesn't understand. In fact, he seems entirely clueless as to the significance of the name Bellini. Spotting the Queen of Hearts in my hand, he's suddenly keen to explain.

'Benedict.' He points at the card and nods.

I over-enunciate. 'Father Benedict gave this to you?'

He points at his heart. '*Amico.*'

Amico. Like 'amigo'? 'Benedict is your amigo?'

'*Amico.*' He nods again.

Stowing the Queen safely in a back pocket, I shake my head a lot. 'Signor, *please* go. Change Paola Aggi's PO box address. The Bellinis are mafiosi. They will find Bambi fast. All of you. This is very bad.'

Longingly, he peers back towards the apartment block he'd been standing by. And I experience a horrifying stab of apprehension.

'Is she *here*?' I mouth at the back of his head, then push past him, running to the building's corner.

Here it forms a junction with a skinny side street – Via Santissima Trinità. I jog on to it. Ten metres in, I find an opening in the side of the building – a large stone arch guarded by iron gates and a padlock.

Inside the railings are parked cars and wheelie bins. Jangling the padlock, I see it's a cheap brand – a cinch for the professional lock-picker, especially when you have the exact implements needed to unfasten it.

A safety pin, for example. I frown down at my feet then kneel to examine the one on the pavement. The end has been shaved. That's sensible, to avoid a serious stab to the thumb. There's also an Allen wrench discarded in the gutter. Somebody has picked the padlock and re-locked it in a hurry.

Or so they want me to think.

Mum has seen the TV shows. We watched them together. When breaking and entering, never leave evidence of your crime behind. Not unless you want to get caught. Or if your plan is to send someone on a wild-chicken chase.

I remember Bambi's particular modus operandi. The homemade posters. A dead paedophile written off as her suicide pal. Her own fabricated childhood and death. Smokescreens are my mother's speciality.

It smarts, the fact she's not ready to see me yet.

Well, that's tough.

I ignore the pin and wrench. Turn around, cross my arms and take in Via Santissima Trinità's scenery. Its street furniture – a bench and one-way signs; its primary land-use – residential, a mixture of apartment blocks and townhouses; the glaring anomaly – a narrow church.

What would Bambi do? The Queen of Hearts may well ask.

I pat my jeans pocket, because it's too easy a conundrum. Bambi Love was a sucker for a power-pray.

The church's entrance is tucked around the side, out of view of the pavement. The lofty wooden doors are ajar and I slip between the gap and into the atrium.

It's as small and cool as a cave. Has room for a congregation of thirty, tops; it's currently empty.

I genuflect before sitting on a pew.

Regardless of your views on creationism, the hypnotic quality of a church is nice. All those unworldly hopes for peace make the most lapsed Catholic feel floaty. When an elderly Italian woman arrives to sweep the floor around my feet, I lift them obligingly and examine her features. It's been a hell of a while since I saw Bambi last. For all I know, she's a master of disguise. An edgy giggle arrives in my abdomen. Reconstructive surgery hasn't come that far – the woman's half a metre too short.

When she and her broom disappear into a back room, I slide forward on to the kneeler, place my palms together and say the most serious thing I have *ever* said to God: 'Where *is* she?' Because now is the perfect time to prove He exists.

Indeed, God manifests himself as a poltergeist. Knocks something over to my right. I pivot on my knees, find myself staring at the confessional. Over-gilded oak, like a royal Portaloo, it has a cupboard for the penitent and a cupboard for the priest.

I slide free of the bench, walk towards the wooden booth, wavering at its two doors. Which side would Bambi hide in – the penitent's or the priest's? The penitent's, of course. For all her cunning, my mother would never have had the impertinence to take the priest's place.

I have the impertinence, though.

Entering the cupboard meant for a cleric, I close the door behind me, nestle into the purple velvet seat. A wooden lattice separates me from the box next door. Shielded by a curtain, I'm unable to confirm whether or not it's occupied.

No matter, I have an ensemble of senses at my disposal.

I inhale the muggy air. It's a heady mix of vintage oak and a synthetic olfactory group known as floral aldehyde, the latter being a combination of scents that include citrus, hyacinth, green leaf, tarragon, peach, cyclamen, carnation, bergamot, lily of the valley, jasmine, rose, sandalwood, vanilla, oakmoss, cedar base notes, aldehyde top notes and musk.

Currently, there are 300 commercial perfumes using those specific ingredients. Charlie by Revlon is one of them, a very feminist cologne whose tagline influenced a generation of women: *Kinda young, kinda now, Charlie! Kinda free, kinda wow! Charlie!*

Every Christmas and birthday I bought my mum a bottle, because it was cheap as chips and you could get it at the chemist's.

Twenty-five years on, my mum sticks within the floral aldehyde bracket, which is excellent evidence of nurture over nature, and something she's going to have to get over if she wants to evade capture. Because women tend towards the same olfactory preferences as their mother, an aroma symbolic of blind love and the epitome of maternal protection.

These days, however, Bambi is wealthier, or has a more generous daughter – she wears the originator of the whole floral aldehyde olfactory group. Chanel No. 5.

Soon as I'm able, I'll explain all this to Noah too, explain the circle of life in perfumery, because that's exactly what I wear on entrapments and first dates.

I don't pull back the curtain. I lean my ear gently against it.

The woman next door struggles to breathe silently. Her sympathetic nervous system is too revved up; breathing leisurely is physiologically tricky. She gives it a go, though. And it barbs at my heart. It's time to put us both out of our misery.

I facilitate the Sacrament of Penance, also known as Reconciliation.

'Hello, there,' I whisper at the curtain. 'My name is Florence Maria Love.' I eliminate doubt on her behalf, 'Your second-born daughter.'

It's a good minute before I hear the most desolate whimper: 'My little Piccolina.'

It feels too intimate when I pull the curtain back, like I'm at a peep show. Especially given the fact she refuses to turn her head and scrutinise me. And the fact she doesn't squeeze her slender fingers through the wooden lattice, desperate to reacquaint herself with my grown-up nose, grown-up eyelashes, grown-up cheeks.

I'm much prettier than I used to be, I want her to notice.

Instead, she studies her knees.

This is how she looks from the side:

Sex: female.

Race/complexion: Italian/a healthy nut-brown.

Build: Charlie's Angel.

Hair colour: A sixty-year-old Jaclyn Smith from *Charlie's Angels*.

Hair length and style: A sixty-year-old Jaclyn Smith from *Charlie's Angels*.

Fashion sense: A sixty-year-old Jaclyn Smith from *Charlie's Angels*.

Fingernails: still long and, I'd bet, as tickly as almonds.

Teeth: the gentlest buck – orthodontic proof that she is benevolent through and through.

So why won't she fucking look at me? Beg for forgiveness? Throw a ton of feeble excuses my way? I'm prepared for that. It's a conversation I've practised over and over in my head.

'The Bellinis know who I am.' I frown at her profile, because she looks exactly the same as when she was my mother; has made no attempt to alter her appearance. 'Trouble is, they know more than me.'

Unlike her husband, she knows the Bellinis all right. I recognise the fear; it manifests itself as an under-bite. I'm not fazed, though. Growing up, I saw it daily. I wonder if her pannacotta-haired lover is as clueless as George Love? Another willing pawn in her game, not privy to the rules.

Things about my mother I don't recognise . . .

The sleep wrinkle on the left-hand side of her nose – a sign of failing collagen and many a night sleeping, restfully, in exactly the same curled position, face squashed peacefully into the pillow.

After she pretended to die, I didn't sleep, not properly, ever again.

Michael's voice bellows from somewhere outside the church; my mother and I do identical gasps.

'Flo!' he shouts, not in a panicked way; in a measured, entirely proactive way.

'The taxi's here,' I mutter at her silhouette.

Only now does she turn to look at me. Snooker-ball eyes, as penetrating as her son's, she fingers the golden horn around her neck – the necklace she didn't leave to me.

'He mustn't see me,' she pleads.

I nod, stare at her lips, because they're just like mine, put a hand to the lattice. We're on the same page.

She forgets to fondle my fingers, again. 'Please, Florrie, get Michael away from here.'

Her Italian accent is richer than I remember. But I spot the vestiges of our secret history – a West Country twang. I wonder if she notices anything about me whatsoever.

You're supposed to be dead, I don't say. Just gawp at her face, as though she's a film star. Someone I have no actual right to, however intrinsic I believe she's been to my personal story. The reality: there's a gut-crushing lack of chemistry from her side.

Relationship fact: complacency is its death knell.

So I make the first move, show her my mettle, prove I'm worthy of her respect. Currently, all she requires of me is that I take absolute charge of Michael. Therefore, my facial expression is unequivocal – you've no need to pity me, touch my grown-up cheeks or worry about my well-being, ever.

'You have my word. I'll make sure Michael is safe.' I nod. 'Now you must do something for me.'

Michael's shouts get closer. 'Flo!'

We hold our breath, staring at our respective doors. Then I tap the grille, get her attention. That's how things worked between us; I looked after her.

'Rocco Bellini has the address of Paola's PO box. Take your family – all of them – and run, or go underground, or whatever it is you do.'

Deep down, we all want to be mothered; look at Bambi's shoulders slump. She stares at me, forsaken; begins to mirror my exact gestures and mannerisms. The rush of validation is electric. Especially when she says the most truthful thing ever: 'Crikey, Piccolina, I'm really in the soup.'

Sweet Jesus, it really is *her*. 'It's OK, Mum.' I nod decisively. 'I'm here now.'

*

Michael is putting our suitcases in the taxi's boot when I sneak up behind him. I jump on his back like a baby monkey, but he fails to see the affection in my violence. Agitatedly, he throws me off. I don't take umbrage – he's eighty per cent bruise.

Checking first that my mother's husband has gone and that Cosmo is nowhere to be seen, I kiss Rosa goodbye. A heartfelt kiss. The type I'd bestow upon a person who's five minutes from death.

Then it's my brother's go. Both he and Rosa sob a little distractedly. Rosa rewards his valediction with 'I love you like my son.'

The short transfer to Trieste is monopolised by Michael's regret at losing a tooth. I rub his back while peering from the rear window in the vain hope that our mother might appear for a final time, panting, waving, demanding that I stay; remembering it's imperative that she examine my ears, teeth, the creases between my fingers, my limb-to-torso ratio; that she enquires after my well-being, then demands Florence Love facts: how did I do in my SATs? Am I happy, fundamentally? Who told me the facts of life? She needs to know that I spoke to her often – childish soliloquies, muttered when I was under the sheets, or in the shower, or on the back of the bus. How, over the years, I've dedicated to her too many songs, the ones regular fifteen-year-olds earmark for their boyfriends. I'll hit Mum with a corker of a closing line: 'That wasn't the other girls' fault – you don't know love, until you've lost your top player.'

Once through Passport Control, Michael and I sit in a room with plastic walls and plastic benches, two vending machines and an entire wall of glass. My brother's chin rests against the panoramic window; nose tipped up, he gazes at planes, homeward-bound.

And I look back towards Passport Control.

Who *on earth* does she think she is?

Tapping Michael's shoulder, I tell him a lie. 'I've left my credit card with Rosa. I have to pop back.'

He sighs, just like our dad. 'You'd forget your head.'

I agree. 'There's an hour until we board. I'll be quick as I can. Worst-case scenario, I'll meet you on the plane.'

I promised Bambi I'd get Michael out of danger. Box ticked. Now I'm owed twenty-five years' worth of love. Before abandoning my brother, I give him clear instructions: 'Practise buckling, unbuckling and re-buckling. Memorise escape routes, and if anybody shouts, "Brace!", soften your knees to an angle of forty-five degrees. Get it?'

'OK. On one condition.' His finger is deadly serious. 'You tell Sébastien the wedding's off.'

The palm I place on my chest is heartfelt. 'Job done, partner.'

Michael doesn't watch me as I weave a route back towards Arrivals.

Retired Entrapment Specialists 101 – Tip #4:
Plans change

OK, so you've broken all the rules. It doesn't matter. You're retired. Some choose a job in B&Q. Others become a lollypop lady. Some PIs like to do genealogy.

Genealogy. The study of families, their lineages and history. It fulfils an evolutionary need to plait one's roots. To love pretend people, who might have been arses yet are biologically you in the making. Their life stories complete, you're safe of their foibles, so romanticise them.

How to do genealogy:

- Demand answers from the living.

- Get a new motivation. Use one of mine if you like . . .

Sometimes, death is the perfect crescendo to the film of your life. See Butch Cassidy and the Sundance Kid, Bonnie and Clyde, Thelma and Louise. *Cinematographically, theirs were deaths worth living for. Fact.*

ACKNOWLEDGEMENTS

I offer my sincerest appreciation and respect to Ray and his colleague, who trusted me with a mind-boggling insight into witness protection, high profile offenders and intergovernmental cooperation. I've *loved* all the stories and look forward, one day, to writing yours.

My editor, Frankie Edwards. A woman so frighteningly sharp, I think she should be writing my books herself. Your enthusiasm makes me feel loved and your organisational skills are enviable. When I grow up I want to be you.

Thanks also to Headline's Fran Gough, Jo Liddiard and Leah Woodburn – it's very liberating being part of a team that's as giggly as me.

The Jo Unwin. Not just a super agent and dear pal, but the owner of a cracking rack.

Lucia Campanella – my Italian tour guide and drinking partner. Our 'research trips' were the best thing about writing this book.

Thank you to my therapists: Jo-Jo O'Keefe, Katie Tadema Knight, Em O'Connor, Trevski O'Grady and Andrea Lee Berry. These guys keep me sane. Well, a couple of them do.

And, finally, I'd like to thank the universe for the real life Tommaso. And then I'd like to thank it again – for *my* beautiful Bambi, Daun.

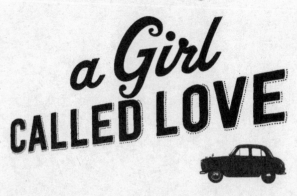

a Girl CALLED LOVE

Scott 'Scat' Delaney is a world-famous jazz singer. He has ample opportunity to stray and his girlfriend, Alice, needs to know she can trust him.

Step up Florence Love, Private Investigator.

Florence has just ten days to entrap an A-Lister. Whilst sticking to her cardinal rule: One kiss, with tongues, five seconds – case closed.

A master of body language, evolutionary science and nifty disguises, her approach is unconventional, her success rate excellent. But targets are rarely as beautiful as Scat. Never fall for the target.

That is very bad form indeed.

Once you've met Florence Love, you'll see the world in glorious technicolour at last.

© Jonathan Ring

Louise Lee was once a Geography teacher. When oxbow lakes no longer floated her boat, she took the next, natural step in her career progression and became a Private Investigator. Memorable cases include a high-functioning bigamist with three wives and six children, who was set to marry a fourth; and losing a target because George Clooney started chatting her up in a bar.

Louise undertook an MA in Creative Writing at Birkbeck, and has had work commissioned by BBC Radio Four. Her debut novel, *A Girl Called Love*, was the first in the Florence Love series which follows the life of an irreverent, thoroughly 'modern' PI who specialises in entrapment. If Louise's mum is reading this, the books are in no way based on her true experiences. Honest.

Louise is currently writing book three in her woman-shed and would love to hear from you – drop her a line on Twitter @louise_lee1.

Get to know Flo a bit better
here as she divulges her
thoughts on some
Very Important Matters . . .

Charlie's Angels, the TV show – a power discussion

Yes, it was 'jiggle TV'. Yes, when the Angels went undercover it was exclusively as sexy people (sexy waitresses, sexy construction workers, sexy clown skaters). And yes, the scripts were sometimes rubbish. Yet it remains in my top five most influential TV shows ever.

The reason: *Charlie's Angels* is a lovely example of socioanthropology working at its most productive. The threesome is so admired because, contrarily, the Angels weren't actually very sexual. Breathtakingly beautiful with excellent fashion sense, maybe, but if they had a libido, biological clock or, indeed, a clitoris, they never threw it in our faces. That was good. I was only five.

In short, *Charlie's Angels* was a show about professionalism and mutual respect, whilst looking hot, which is exactly what girls wanted in the late seventies/early eighties. That desire, for me, still stands today. Most especially, the chance to dress up whilst going deep undercover.

Disclaimer . . . Feminism is a big subject. I'm not always entirely clear what one is. But the Barrymore Angels are a travesty. I wouldn't trust one of them with my boyfriend, which was the entire essence of the original TV show's charm.

Women I admire

- Anybody who played a **Charlie's Angel** between 1976 and 1981. (Except Shelley Hack who didn't cut the mustard.)

- **Saint Rita of Cascia**. In the absence of a mother, this statue gives me disappointed looks from the top of my wardrobe. I'm too confused to be religious, yet the patron saint of women and lost causes seems especially interested in me. I get it. Our chemistry is palpable. Now and then, I whisper a prayer her way because it's savvy to cover all the spiritual bases.

- **Daenerys of House Targaryen** aka **Khaleesi**. She has conquered *a lot* of people, is the mother of dragons and a strong contender for the new queen of the Seven Kingdoms of Westeros. In a non-lesbianic way, I'm hook, line and sinker in lust.

- The real-life Queen aka **Queen Elizabeth II**. Monarchist or republican, no one can deny that this small woman has the stamina of an X-Man.

- All Taurean women, including **Catherine the Great**, **Charlotte Brontë**, **Tina Fey** and the real-life Queen aka **Queen Elizabeth II**. These gals have no regrets about anything they say, ever. Christ, I envy that. I'm a Cancerian. If I upset people, I must explain myself fully. Being that emotionally obsequious is exhausting.